A JEWISH REFUGEE IN NEW YORK

THE MODERN JEWISH EXPERIENCE

Deborah Dash Moore and Marsha L. Rozenblit, editors
Paula Hyman, founding coeditor

A JEWISH REFUGEE IN NEW YORK

Rivke Zilberg's Journal

Kadya Molodovsky
Translated by Anita Norich

INDIANA UNIVERSITY PRESS

This book is a publication of

Indiana University Press
Office of Scholarly Publishing
Herman B Wells Library 350
1320 East 10th Street
Bloomington, Indiana 47405 USA

iupress.indiana.edu

© 2019 by Anita Norich

All rights reserved

Manufactured in the United States of America

ISBN 978-0-253-04075-6 (hardback)
ISBN 978-0-253-04076-3 (paperback)
ISBN 978-0-253-04079-4 (ebook)

1 2 3 4 5   23 22 21 20 19

CONTENTS

INTRODUCTION

O N MAY 30, 1941, THE FIRST INSTALLMENT OF a serialized novel appeared in the New York Yiddish newspaper *Morgn-zhurnal* (Morning journal). Entitled *Fun Lublin biz Nyu-york: Togbukh fun Rivke Zilberg* (From Lublin to New York: The diary of Rivke Zilberg), the novel tells the story of a twenty-year-old refugee who flees the Nazis and comes to live at her aunt's home in New York. Rivke keeps a journal that begins on December 15, 1939, and ends ten months later on October 6, 1940. In her 107 entries, Rivke looks back to Poland and forward to possibilities in the United States. Knowing of her mother's death in the German bombing of Lublin,[1] and unsure of the fate of her father, brothers, or the man she was to marry, Rivke must now contend with the difficulties of immigration. Her fiancé, she learns after months of uncertainty, has made his way to Palestine and urges her to join him. But having been pursued by two young, rather self-satisfied American Jews, she settles on one and remains in the United States. Yet her views of American Jewry are hardly flattering. One Yiddish reviewer of the book wrote that Molodovsky saw "the tragic loneliness of American Jews . . . that hides itself behind the three foundations of Jewish life here: making money, spending money, and the 'good times' of parties, movies, card games."[2]

Fun Lublin biz Nyu-york, or *A Jewish Refugee in New York*, as it is called in this English translation, is not a novel about the Holocaust in the familiar sense, but it is written under its palpable shadow. The story illustrates the mundane, ongoing lives of those not directly in the line of fire as well as the undercurrent of horror and uncertainty with which those lives were lived. Nor is this a love story in any traditional sense. It is the story of a young woman shaped by historical crises, trying to make sense of her place in a bewildering, threatening world. Rivke seems alternately callow and thoughtful; she is as likely to comment on her cousin's hairstyle and her desire for nicer shoes as on the effects of American assimilation or the fear of what is happening in Europe. Throughout her reflections, Lublin—invaded, devastated, the site of death and massive destruction—remains "home." Rivke's refrain of "I don't know" or "Who knows?" is both a question and a plea voiced by a woman bereft of everything familiar. Frequent metaphoric uses of fire, conflagration, and burning point the reader beyond the symbol to the real inferno. The book confronts us with a protagonist whom we may or may not like or admire but with whom we are compelled to sympathize.

The novel was serialized daily (except Saturday, when the newspaper did not print) until August 11, 1941, and appeared as a book in 1942 under the imprimatur Papirene brik (paper bridge), which Molodovsky and her husband Simcha Lev, a printer, used when they published some of her works.[3] (The paper bridge is a reference to poems in Molodovsky's oeuvre and to a legend about messianic days when Jews will cross into the Promised Land on a paper bridge made of Torah and learning.) The serialized version followed the exigencies of newspaper publication, including the amount of space the paper had on a given day; dated entries and even paragraphs of the journal could be spread out over two or more issues of the newspaper. Molodovsky (or Lev, the printer) made some editorial emendations when they published the book. Spelling was standardized, most Yiddish translations of the newspaper's transliterated English were dropped, errors in dating were corrected, and, infrequently, a sentence was added or deleted. They also made more substantive changes. In the book, titles were added to each journal entry, as if to highlight the fact that this was, in fact, a novel. More significantly, the subtitle was changed from *Dos togbukh fun a yidish flikhtling-meydl* (The diary of a Jewish refugee girl) to *Togbukh fun Rivke Zilberg* (Diary of Rivke Zilberg). The earlier version is more compelling and is resonant of the novel's major themes and character. Because neither Molodovsky nor Lev left any explanation for the changes that were made, we can only speculate about their motives. Perhaps *refugee* implied some hope for those who needed refuge, a hope that had been betrayed in the months separating the two publications. Perhaps a focus on Rivke in New York suggested a future that was difficult but necessary to imagine for those who were painfully conscious of the devastated past. Molodovsky and other Yiddish writers from Eastern Europe, living in the United States as the war unfolded, wrote about that past, mourning the people and places that were being destroyed while they were safe in New York. Yet they also imagined what it would mean to prepare a future for Yiddish and for those who might be saved.[4]

Although Rivke reflects primarily on the events of the war affecting her immediate family, Molodovsky was writing with a broader and more remained unfinished for the same reasons that Molodovsky stopped editing *Svive*. In addition to her desperate worry about Poland's Jews, she faced financial pressures and health concerns, including surgery on her hand. In 1948, in the same daily in which *Fun Lublin biz Nyu-york* had appeared, she published another novel, entitled *Zeydes un eyniklekh* (Grandfathers and grandchildren).[9] She had hoped to publish the novel in book form, but her emigration to Israel just after the novel's serialization may have put an end to that plan.

Like the earlier novel, these later works take place in New York, with characters who have lost their families and communities to Nazi horrors. In all three of the novels Molodovsky wrote in the 1940s, Europeans who have fled or survived the Nazis meet American Jews who express sorrow and a rather condescending pity for what these survivors endured. Molodovsky's primary concern, as these works and her later memoir make clear, is the meaning of *yerushe*, meaning *inheritance* or *legacy*—not in the sense of material things, but of values, beliefs, and what may remain after destruction. In its exploration of a Jewish future, *Zeydes un eyniklekh* includes the nascent kibbutz movement in Israel. Taken together, these novels are clear evidence that writing about the war during and immediately after it occurred was inescapable for Yiddish writers.

In 1949 Molodovsky and her husband went to the newly established State of Israel, but a combination of personal and national financial hardships, as well as limited opportunities for Yiddish, brought them back to New York three years later. She wrote that it was difficult to leave Israel and she remained committed to the Zionist ideal, but her frustrations were clear. Her editorial work meant that she had no time to write. She was unpleasantly surprised when she was interrupted during a public speech and told to speak Hebrew instead of Yiddish.[10] She combined praise for the newly emerging state with a deep sense of disappointment that, in trying to erase Yiddish, it was erasing hundreds of years of *yerushe*. She edited a journal called *Heym* (Home), but she did not feel at home. Ironically, Molodovsky's fame today rests primarily on Hebrew translations of her poetry by such prominent writers as Lea Goldberg and Natan Alterman. Some of her poems for children have become a staple of Israeli schools, although their Yiddish origins are often unacknowledged and even unknown to both students and teachers.

* * *

A Jewish Refugee in New York—and its existence as a novel—challenges longstanding assumptions about gender divisions within both Yiddish literature and literature by women. Yiddish—known at various times as merely *dzhargon* (jargon) or, also problematically, as *mame loshn* (mother tongue)—was historically feminized and its status diminished. The domestication of Yiddish implied in this designation belied the development of Yiddish literature as an outgrowth of the Haskalah, the Jewish Enlightenment movement of the nineteenth century, and of the modernist sensibilities and cultural experiments of its most active practitioners, Molodovsky among them. Yiddish, of course, was never a "woman's language" or a language used primarily by women, but its matrilineal associations were emphasized in contrast to the patrilineal religious and literary authority of Hebrew. Yiddish was increasingly figured as the language of home in the modern, post-Haskalah period. "To be a Jew in the home and a human being in the street," as the Haskalah enjoined, meant confining the distinctive customs, appearance, and language of the Jew behind closed doors, while seeming and sounding like everyone else in public. Men writing in Yiddish sought to distance themselves from these feminized images, as Sholem Aleichem did when he established a Yiddish literary genealogy that was adamantly patrilineal, beginning with Mendele Moykher Sforim, whom he called *der zeyde* (the grandfather). The language, in other words, was coded as feminine while the literature that emerged from it was coded as masculine.[11] Yiddish expressions about storytelling also reveal a distinct gendered bias. Men are said to tell stories *tsvishn minkhe un mayrev* (between afternoon and evening prayers), a sanctioned time for study and storytelling from which women were excluded. Women, on the other hand, are said to have *nayn mos reyd* (nine measures of talk), suggesting that they talk too much.[12] When acknowledged at all, women writers tended to be admitted into the Yiddish literary canon as writers of verse, not of prose.

The question of "women's writing"—what, how, and why women wrote—worried many of Molodovsky's contemporaries, and they propagated the notion that women were more sensitive than men or more likely to write love poetry. In her writing and public statements, she dismissed such beliefs, which recalled to her the presence of the women's section in synagogues; women might peer out behind a curtain and watch the public world of men, but their voices were not allowed to cross that barrier. She disdained the notion of "women's literature," and dismissed the idea that one could discern a "woman's voice" in literary texts. This is evident in her 1955 interview with the Yiddish critic Avrom Tabachnik when, despite his insistent questions, she rejected such terms, referring to articles she had written decades earlier in response to no doubt well-meaning calls by famous male poets for the inclusion of women in considerations of Yiddish literature.[13] In 1915, the young poet Aaron Glanz (1889–1966) lamented the absence of a female presence in Yiddish literature; women, he claimed, were more intuitive and emotional and thus a necessary addition to men's voices.[14] Melekh Ravitch (1893–1976) wrote an essay entitled "Meydlekh, froyen, vayber—yidishe dikhterins" (Girls, women, wives—Yiddish poetesses) in 1927. Ravitch sexualized his praise of women writers, explicitly referring to chastity, seduction, flirtation, and fecundity.[15] In the next issue of the same journal, Molodovsky rejected such terms with the sarcastically titled "Meydlekh, froyen, vayber, un . . . nevue" (Girls, women, wives, and . . . prophecy).[16] In 1928, Ezra Korman published an anthology of poetry devoted to *Yidishe dikhterins* (Yiddish poetesses).[17] Responding in 1936 to a number of articles and cultural events honoring women writers, Molodovsky dismissed such events as condescending and accused them of marginalizing women's writings. She saw the feminine ending added to *writer* and *poet* as patronizing, relegating women to the status of "tsarte, oftmol ekzotishe blumen in literarishn gortn" (dainty, often exotic flowers in the literary garden).[18] Increasingly frightening events in Europe would soon overshadow questions about the role of women in Yiddish literature, but for decades they mattered deeply to Molodovsky and other Yiddish writers.[19]

Contrary to her male colleagues' expectations, Molodovsky's own oeuvre extends well beyond gendered categories. In addition to publishing collections of poetry, she was the author of novels, memoirs, plays, essays, and reviews. A prominent figure among modern Yiddish writers in Poland, Russia, the United States, and Israel, she also has the distinction of being the only woman in the history of Yiddish literature to edit a major literary journal, *Svive*, published as a bimonthly in New York from January/February 1943 to April/May 1944 and then again as a quarterly from November 1960 to September 1974. From 1934 to 1936, she served as editor of the literary pages of the Warsaw Communist daily *Fraynt* (Friend), and from 1950 to 1952 of *Heym: dos vort fun der arbetndiker froy in Yisroel* (Home: The word of the working woman in Israel) in Tel Aviv.[20]

In keeping with Molodovsky's polemical and professional stance, *A Jewish Refugee in New York* also challenges us to contemplate questions of genre and gender. The novel invites a reconsideration of fragmented or nonlinear genres like diaries, letters, and poetry as being somehow particularly apt for women writers because they do not presuppose a coherent, expansive consideration of the sociohistorical milieu in which they were written—a milieu that women have been said to inhabit only in the margins, as it were. Molodovsky's novel rejects all such essentialist, marginalizing categorizations. This novel asserts its dual focus on journalistic and fictional writing from the moment we encounter its title and geographical expanse and from its original table of contents, which cited not dates but chapter headings, as they would appear in a novel. Conversations are not paraphrased but recorded verbatim, echoing the conventions of novel writing rather than those of diaries in which such a precise memory would be suspect. (English novel readers may be reminded of the equally impossibly precise recall, conveyed in the present tense, found in the letters of Samuel Richardson's *Pamela* or *Clarissa*.) The work's self-proclaimed designation as a *togbukh*—literally, a daybook—does not mean that there are daily entries recording the diarist's movements. In the first and final months of writing, Rivke skips days, and at one point late in the work, a two-week period. Facing the Yiddish title in the printed book is an English translation that reads: "From Lublin to New York: Diary of Rivke Zilberg." I have chosen to translate *togbukh* as *journal* instead of *diary* in order to distance the novel from the too-familiar sting of "women's genres." Both journal and diary derive from *day* (the former through the French *jour* or Old French *jurnal*, and the latter through the Latin *dies* or *diarium*), but a journal is generally regarded as a more contemplative genre, less a compendium of the day's activities and more an analysis of actions, feelings, and events—just what Molodovsky aims at in this work.

Consider, in juxtaposition, the most famous "daybook" (*dagboekbrieven* in Dutch) of the twentieth century, *The Diary of Anne Frank*, a work begun the year in which Molodovsky's novel was published.[21] Anne Frank addressed her writing to "Dear Kitty" (and in its earliest entries, to other names as well) and crafted it for a broader audience she hoped would read it after the war. Unlike a diary one writes for oneself, thirteen-year-old Frank always had a public audience in mind. Its petty details and confessional musings, its soul-searching questions and descriptions of daily life were not just the product of self-reflection but were self-conscious stories constructed for that audience. Her writing bore witness to the experiences of a particular time and place—and to an author's desire to communicate that experience to hoped-for readers. This, too, is the kind of text we have in *A Jewish Refugee in New York*. Deliberately blurring the fictive and memoirist modes, Molodovsky offers a view of the material and inner life of its central figure—her feelings and thoughts about work, money, fashion, and Jewish Americans and the yearning for the physical reality of a home. Addressed to an audience that, its author hoped, would care about these things and respond to them sympathetically and pragmatically, the book is an invocation of the power of memory alongside a call to action. For Molodovsky herself, "action" took the form of Zionist and socialist causes and work for social and educational reform. The evidence of this book also made it clear that immigration reform was necessary and that much more must be done not only to evoke sympathy for the Jews caught up in the Nazis' horror but also to aid them in more substantive ways.

* * *

More than a decade after the publication of *Fun Lublin biz Nyu-york*, Molodovsky returned to Rivke Zilberg. Her play *A hoyz af grend strit* (A house on Grand Street) was a dramatic reworking of Rivke's story. It premiered on October 9, 1953, at the President Theater on West Forty-Ninth Street in Manhattan and was favorably reviewed by English-language publications including *Variety* and the *New York Times*.[22] Molodovsky also wrote a column about famous women for the daily Yiddish newspaper *Forverts* (Forward) using the name Rivke Zilberg. Entitled Portretn fun froyen (Portraits of women), Rivke Zilberg's column appeared between 1954 and 1956. In using the same name for the young protagonist and the older columnist, Molodovsky seems to hint at what the twenty-year-old refugee might have become ten or fifteen years later: a journalist and an intellectual interested in questions about the condition of women. The column, like much of Molodovsky's poetry, has a protofeminist perspective that the novel seemed to share, though in a less developed or articulate way. Note, for example, the younger Rivke's musings in her August 6 journal entry asking why her grandfather is remembered and praised by all who knew him whereas her grandmother is entirely ignored.

It may be tempting to see the name Rivke Zilberg as a pseudonym used by Molodovsky to distance the poet and novelist from occasional journalistic essays. Yiddish writers often used pseudonyms to distinguish their fiction from nonfiction. (Isaac Bashevis Singer is only one of many famous examples.) But Molodovsky had written and would continue to write essays under her own name. Rivke Zilberg can be better understood as a persona—a character created and developed by Molodovsky over several years—rather than a pseudonym.[23] (Again, examples in Yiddish literature abound; Sholem Aleichem and Mendele Moykher Sforim are the most familiar of them.) A pseudonym ostensibly disguises the identity of the author, but it is often the worst kept secret in the Yiddish literary world and thus erases the distinction between the biographical author and the putative author of the piece. If Zilberg, the columnist, and Molodovsky, the novelist, are merely two names for the same person, then the earlier novel is more likely to be seen as a semiautobiographical work.[24] Understanding instead that Rivke is a persona resists the conflation of the novel's immature young woman with the renowned author. Although they share a country (but not city) of origin, Molodovsky was twice Rivke's age when she came to the United States. She came before the war, when she was forty-one years old, and she wrote the novel seven years later, but not as a self-portrait of the artist as a young woman. Rivke's writing is compelling because of her subject, but she is not a literary stylist. Her text is full of repetitions, digressions, shifts in tense, short, choppy sentences, and ellipses. She often omits necessary paragraph breaks and quotation marks (which I have reinserted in this translation). She expresses no interest in the craft of writing or in varying modes of expression, though she expresses acute awareness of the difficulties of learning a language. Rivke is writing the kind of genre—the journal—that Molodovsky, the novelist, essayist and poet, did not write. Her story ends with her impending marriage, though Molodovsky's certainly does not. Conflating the author and the character risks diminishing the imaginative work of novel writing and removing Molodovsky from any canon of Yiddish novelists, confining her, instead, to those genres assumed to be more appropriate to literature written by and for women.

Still, Rivke shares a number of recurring concerns that Molodovsky expresses in her letters, essays, and poems. Both character and author shared the immigrant's infantilizing experience of being unable to express themselves in English. Central to this story, and a particular challenge for translation, is Molodovsky's careful attention to the nuances of English words and to Rivke's struggle to acquire a new language. A foreignized English—transliterated into Yiddish—appears on nearly every page of this 280-page book, sometimes translated into Yiddish and sometimes left to be understood by context alone. Molodovsky thus presents her reader with challenges similar to the ones faced by her main character, who arrives in New York knowing no English and uncertain of her ability to learn it. I have sought to maintain that foreignness in this translation, transliterating English words found in the original Yiddish not with standard Yiddish transliteration, but by reproducing the sounds so that English readers can experience the words Rivke would have heard or misheard as she tried to learn this new language. For example, the word *crazy* is here rendered as *krayzee*, *party* as *partee*, *cake* as *kayk*, and so on. The English words Rivke attempts to understand and learn, her difficulties reading the endlessly foreign signs—linguistic and nonlinguistic alike—are mirrored by our own experience of reading her journal and, no doubt, by Molodovsky's own immigrant experience.

Indeed, archival sources hold ample evidence in the form of grammar lessons, exercise books, and letters that make evident Molodovsky's struggles upon arriving in the United States in 1935 and her determination to learn a new language. Molodovsky used composition notebooks for her language drills, labeling the pages "conversation, pronunciation, vocabulary, grammar." On one side of the pages of these composition books, we find language exercises; on the other side, neatly clipped and pasted, are the serialized pages of her novel *Zeydes un eyniklekh*, gathered together as if in preparation for the book publication that never appeared. Writing in a neat though labored hand, slanting her letters to the left, Molodovsky practiced *th* sounds by writing "mouse-mouth; frill-thrill; tick-thick; tie-thigh; lather, leather, ladder," and so forth. Her vocabulary exercises included definitions and sentences for words such as *fickle*, *clutch*, *wizened*, and *shabby*. She practiced tenses and idioms ("I shall, we shall, you will"; "My books lie here every day. The baby lay on the floor yesterday. My coat has lain there all day.") She reminded herself about the use of prepositions—the part of speech that is most difficult to master in another language ("angry at things; annoyed with people").[25] (See figs. 0.2–0.4.) Her character, Rivke, is not nearly as systematic in her studies, though she is equally committed to understanding and being understood in English.

Fig. 0.1 Kadya Molodovsky, circa 1930s. Reprinted by permission of YIVO Institute for Jewish Research.

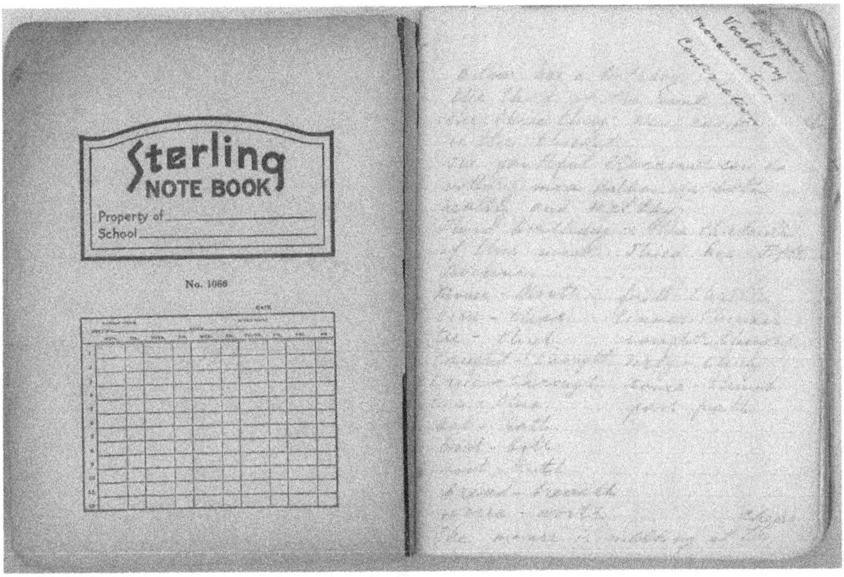

Fig. 0.2 Inside cover and first page of Molodovsky's English exercise book. Reprinted by permission of YIVO Institute for Jewish Research.

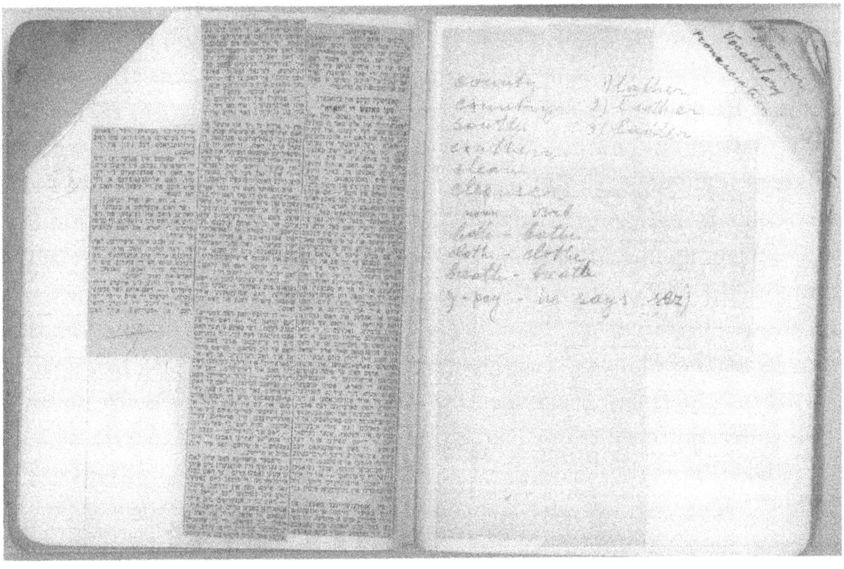

Fig. 0.3 Molodovsky's English exercises with facing page of clippings from the novel *Zeydes un eyniklekh*. Reprinted by permission of YIVO Institute for Jewish Research.

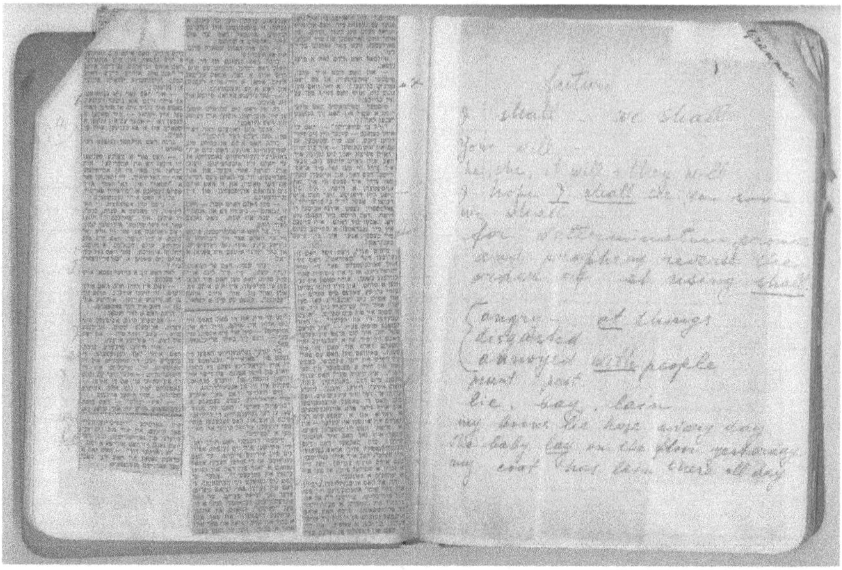

Fig. 0.4 Molodovsky's English exercises with facing page of clippings from the novel *Zeydes un eyniklekh*. Reprinted by permission of YIVO Institute for Jewish Research.

Alongside the struggles with language that she and her protagonist share, Molodovsky lamented the uncertainty and despair wrought by the situation in Europe and explored the sense of disorientation caused by immigration. Just months before her death, Molodovsky wrote that the difficulties faced by immigrants was one of her main concerns in *Fun Lublin biz Nyu-york*. "I knew how hard it was to get used to a new milieu, with an unknown language. In those days it was a desirable subject because those who came from Europe struggled hard before they were able to fit into this new environment."[26] In addition to learning English, Rivke must learn the mores of her new culture, including the expectations of women in the United States. She discovers that it is easier to find a husband than a job, that movies are the arbiters of relationships, and that she must learn how to flirt. To her bewilderment, American Jews and the world they inhabit are radically different from the one left behind.

Rivke Zilberg's journal does not explicitly engage the questions about Yiddish, genre, and gender I have outlined here, focusing instead on the pressing personal and historical crises with which she must grapple. But Molodovsky does engage them, and they are a significant part of the story she is telling. In *A Jewish Refugee in New York*, she addresses an extraordinary range of issues concerning immigration, the Holocaust, displacement, economics, language, romance, acculturation, and more. The novel asks us to consider the meaning of *home* and *domesticity*—purportedly the concern of women—and suggests that establishing or reestablishing a home is both a domestic and a sociopolitical act. The novel, in which we encounter one young woman's struggles with these questions, exposes the social, political, and cultural tensions of the time and place in which it was written—and of our own. These tensions, too, are part of the *yerushe*—the legacy—of the past. But Molodovsky's writing also asks us to consider the ethics and ideals we may inherit: the legacy of Jewish learning and culture, of social commitments and political strategies, of ethics, and of humane and humanistic values.

Notes

1. At the outbreak of the war, Jews constituted about one-third of Lublin's population of more than 120,000 people. In Lublin province, the Nazis would build the infamous Majdenek concentration camp in late 1941.

2. Avrom Golomb, "Shtiler, a mentsh iz untergegangen" [Quieter, someone has gone under], *Afn shvel* [At the threshold], May–June 1942, 9. "Zi hot derzen dem gantsn tragishn elnt fun amerikaner yidn, dem tifn, tifn tsar un shtume benkenish, vos bahalt zikh hinter di dray yesoydos fun yidishn lebn do: makhn gelt, oysbrengen gelt, un 'gut taym' fun 'parties,' muvies, kortn."

3. In addition to the novel, works published by Papirene brik include Molodovsky's *Der meylekh Dovid aleyn iz geblibn* [Only King David remained] (1946), *Nokhn got fun midber: drame* [After the god of the desert: a play] (1949), and *In yerushalayim kumen malokhim: lider* [Angels come to Jerusalem: poems] (1952).

4. I have addressed those writings in my book *Discovering Exile: Yiddish and Jewish American Literature during the Holocaust* (Stanford: Stanford University Press, 2007).

5. "Kadya Molodovsky (a por verter tsu ir opforn keyn amerike)" [Kadya Molodovsky (a few words on the occasion of her trip to America)], *Literarishe bleter* [Literary pages], June 14, 1935.

6. "El khanun," *Der yidisher kemfer* [The Jewish fighter], October 13, 1944, 3.

7. These novels are cited in a Hebrew MA thesis written under the direction of Avrom Nowerstern: Amir Shomroni, "Kadya Molodovsky: Amerike b'yetsirata b'shanim, 1935–1954" [Kadya Molodovsky: America in her writings between 1935 and 1954] (master's thesis, Hebrew University of Jerusalem, 2014). I thank them, as well as Kathryn Hellerstein and Zelda Newman, for graciously providing valuable resources.

8. *Di yerushe*, *Svive*, May–June and November–December, 1943; *Di yerushe*, *Der yidisher kemfer*, sporadically, February 18, 1944–February 2, 1945; *Di yerushe*, Molodovsky archive, YIVO Institute for Jewish Research, New York, RG703, folder 119.

9. *Zeydes un eyniklekh, Morgn-zhurnal,* October 13–December 28, 1948.

10. "In yisroel un tsurik in amerike" [In Israel and back in America], Molodovsky archive, YIVO Institute for Jewish Research, New York, RG703, folder 64.

11. See Naomi Seidman, *A Marriage Made in Heaven* (Berkeley: University of California Press, 1997); and Kathryn Hellerstein, *A Question of Tradition: Women Poets in Yiddish, 1586–1987* (Stanford: Stanford University Press, 2014). See also Anita Norich, "Yiddish Literature in the United States," in *Jewish Women: A Comprehensive Historical Encyclopedia,* Jewish Women's Archive, March 20, 2009, https://jwa.org/encyclopedia/article/yiddish-literature-in-united-states; Norich, "Jewish Literatures and Feminist Criticism: An Introduction," in *Gender and Text in Modern Hebrew and Yiddish Literature,* ed. Naomi Sokoloff, Anne Lerner, and Anita Norich, 1–15 (New York: Jewish Theological Seminary, 1992); and Irena Klepfisz, "Di Mames, dos Loshn/The Mothers, the Language: Feminism, *Yidishkayt,* and the Politics of Memory," *Bridges* 4, no. 1 (Winter/Spring 1994): 12–47.

12. The expression comes from the Talmud (Kiddushin 49b), which says "Ten measures of talk came down into the world; women took nine and the rest of the world took one."

13. The interview was conducted at the Jewish Public Library of Montreal and digitized by the National Yiddish Book Center. There is no date on the book center's recording, but the original tapes, in Tabachnik's handwriting, carry the date 1955. My thanks to Saul Hankin for tracking down the date. See "Kadia Molodowsky: A Conversation with Abraham Tabachnick," Yiddish Book Center, accessed October 12, 2014, https://www.yiddishbookcenter.org/collections/archival-recordings/fbr-188_4188 (original interview at Montreal Jewish Library, 1955).

14. Aaron Glanz, "Kultur un di froy" [Culture and women], *Di fraye arbeter shtime,* October 30, 1915.

15. Melekh Ravitch, "Meydlekh, froyen, vayber—yidishe dikhterins" [Girls, women, wives—Yiddish poetesses], *Literarishe bleter,* May 27, 1927, 395–96.

16. Kadya Molodovsky, "Meydlekh, froyen, vayber, un . . . nevue" [Girls, women, wives, and . . . prophecy], *Literarishe bleter,* June 3, 1927, 416.

17. Ezra Korman, *Yidishe dikhterins* [Yiddish poetesses] (Chicago: L. M. Shtayn, 1928).

18. Kadya Molodovksy, "A por verter vegn froyen dikhterins" [A few words about women poetesses], *Signal* 6, June 1936, 23.

19. It would take decades before critics returned to these questions. In 1966, Shmuel Rozhansky published *Di froy in der yidisher poezye* [The woman in Yiddish poetry] as volume 29 of his *Musterverk fun der yidisher literatur,* a monumental project of canon formation. This volume included 136 poets, of whom about one-third were women. In 1973, Ber Grin, using the same title as Ezra Korman, published a series of articles presenting short biographical and bibliographical information about twenty-four women poets. See Korman, *Yidishe dikhterins*; Ber Grin, Yidishe dikhterins [Yiddish poetesses], *Yidishe kultur,* December 1973, January 1974, March 1974, April–May 1974; Shmuel Rozhansky, ed., *Di froy in der yidisher poezye* [The woman in Yiddish poetry], vol. 29, *Musterverk fun der yidisher literatur* (Buenos Aires: Kultur Kongres, 1966).

20. Biographical and bibliographical sources include Anna Fishman Gonshor, "Kadye Molodovsky in *Literarishe Bleter,* 1925–35: Annotated Bibliography" (master's thesis, McGill University, 1997); Kathryn Hellerstein, *Paper Bridges: Selected Poems of Kadya Molodowsky* (Detroit: Wayne State University Press, 1999); Berl Kagan, *Leksikon fun yidish shraybers* [Encyclopedia of Yiddish writers] (New York: R. Ilman-Kohen, 1986); "Kadia Molodowsky:

A Conversation with Abraham Tabachnick"; Zelda Newman, "The Molodowsky-Korn Correspondence," *Women in Judaism: A Multidisciplinary Journal* 8, no. 1 (Spring 2011): 1–26; Newman, "Kadya Molodowsky: Clearing the Mist," *Mendele Review* 12, no. 11 (May 18, 2008), http://yiddish.haifa.ac.il/tmr/tmr12/tmr12011.htm#12; Shomroni, "Kadya Molodovsky"; and Molodovsky's memoir, *Fun mayn elter-zeydes yerushe* [From my great-grandfather's legacy], *Svive*, 1965–1974. Archival materials including letters and manuscripts can be found at YIVO Institute for Jewish Research, New York, and the Lavon (Labor Zionist) Archive, Tel Aviv.

21. In its first Dutch publication in 1947, the work was entitled *Het Achterhuis: Dagboek-brieven 14 Juni 1942–1 Augustus 1944* [The annex: daybook letters, June 14, 1942–August 1, 1944] (Amsterdam: Contact Publishing, 1947).

22. "Yiddish Plays: House on Grand Street," *Variety*, October 14, 1953, 92; "Entertaining Yiddish Drama by Kadia Molodowsky Has Premiere at the President Theatre," *New York Times*, October 10, 1953, 12. In addition to playing on Broadway—a unique venue for Yiddish theatrical productions—*A hoyz af grend strit* was read on WEVD, the Yiddish-speaking radio station in New York. Manuscripts can be found in the Lavon Archive and YIVO.

23. Previous bibliographies that have mentioned this column have mistakenly attributed it to sometime in the 1940s, perhaps leading to the view of Rivke Zilberg as a pseudonym.

24. In a review of the novel, the Yiddish critic Shmuel Niger referred to Rivke as Kadya Molodovsky's "alter ego"; see Shmuel Niger, *Der tog* [The day], May 16, 1942, 4. Zelda Newman calls the novel "a fictive biography" that may be seen "as in some sense Molodovsky's own story"; see Newman, "Kadya Molodowsky: Clearing the Mist."

25. Molodovsky archive, YIVO Institute for Jewish Research, New York, folder 147. On the cover of the first notebook is one of the few uses of her married name: "Mrs. K. Lew, 62 E. 170th Street, Bronx." (The second notebook is under the name K. Molodowsky.) A different, more poignant use of her married name is in a certificate issued when she completed her English class: "This is to certify that Kadia Lew attended classes in English to the Foreign Born at P.S. 149, Sutter and Vermont St., January to July 1941 for 200 hours" (see folder 173 in the same archive).

26. Molodovsky archive, YIVO Institute for Jewish Research, New York, RG703, folder 64. When published in *Svive*, this sentence was changed as follows: "Es iz mir geleygn afn hartsn der ibergang fun ayn land in a tsveytn land un di shverkayt fun tsupasn zikh tsu naye badingungen" [The difficulties of going from one country to another and of fitting into new conditions lay heavy on my heart]. Molodovsky, *Fun mayn elter-zeydes yerushe* [From my great-grandfather's legacy], *Svive*, no. 38, January 1973, 59.

A JEWISH REFUGEE IN NEW YORK

My First Day in New York

December 15, 1939

I arrived on a beautiful day. Perhaps this was a sign that things would go well for me in America.

My aunt looks just like my mother, may she rest in peace, but her smile is not as nice as my mother's was. My uncle is silent and doesn't seem so happy that I've come. Selma is exactly my age and height. She spoke a few Yiddish words to me today: "How are you feeling?" and "You're my cousin." She says that she doesn't know more Yiddish than that. Marvin is eighteen years old. All he said was *hallo* and then he left the house. My aunt looked over my things, and she and Selma laughed at my stockings, shirts, and dresses. In Lublin I was well dressed. Will I always be laughed at in America?

My aunt picked up all of my dresses and said, "Rags! We need to buy her a *dres* and a *het*." I could barely keep from crying. They greeted me as though I were some poor relative. Maybe it would have been better if I had stayed at home. I don't know what I'll do here. They all speak English, and I don't understand a word. I think they're talking about me, and it's as if, at the age of twenty, I've suddenly become deaf.

This evening, some neighbors came over to hear about the "old country." They all had painted cheeks and painted lips. It's not a nice thing to say, but to me they all looked like loose women. Even forty- and fifty-year-old women wear makeup here. Every one of them talked about her home, asking me very little. It seems that they were interested in me only so that they could have an audience for their own stories about the old country.

One of the neighbors, who my aunt calls Betty or Mrs. Shore, told a story about how she lost her fiancé on the way to America. She spoke lightheartedly about being on the ship with her fiancé and a family from Bessarabia. The family had been traveling with a lot of hard cheese and shared it with their ship brothers and sisters. Her fiancé didn't like the cheese at first but then he became very fond of it, and from time to time he would disappear, finding his way to the Bessarabian family with the tasty cheese. The woman in that family was a twenty-eight- or thirty-year-old widow whose husband had died in America, and she and her two children were going to join her father-in-law there. She liked to laugh, and she liked to treat Betty's fiancé to cheese, calling him the nosher, the cheese-snacker. She promised him a cheesy paradise. Betty used to laugh along with her Bessarabian ship sister, but in New York it became clear that her intended bridegroom had become restless. He often went off on his own, and he finally told Betty that he didn't want to get married just yet; he was too young and unsettled. In the end, he married that Bessarabian woman! Mrs. Shore told the story without bitterness. I wondered about that a lot. I would certainly have been too embarrassed to breathe a word of it if such a thing had happened to me, but Betty just bragged that her former fiancé was as poor today as he had been then and that she had escaped from a bad situation.

The women talked a lot about themselves and didn't give me the slightest opportunity to tell them how I came to be a refugee. Mrs. Shore's story really upset me. I think it can't be a good sign that the very first story I heard in America was about cheating and misfortune. Who knows what will become of me here?

Some People's Sweetness

December 20

Today I noticed, quite by accident, that my aunt was watering down my *orandg juws*. I was standing opposite the mirror and saw how she added some water into one of the glasses and then handed me that very glass. "Drink," she said, "orange juice is good for you." But it certainly was not good for me. I could barely swallow it. My mother, may she rest in peace, used to say that the bitterest things that come from God are better than the sweetest from people. So, today's orange juice really was my taste of someone's sweetness.

I have one more thing to write about today: Marvin can speak Yiddish, but I can't figure out what kind of Yiddish it is. Yesterday, he left his shoes near my bed, and when he came to pick them up this morning, he said something I couldn't really understand: *"Dos iz a khazeray."* It's a mess. What could he have meant? Did he think I would shine his shoes? Whatever it was that he meant, he said it in some sort of incomprehensible Yiddish. My aunt answered him in English. I heard the word *shee* several times. Marvin and my aunt kept *shee*-ing. *"Shee"* and *"shee"* and again *"shee."* I'll ask Mrs. Shore what *shee* means. I thought they were talking about the shoes and about me because after their conversation my aunt turned to me and smiled, saying "Rivke, go eat something."

If only I wasn't a refugee!

Eddie

December 25

I saw Selma's *boy* today. He's tall and thin, and his pants are very neatly pressed. When we were introduced, he said a few words in Yiddish: "How do you like America?" (Everybody asks the same thing.) He talks like a gentile, just like Pan Stefanovski, who used to come to my father to discuss business matters and would try to start a Yiddish conversation with me. I started laughing when I remembered Pan Stefanovski. My aunt said, "Better you should learn English, Rivke, and not laugh like that. You're not in Lublin. Here everybody speaks English." Selma's *boy* defended me. I didn't understand what he said, but I saw that he kept looking at me and smiling. I really liked that, and I was sorry when he and Selma left to go to the *moovees.*

My aunt said that she would register me in a *skool* so I can learn English.

I met Mrs. Shore on the staircase today and I asked her what *shee* means. She told me that a girl is *shee*, a boy is *hee*, and *iy* refers to me. So they really were talking about me, and Marvin really did want me to polish his shoes. No, I won't do that! Who does he think he is? He's putting on airs, but he can shine his own shoes.

The New Year

January 1

Last night everyone went out to *hev a gud tiym.* My aunt and uncle went to play cards at Mrs. Shore's apartment. Selma and her *boy* went off to dance.

Marvin went to Times Square. I didn't want to go anywhere. It's a dreadful day for me. A year ago my mother was alive. She made potato pancakes for us, but not because it was New Year's Day. We never made a big deal about New Year's. She made them because Uncle Zaydl had come to take us out on a sleigh ride. Mama, may she rest in peace, didn't want to let him go without some food. "Food?" Uncle Zaydl said. "If we're talking food, then let's have some potato pancakes." So . . . we ate potato pancakes. In the end, we didn't really have such a good time. As soon as we got onto the broad street, our sleigh was attacked by snow. At first we thought we were being stoned, but then it turned out that they were snowballs thrown by some hooligans, may a plague strike them, who were cursing and whistling at us. We turned back home all wet and dirty. Uncle Zaydl wished them a miserable end, and I nearly cried out of disappointment. But still, there was a home with a mother, with Lublin, and also with Layzer. I never imagined then that within a year I would be in a strange house, alone, living on charity, or that I wouldn't even know what happened to my father, my brother, or my home. I never imagined that I would be a refugee. What a horrible word: *refugee*. The word is a curse. It probably comes from *refuse*, garbage. A refugee is truly cursed, discarded, and worthless. In any case, I didn't go anywhere today. For me, this New Year is not a time for celebration. It would have been better if the last New Year had never ended—or perhaps had ended for me as it did for my mother, may she rest in peace.

A Comfort

January 5

For the last few days my aunt and uncle have been talking to one another in English and often using the word *shee*. I already know that they're talking about me: *Shee. Shee.* It seems that they've decided to dismiss the colored girl who comes every day to do housework. Today my aunt gave me some washing to do—dresses, slips, and socks that belong to her, Selma, and me. She helped me, but I felt as if I were becoming a maid in the house. The work wasn't hard, but my heart felt as heavy as a stone. My aunt said that the girl was ill and it was impossible to know when she would be able to return to work. I would rather have washed the cobblestone streets back home than be here washing Selma's dresses. And often I think about the fact that I have no idea what's going on at home now. Maybe being here and washing dresses using something called Lux is really a paradise because my home in Lublin is now a hellish place. My one comfort is that I'm going to *skool*. The teacher there often comes over to my desk to look at my writing. I think she must be a Jew, but I can't ask her that. Other than a few words that we learned in *skool*, I still can't speak English. It's such a hard language to learn. Who knows if I'll ever be able to speak it?

Mendl Pushcart

January 8

The cleaning girl still hasn't returned. She's sick, and no one knows when she'll be well. Yesterday there was a *kard partey* here. My uncle becomes a totally different person when he plays cards. He talks and makes jokes. Maybe he was in such a good mood because he won a dollar. I served tea because my aunt said, "Since you don't play cards, you can at least bring tea to the table; a person has to do something." Mendl Pushcart bothered me more than anyone else. (I'm using his name on purpose; let there be no mistake about who I mean.) He drank at least five or six or even more glasses of tea. He poured it in as if into a well, and every single time, he winked at me to signal that I should bring more. He treated me as if he was paying me a salary, and I started to hate him as much as I hate even the thought of pork. I came to understand that you never know what a person can turn into.

Besides drinking tea, Mendl Pushcart told stories. He never let anyone else get a word in; words just poured out of him constantly. He told everyone about the award his daughter received for playing the violin and how people made a fuss over her after every concert. He said she was now the greatest musical connoisseur and that all the great music professors came to her for advice. Then he said that his daughter, the very same violinist, can fry *peetches* better than anyone in the world and that professors take it as a great honor to be invited to taste her *peetches*. If he only had the money that he had spent on his daughter's studies, he would now be a very rich man and wouldn't be living on Grand Street. Then he said that twenty years ago, before they came to America, his daughter spoke Russian fluently. Once, a general wanted to arrest her because she was traveling without a passport. When she said to him, "Your Excellency, a good person is always good," the general was so pleased with her that he shook her hand. Mendl Pushcart's face shone and drops of sweat formed on his forehead when he told these stories.

In the beginning, I believed him, but then, when he kept winking at me about the tea, I realized what kind of man he was, and I didn't believe another word that came out of his mouth. By his sixth glass of tea, I couldn't take it anymore, and when he winked at me again and then at his glass, I don't know where I got the nerve, but I addressed him just as his daughter had addressed the general—"Your Excellency," and then I added, "go get your own tea." Everyone burst out laughing, and it was my aunt who went to get him tea. Mendl Pushcart looked at me and said, "Aha, she's not so green after all." I felt as if I was about to cry, and to keep everyone from seeing it, I left the room and went to bed. I couldn't sleep because my heart was pounding. When my aunt came in, bringing me a piece of orange, she saw the tears pouring from my eyes. "*Don' bee foolish*," she said, and she left the room. What does that mean? Are these curse words or words of comfort? Who knows what this means in America?

The World Is Not Entirely Closed to Me

January 10

I just got back from going to the *moovees* with Selma and her *boy*. He brought complimentary *tikets* and invited me to join them. Selma had no choice, adding, "Come, what do you have to lose?" But I saw that she was not at all pleased. When Selma gets annoyed, her chin falls and seems to swell, and her mouth turns down even though she's smiling. I saw it all on her face. My aunt was silent. They started fixing me up to go to the movies. I put on my *dres*, and Selma lent me one of her hats. She said: "You see, Ma, it even looks good on Rivke." I pretended not to hear or understand because if I paid attention to everything that people said, I'd have to pack up and leave this house. Where would I go? To Lublin? To my mother in her grave? The *boy* walked between me and Selma, with Selma holding onto his arm. I walked alongside, but then he took my arm also. Selma looked at us but didn't say a word. Once again, I saw how her chin fell and her face got wider. It doesn't make her look good; in fact, she looks really ugly.

The *boy*'s name is Eddie. He and Selma spoke English, and I kept silent the entire time. But Eddie smiled at me nicely and said, "You don't understand." Selma said she was tired and didn't want to go out for ice cream, so we went home. Today, my heart is a little lighter. It feels as if the world is not entirely closed to me.

The Anniversary of My Grandfather's Death

January 20

Today is the anniversary of my grandfather's death. My aunt lit a tall memorial candle in the kitchen so that it could burn for the whole day. She walked around sighing, remembering her father. Maybe that's why I felt closer to her and the house seemed homier. It was clear that she felt something too, and she even cried about my mother's death. "This is how," she said, "a family is destroyed." As she stood there wiping her nose with a flowered handkerchief, she seemed more like a woman from Lublin than one of these New York women. But in the middle of the day, she combed her hair, put on rouge and lipstick as usual, and went out. I stayed home to clean the apartment. The cleaning girl has not returned; she seems to be eternally ill.

Just as my aunt left, Mrs. Shore came in. It's hard to tell if she's a good person or not, but she's certainly an odd one. "What's this? Your colored girl isn't coming anymore?" she asked. When I told her she was sick, Mrs. Shore snorted, barely containing her laughter. "So, there are no other colored girls in the United States? Never mind. Your aunt just wants to save money since she's supporting a refugee in her home." She said that and then she took a cigarette out of her purse and smoked it. Mrs. Shore smokes and exhales slowly through her nostrils. Since I don't smoke, she gave me *tchuinkgum* instead, saying that chewing it helps calm the nerves when times are hard. And as she said that, she winked at me knowingly. I've noticed that when Americans tell you something that's hard to take or when they do something nasty, they sweeten it afterward with a piece of orange or this *tchuinkgum*. That's what both my aunt and Mrs. Shore do.

Selma

January 24

Selma was really nervous today, and my uncle was even more quiet than usual. I like him better than anyone in the house. Even though my aunt is my mother's (may she rest in peace) sister, he feels closer to me than she does. He's not a sullen man, even though he rarely speaks except when he's playing cards. At home, in Lublin, he was considered learned and even had rabbinical training. But he didn't want to be a rabbi, and he left for America. Here, he's an insurance agent, but I still think it would be more fitting for him to be a rabbi.

Selma suddenly starting crying today. When she got dressed to go out, she just couldn't decide whether to put on black shoes or brown ones or yellow ones. My uncle, smiling knowingly, just like a rabbi, said, "That would be a difficult question even for our sages." He shook his head, saying, "If the head isn't working, the shoes won't help." My aunt yelled, "Leave the child alone. This isn't Europe!" Selma cried. I don't understand the whole mess, but there's something going on in the house that I don't know about that concerns Selma.

Seventy-Five Cents a Day (I Want to Cry)

January 25

Marvin has decided to learn how to dance like Benny Goodman. He turns on the radio and dances for hours on end. He changes channels and dances. Dances and changes channels. It gives me a headache. When he dances, all I can think about is that my mother was killed by a bomb, and I don't know what's happening with my brothers, although I'm sure they're not dancing now. I have no idea what's become of my father either. I'd go to the ends of the earth to avoid Marvin's dancing, but where can I go?

In the evening Mrs. Shore came to visit and once again gave me chewing gum while I waited for her to ask, "Still no cleaning girl?" A little later she said, "I met your girl on the street today. She's not sick at all, but your aunt wants to save the seventy-five cents she pays her daily and *dat's awl*. Rivke, if you'd like to come to me, I'd actually pay you. Why not? I wouldn't have to worry about anything being stolen." I don't know if I slipped on something or if my legs just gave out, but at that very moment I fell down. I didn't hurt myself, but I really felt like crying. My aunt came and said something in English to which Mrs. Shore immediately replied with a lie: "I think that *nees* of yours is homesick." My aunt saw that I was really upset, and when she felt my head, she said that it was hot. I lay down and took some aspirin, and I was grateful that my aunt said I was sick. I stayed in bed for the rest of the day.

A World That Disappeared

January 28

Selma cries and Marvin dances. I feel so out of place in this house. It's a good thing that I leave every evening to spend two hours in school. The teacher noticed that I was worried about something, and I guess she wanted to comfort me. "*Yur yung*," she said. It's true that I'm young, but I've lived through a lot. The teacher knows nothing of Lublin, mother, father, brothers, Layzer and our walks in the woods, Uncle Zaydl with his horse and carriage or his sleigh. Now there is nothing. I was cut off from my world, and that world disappeared. What good does it do me to be young?

Lublin Still Exists

February 2

Lublin still exists! I received a postcard from my father today. He's alive, and so is my brother. He didn't say anything about my mother, and even though I knew her fate, I was still heartbroken that there was no word about her. But Lublin is still there. The city, my home, the woods still exist. There was no word about Layzer either, and I don't know what's become of him. I try not to think about it. What is there to think about? I'll probably never see him again, but I'd still like to know if he's alive. Today, it didn't even bother me when Marvin once again left his shoes near my bed. What do I care? The postcard arrived first thing in the morning, so I polished Marvin's shoes. As long as there is once again a city, a sign of home, then my world still exists and someday I'll get rid of Marvin's shoes.

It's Friday and my aunt made gefilte fish and baked *kookees*. Here, Friday night has more of the feel of Shabbos than the Sabbath day itself. Later in the evening, they play cards, but first my aunt lights the Sabbath candles. She's worried about Selma tonight. Selma isn't well and needs an operation. She's worried too. It seems that everyone is afraid when it comes to their own lives. And what about my mother? The postcard said nothing about her. I would have wanted to at least see her resting place and read her name on a tombstone.

My Ears

February 3

My mother, may she rest in peace, used to yell at me for eavesdropping. "No one needs to know everything that's going on," she would say. But what can I do if I have the kind of ears that don't listen but still hear everything? At night, I heard my uncle in the next room, saying, "All I need is bastards in the house!" My aunt shushed him and said something in English and then I heard them once again saying *shee* this and *shee* that. This time, though, they weren't talking about me but about Selma. Something's wrong with her, and it looks like her operation is not just any operation. I think that Selma is in real trouble and that's why Eddie doesn't come around. He hasn't been here for at least ten days. Selma is my cousin, and we share a name—Sara Rivke, Selma in English. I'd like to be sympathetic, and yet I can't be. She has such nice clothing and handbags and shoes. She takes whatever she needs out of her bag: makeup, a nail file, a comb, a handkerchief, a hairpin, a brooch, a ribbon, an address. I think that no matter what happens to Selma, she'll quickly pull something out of her handbag that will help her out. Even advice or a cure can be found in her nice handbags, so how can I possibly feel sorry for her? Still, she keeps on crying. Today I heard her talking to Eddie on the telephone, repeating his name many times. I don't know what she said. English. But after her conversation she went into her room, and once again my poor ears heard her blowing her nose and crying.

At My Aunt's House on Grand Street

February 5

It's silly of me to think about Layzer, but I can't help it. I think about how we used to walk among the pine trees in the forest. Because of my father's postcard, I know that something still remains of Lublin. Maybe the pine forest is still there too. But Layzer? Where is he now? Did he go with the Poles to Romania? Is he in German hands? Maybe he's in Lublin? He had wanted to go to Palestine. Maybe he went there. Is he even alive? I'll ask my father; maybe he'll answer.

I learned some new words in school today. I understand a little English when it's spoken slowly, but when Marvin speaks, I can't understand a word.

Mrs. Shore came over again today when my aunt wasn't home. She wanted to take me to the Lublin Association. "You need to get out more," she said. "What good will it do you to sit here on Grand Street?" Mrs. Shore is an odd person. She has blue eyes, one larger than the other, and she always looks like she's squinting. She doesn't always seem like a good person, but still, when she comes over I feel better, more *heymish*, at home. Today she said to me, "You're already twenty years old. In America, you're supposed to be married by now. Here, an unmarried twenty-year-old is almost considered an old maid." And she laughed. My heart started pounding. I remembered that Layzer once promised to marry me when he got to be twenty-five and I was twenty-two. And here I'm already an old maid at twenty! I don't know if Layzer is alive. Lublin is at the other end of the world. I'm in America, living with my aunt on Grand Street, polishing shoes for Marvin. Because of me, they've let the colored girl go. Oh! I'm much older than twenty. More like thirty, forty, or even older. I'm old, very old, even though I'm exactly Selma's age. Still, Selma is to be pitied too.

I Go to Meet People from Home

February 11

Selma came home from the hospital yesterday after a two-day stay. Eddie came in the evening. He said *Hallo, Greenhorn* to me and ruffled my hair. I saw that it upset Selma. She smiled, but once again her chin fell and her face got wider. My aunt remembered that she had to go to a meeting of the Lublin Association Ladies' Society and asked me to go with her. "Come and you'll see other people from Lublin," she said. I put on my *dres*, my aunt gave me a hat, and Selma gave me a handbag. We took the subway. I just can't get used to that. The subway made me feel sick, but I didn't want to tell my aunt. I'm already too much of a greenhorn as it is. Instead, I sat with my ears ringing, and I barely made it out into the fresh air.

"Your mother—may you have a longer life—was also weak," she said to me. "I see that the subway makes you wheeze."

"No, I just don't feel well," I answered quickly. I don't even understand why I lied, but that's what I felt like saying.

We got to the meeting, and there were about fifty women there, almost all of them gray haired. There were just a few younger women and a few men. The women were dressed up with brooches on their clothes, and many had gold watches on their wrists. At home, I never saw older women dressed like that.

I don't understand why they called this *miting*. They spent almost the whole evening drinking coffee and eating cake. The chairwoman spoke in

English, and I didn't understand what she was talking about, but in the middle of it all, she'd erupt with a few Yiddish words. "Whoever doesn't obey will pay more." Or, "Leave the food for later." Or, "The best *kayk* will win a kiss." They clapped and started asking, "From who? A kiss from who?" The chairwoman explained something else to them in English and again shot out in Yiddish: "Whoever brings a bottle of Palestinian wine will certainly not be thrown out." I thought that they were getting ready for a Purim ball, but they explained that they were planning an event for war victims. I couldn't believe how happy they were. They joked and talked and ate *kayk*. No matter what's going on, there's always cake. If they're having a card party—cake; a birthday—cake; a collection for those suffering in the war—more cake. They told me that even when somebody dies, cake is served after the funeral, but I won't believe that unless I see it with my own two eyes. And the women tasted every single cake. First they had a piece of honey cake, then a piece of cheesecake, then a coffee cake, and then *kookees*. They chewed and chewed, sighing all along about how bad things were in the old country. And they chewed on that along with a piece of coffee cake. Then they played cards. All the proceeds will be sent to Lublin.

I met Khanke the baker at the meeting. I had heard lots of stories about her at home. She had once been really beautiful. She married at a very young age and then divorced her husband and took up political activities and became a great speaker and activist. She was arrested at a meeting and sent to prison, but she escaped and came to America. Khanke brought the best *kookees* to the meeting. She was delighted when I told her that people still told stories about her in Lublin. Now, she said, she could still claim to be good at something since she was the best poker player in the Lublin Association. (Poker is a card game.)

Eddie was still there when we got back home. When I stood off to one side and put Selma's hat back in its box (she keeps all her hats in boxes, and her room has a whole shelf just for hatboxes), Eddie came over to me and said in a loud voice: "So, you've seen your townspeople?" And quietly he added, "You're so pretty." It unsettled me, and I was afraid that my aunt or Selma would hear him. They didn't, but still my aunt came over to us and said, "We *endjoyet* ourselves very much." Before he left, Eddie squeezed my finger tightly, and afterward I felt the pressure of that finger for a long time, although he certainly hadn't hurt it. Still, until I fell asleep, I felt that finger burning.

A Borrowed World

February 14

Living on charity is a bitter fate. Selma doesn't look at me at all, and my aunt has become hard and stiff. She does speak to me, but it's as if she has some complaint. I don't refuse any kind of work. I clean Marvin's shoes, and I prepare the vegetables for dinner even before I'm asked. Still, it's as if the whole household has something against me. At night I even dream that I am in the middle of the room and all of them are standing around me and yelling, "Get out of this house. Get out!" Selma's double chin looks as swollen as a cow's udder. These dreams are silly, and when I awake, my heart aches, but I am happy to see that it is all a dream. Because where would I go?

My aunt must have said something to Mrs. Shore because when I met her on the staircase, it seemed like she had been waiting for me. She put her arm around my waist and invited me into her apartment, where she sat me down on the couch and made it clear that she wanted to talk to me about something very important.

On the wall opposite me, I saw a picture of a Turkish princess with a crown on her head surrounded by attendants who sat at her feet and handed her fruit. Mrs. Shore gave me some chewing gum and took a cigarette for herself. Then she said: "Listen, Rivke, in America, your best friend is the dollar, and you're your own closest relative. Why do you need to sit in your aunt's house? Selma is a girl; you're a girl. Two cats in one sack can't be good. It would be better for you to find work, and then you could have your own money and the whole world would be open to you."

I listened and felt my heart hammering. Where should I go look for work? What kind of work? I thought that if Mrs. Shore had invited me into her apartment so she could talk to me, she probably knew what she was talking about. I suddenly felt as if I were living on borrowed time. I was borrowing Mrs. Shore's couch to sit on for a while. I was borrowing my bed for a few nights. Even the stairs were borrowed so that I could go up and down a few times until I could go down without returning back up. Borrowed time is just as awful as a borrowed dress or shoes. It's not yours and has to be returned. Where on earth will I be able to find permanence? Where should I go? I don't know how long I sat with my head bowed. I didn't even notice when Mrs. Shore went into the kitchen and brought us coffee and *kookees*. She lifted my head up and said: "Don't worry; there's a big world out there."

Mrs. Rubin

February 16

I've decided that the first thing I should do is go see my mother's friend, Mrs. Rubin. At the meeting, when I told her that my mother was no longer alive, she wept. I could see that she was one of us. My aunt saw me put on my *dres* and asked me where I was going. From the way she asked, I could tell that she knew very well where I was going but was pretending not to know. I told her that I wanted to go get a library card in order to borrow books.

"Borrow books if you want books," she said in a resigned voice, "but don't come back too late."

Mrs. Rubin looked very different at home than at the meeting. First of all, she had some kind of little mechanical things all over her head that were for curling her hair. She looked like she had a whole lot of horns on her head, all over the front, back, and sides. Her face looked a lot older, and she was wearing an apron that flattened her out from top to bottom like a sack of straw. No waist, no bust, no sides, nothing. A big sack of straw with horns on top and a pair of slippers below. She was surprised to see that I had come alone, leaving my aunt at home in the middle of a busy Friday. I waited for her to speak again of her friendship with my mother, may she rest in peace. If she had, it would have been easier to tell her that I needed to ask her a favor, that I needed her to help me find a job. But, as if in spite, she didn't say a word about my mother, speaking only of my aunt and what a good woman she was and how lucky I was that she had taken me in. I couldn't find an opportunity to speak openly to her. It's so hard to ask for favors. I ate an apple, drank a glass of tea, and saw that it was time to go home. It took all my strength to say, "Mrs. Rubin, I've come to you because you were my mother's friend, may she rest in peace. I feel close to you . . ."

Mrs. Rubin became serious, almost scared. I didn't know what else to say, and to my great sorrow, tears welled up and my throat tightened as though I were choking. In order not to start crying, I picked up my glass of tea. Mrs. Shore pretended not to notice that my eyes were full of tears. She was silent, and I quietly sipped my tea. Then I finally told her that I wanted to leave my aunt's house, and I didn't know what kind of work I could get.

"It's easy to leave," Mrs. Rubin said, "but it's hard if, God forbid, you want to return. Don't leave. It's best to pretend that there's nothing wrong, even if something is bothering you. When my Harry comes home, I'll talk to him. Maybe he'll find some work for you in his glove business."

It was very nice of Mrs. Rubin to invite me for supper, but I was so tired from our conversation that I just wanted to get away and rest.

Insurance

February 19

My uncle came home with a headache today. Things are awful at home because a Mrs. Rabkin, who was supposed to take out an insurance policy for her children, suddenly got cold feet. She said she didn't want to insure them just yet. And it seemed that it was all because my aunt hadn't voted for her when she ran for treasurer of the Ladies' Society. My aunt swore that she had voted for no one at all because she had a headache that day and sat at the meeting in a fog without even hearing what they were blabbering about.

"Forget your head! Who cares about your head?" my uncle said. "What kind of business is this when the stakes are so high?"

My aunt protested that no one had reminded her that her husband was getting ready to write an insurance policy for the Rabkins. And he argued back that she should have remembered without being reminded. In the end, my aunt walked around with cold compresses on her head, swallowing aspirin until Mrs. Shore and Mendl Pushcart came in and they all started playing pinochle. Pinochle can rescue my uncle from all sorts of troubles, and I was glad that he sat down to play even though, whenever he thought about it for a minute, he looked like he was resolving a deep rabbinic dilemma.

At around eight o'clock, my aunt gave me a quarter and sent me to the movies, saying that it would help me learn English. I know that when she sends me away in the evening, it means that she is expecting Eddie to come and she doesn't want me in the house. Selma always seems really unhappy when Eddie says a word to me. And I'm happy not to be seeing him. Whenever I do, things get so strained in the house that I feel as if they're all watching to make sure I don't steal anything.

The movie was about a woman who was cheating on four men at once. She was quite a good actress, and I learned something from her. What did I learn? I learned that you don't need to be honest with men; you need to fool them constantly, promise things and not keep your word. That's what they like. I thought that if every woman behaved like this actress, every man in the world would be deceived. I'll never be able to do that because you need to say one lie after another, but if I lie, it immediately shows on my face. Still, I wish I could be just like her.

When I was at the movies, Mrs. Rubin came to visit me. It's too bad that I missed her. My heart started pounding when my aunt gave me the message that Mrs. Rubin said I should come see her tomorrow. Maybe a job will come out of all this and the world will open up for me.

Mr. Rubin

February 20

I've noticed that people are different when they're at home and when they're at the Lublin Association. When he's at the association, Mr. Rubin looks like everyone else. When he's at home, he looks like the lord of the manor. He sits there with his cigar in his mouth giving me advice. (By the way, he smokes his cigar in an odd way. He hardly smokes it at all. Every once in a great while, he pulls on it and puckers up his lips, and three or four circles of smoke come out of the cigar. And then nothing. He doesn't light it again, and there's no more smoke.)

It's impossible to get work at his *glov faktoree*, he said, because he can't take on any more apprentices and there's no other work for me to do there since I don't speak English. Then he puffed on his cigar and four rings of smoke came out of it and Mr. Rubin came up with a plan for me: the best thing for a girl my age who comes to America . . . is to get married.

"It's harder for a girl to find work than to find a husband," he said.

Mrs. Rubin mixed in and said, "What's the matter with you? The girl needs a *dzshob*. What kind of advice is that to give a girl? Get married!" I saw that Mrs. Rubin really was my mother's friend and wanted to stand by me in these hard times.

Then Mr. Rubin took another drag on his cigar while I held my breath, and when he let out the rings of smoke, he offered a different suggestion. "Since the vice president of the Refugee Aid Society is from Lublin too, the best thing would be to go to him and have him figure out something for you to do. But in order for him to want to do anything, you need to bring him a letter from someone." Mr. Rubin thought about it for a long time. A letter from who? His cigar let out a few rings of smoke every now and then, and in the end, Mr. Rubin said, "Since Rabbi Finkel is also from Lublin, it would be best to get a letter from him. If the vice president gets a letter from Rabbi Finkel, he'll have no choice but to do something on behalf of a refugee. How do you get a letter from Rabbi Finkel? Simple: you go get it. You don't need connections in order to go see a rabbi." Mr. Rubin was sure that he had come up with the best plan, and he gave me addresses for Rabbi Finkel and for the vice president. (He must have a million addresses to give out.) He wrote each address on a separate piece of paper.

Mrs. Rubin served the very same cookies as last time and a *kup koffee* and fruit on a green plate. When I left their house, I felt as if finding work really was harder than finding a husband. The street was lively, with cars going in all directions, people rushing by, and crowds everywhere. It felt as if I needed to push all those people aside in order to find a place for myself, and then I could hurry off somewhere just like they were doing. My hands felt weak, and I was afraid that I'd never be able to push myself through.

When I came home and told my aunt about Mr. Rubin's advice, she flicked it away with her hand and said, "Cold comfort, a cold fish. But still it's worth a try."

Rabbi Finkel

February 21

I've got the letter from Rabbi Finkel! He's a man who sits on a raised chair that seems higher than a normal chair, and he looks like he never gets off of it. He sits and gives advice. There's a small ark opposite him, covered by a velvet curtain adorned with silver fringes. Women come to ask his advice and leave a dollar or two on the table. Rabbi Finkel doesn't take the money; he pushes it aside and puts it under one of the books. "What kind of advice do you need?" he asked Mrs. Shore and me when it was our turn to approach his desk. I was a little overwhelmed and didn't know where to begin, but Mrs. Shore took the opportunity to say, pointing at me, "She's from Lublin. She wants a letter."

"Let her speak for herself. Who are you?" he asked me, even before I had time to say a word.

"I am Shimon Zilberg's daughter."

He didn't budge at all but raised his eyes and said, "You are Reb Mottele Zilberg's grandchild? Who do you want me to write to?"

When I told him that I wanted a letter to the vice president of the Refugee Aid Society, he repeated, "Vice president, vice president. . . . You need a letter to Velvel Khomut, the matzoh cutter. Vice president!" It turns out that my grandfather, Reb Mottele Zilberg, was a lot more important to Rabbi Finkel than Velvel the matzoh cutter was. He sighed before dipping his pen in the deep inkwell and once again raised his eyes.

"What do you want from him? A favor?"

"I'm looking for work. I want him . . ."

"A favor, a favor," he said, interrupting me. He wrote a long salutation and a short letter and stamped a Hebrew seal on it. He gave me the letter, and before I had a chance to thank him, another woman was already standing at his table wearing a feather in her hat and asking for advice. When we left his room, Mrs. Shore and I read the letter he had written. The long salutation was stuffed full of Hebrew words that neither of us, truth be told, could understand. After that, Rabbi Finkel had written, "In the name of the Holy One, blessed be He, help this child of our city, a daughter of the Zilberg family. May all her paths find success." And then there was another line with Hebrew acronyms and then a signature. Mrs. Shore was mad at the rabbi. "A cheapskate with words!" she said. "He doesn't say anything, and he doesn't let anybody else say anything either. He's a *statchu*," she said, and she put the letter into her pocketbook so that I wouldn't lose it. The whole way home she complained that she had never in her life seen such a rabbi, not in the old country and not in America. "*A statchu an' dat's awl.*" I don't care whether or not he's a statue as long as I finally have the letter.

Mr. Shamut

February 23

My aunt seemed annoyed that Mrs. Shore went to Reb Finkel with me and then told everyone that Reb Finkel had written a laughably short letter and that we could only hope it would help.

"So, what's with your *biznes*?" my aunt asked me, a little sarcastically. I told her that I was going to give Reb Finkel's letter to the vice president of the Refugee Aid Society.

"And here I thought you were keeping it a *seekrit* from me," she said.

It's an odd thing: since I've been here, I've gotten used to keeping every sign of anger bottled up inside. My aunt's words made my heart ache. Why should she reproach me? For what? She was the first one to go to Mrs. Shore to ask for advice about how to get rid of a refugee, and now she's accusing me of having a *seekrit*. But I buried the heartache and anger deep within me and spoke to her calmly. She said she would go with me to the vice president. Why should we bother people who are not in the family? When I went to Mrs. Shore to get Reb Finkel's letter, she opened her *poketbuk*, took out the letter, and said, "It was your aunt herself who asked me to help you find work, and now she's insisting on going to the vice president herself. She's the one who asked me for help."

Mrs. Shore said this quietly, almost whispering, with one eye half-closed. I think the story of the hard cheese and the Bessarabian woman who took away her fiancé taught her a life lesson: don't believe anyone, including my aunt. Maybe that's why Mrs. Shore always seems to be squinting, looking oddly at people. In the end, we decided that all three of us would go to the vice president even though it was pointless to have Mrs. Shore go with us because no more than two people are allowed into his office at a time. Mrs. Shore was left to smoke a cigarette in the waiting room. As a jab at the vice president, she repeated what she had heard from Reb Finkel: "Velvel, the one who put the holes in matzohs at Passover! Look who thinks he's a somebody! He doesn't receive more than two people at a time—matzoh cutter!"

My aunt and I went in to see the vice president. There were large black letters in Yiddish and English on his door, with the name "William Shamut." He had such a round face that he looked more like a middle-aged woman than a vice president of anything. He seemed happy with Reb Finkel's letter and especially with the salutation full of Hebrew acronyms he couldn't really decipher. He merely put the letter on the table and tapped the long salutation a few times with his fingers. I don't know why, but my heart was hammering away the whole time that I sat in his office. It wasn't out of fear, but sorrow. What if he didn't want to do anything for me, even though I came from Lublin?

When Mr. Shamut was done with the letter, he banged on the table and said, "Exactly who are you from Lublin? Are you really a member of the Zilberg family?"

The rabbi hadn't asked a thing or wanted to know a thing, but Mr. William Shamut was just the opposite, asking everything and wanting to know everything.

"You're Reb Mottele's grandchild? And whatever happened to Reb Mottele's lovely daughter, Simele? I think she was called Simele, wasn't she?"

I told him that I was Simele's daughter and that my mother (may she rest in peace) died when the Germans bombed Lublin.

Mr. Shamut had already heard lots of stories about the troubles of Jews "on the other side." He didn't react in the slightest way when he heard of my mother's death.

"She was a lovely girl," he said. "And you're a refugee . . ."

Mr. Shamut smiled, as if being a refugee was a joyful thing. For a while I thought that he resembled our Lublin cantor's wife, and I simply couldn't understand how that was possible. All of a sudden there was a loud ringing in the room, and I looked around at all the doors, but Mr. Shamut quietly picked up the telephone receiver and said, "I'll be done in a few minutes. Yes, I'll be right there." I felt faint. What had we accomplished with our visit and Rabbi Finkel's letter? What was to become of me? Mr. Shamut touched the clock sitting on his desk and took my hand.

"Listen, dear, I've got a meeting now and must go." (He had already stood up.) "Come to me on Monday and, one way or another, we'll figure out what to do for someone from Lublin."

Mr. Shamut once again took my hand, and we all left his office. A few days ago, when Eddie squeezed my finger before leaving, that finger burned until I fell asleep, and this time, when Mr. Shamut took my hand, I felt a dampness, and if I had not been worried about embarrassing myself in my aunt's presence, I would have wiped my hand with a handkerchief. But I realized that it was better to keep still and not make a big deal over this. Never mind; my hand would dry.

Mrs. Shore was impatient. "Well, what did the matzoh cutter say?" she asked.

"Sh-sh-sh!" My aunt shushed her. "Sh, we need to come again on Monday."

I've already learned how to ride the subway. My head aches a little, but I can ride it like all the other passengers.

I Meet My Teacher, Sheinfeld

Monday, February 26

Once again, I saw that Mr. Rubin was right when he said that it's easier to find a husband than a job. I could barely wait for Monday in order to go see the vice president, Mr. William Shamut, and to hear what he would do for me. And when I went to him today, he wasn't there.

"Caught a cold," the receptionist said.

"When will he be back?" I asked her. First she said something in English with her painted, fiery-red lips, and I didn't understand a single word. How could I leave when I didn't know when to come back? So I stood there waiting and hoping that she would say something else. She was sitting, and I was standing. Then those red lips again said something: *"Ay told yu,"* and then a few words that I didn't begin to understand. "I told you" I do understand; I hear it at home all the time. My aunt must say "I told you" fifteen times a day; Selma says "I told you" constantly; Marvin says "I told you." (My uncle is the only one who never says it.) And even though I know exactly what the words mean, I always think that its real intention is to say, "Stop bothering me." But, still, I was disappointed with this girl. She could see that I didn't understand her and still she just repeated the same words with an additional "I told you." So I kept standing there not wanting to leave because I still didn't know when to come back. Finally the girl opened up her fiery-red lips and said to me in Yiddish, "I've told you that Mr. Shamut *ketched a kold*, and he didn't say when he'd be back."

The truth is that I felt no anger toward this girl, but really those lips looked much too red to me, and I wanted to take out my handkerchief and wipe away some of the color. But I didn't do that. Fortunately, I heard someone calling my name and, though the voice was familiar because I had heard it often, I just couldn't remember who it belonged to. I never imagined that I would meet my teacher, Sheinfeld, here. He shook hands with me, and the first thing I noticed was how terribly changed his hands were. I remembered clearly how he used to stand at the blackboard, drawing geometric shapes. His wonderful triangles were always so nice and straight. And now he was extending a hand with blackened fingernails. He had also come to Mr. Shamut about work, although he already had a bit of a *dzshob*: he washed old spoons in a factory where they were made to look like new. *Sekondhenders*, he called them. When he noticed that I was staring at his fingers, he told me that he washed the spoons with some kind of chemical that made his nails turn black. He said that he wanted to learn English but had no time or energy to do that after a day's work. "I'm not a young man," he said plainly, as if speaking to his own sister. And he added: "You'll be fine; you're still young." He says I'm young and Mrs. Shore says that I'm already an old maid in America and I say that, either way, things are far from fine.

A New Problem

Wednesday, February 28

Selma's boyfriend, Eddie, is an additional new problem for me. He came up today to test my English. "How do you spell a *teybl*?" and "How do you spell a *tcher*?" At first I answered him, but then I saw that the whole house was in an uproar. Selma was on fire. She started looking for some kind of scissors and threw her boxes around with such force that the whole house shook. My aunt kept saying, "The *teetsherke* will take care of teaching her, *don' boder.*" Then, thank God, Mrs. Shore called me to help her with something. I ran from the house, feeling as if every limb on my body was on fire. I heard my aunt slamming doors and wondered if she had asked Mrs. Shore to call me away. I noticed that Eddie was furious when Mrs. Shore called me; he turned the radio dials, making loud scratching noises. My uncle, who was reading the newspaper and taking a "*vakayshon*" from talking, sighed. My heart ached, although deep down I was actually pleased that Eddie hadn't wanted me to leave.

Mrs. Shore needed me for absolutely nothing at all. She told me that she planned to go to a *sayl* (sale) tomorrow and that I should go with her and stop off to see if Mr. Shamut was back in his office. She asked me to sit awhile, and she went into the kitchen, busying herself with something. I sat facing the picture she has of the Turkish princess and her crown. I feel like I always see that crowned Turkish princess when things aren't going well with me. She comforts me by letting me know that she, too, is trapped in Mrs. Shore's house.

Mrs. Shore came back with a cigarette in her mouth. As usual, she squinted a little and said, sounding like she was pleading, "Rivkele, don't have too much to do with Eddie."

Oh, great! Here we go with a new mess, I thought to myself. Mrs. Shore went on: "He is a *jereebug*, that's what he is. Here today, there tomorrow, always prancing around. You don't know these American *boyes*."

My face turned red and my whole body shook. How is it my fault if Eddie wants to teach me English spelling?

"What's a *jereebug*?" I asked Mrs. Shore.

"Don't ask," she said, "it's certainly no saint. *A jereebug iz a jereebug.*"

I couldn't ask anything after that, but I understood that no good can come of being friends with a *jereebug*. I don't know if I'm angry at Mrs. Shore or not, but I do know that this world feels as tight as my heart. Whatever I do is wrong. And Eddie is now a new addition to my troubles.

Still, I'd really like to know what a *jereebug* is.

Turning This Way and That and Going Nowhere

Thursday, February 29

What a crazy day! Mr. Shamut is, thank God, healthy again. Mrs. Shore went with me to see him. He opened his office door himself and motioned to me to come in. Mrs. Shore stayed seated, then stood up, and then sat down again.

"Come on in, both of you," Mr. Shamut said. When we entered, he pointed to his throat and said, "A *kold*. I should have stayed home another day, but that's impossible with all I have to do in the office." The first thing Mr. Shamut did was to call Rabbi Finkl and throw fancy Hebrew words into the conversation: "Your emissary is here," he said. "Reb Mottele Zilberg's grandchild. I'll send her to Pinchas Hersh, the butcher's son. . . . Yeah, yeah, he's filthy rich. He owns a glove factory. Kindly call him up. Yeah . . . on the phone. . . . He respects you. . . . I'll write him a letter. . . . Let's hope it works . . ."

"OK, Rabbi Finkl will help too," Mr. Shamut said to me. Do you know who we're sending you to? Also someone from Lublin. A scoundrel if ever there was one. At home he was a butcher, and here he's become filthy rich. You hear?" Mr. Shamut took my hand and laughed loudly. At the same time, he moved the clock sitting on his desk. (He still had some time.) "You hear me? In Lublin, this Pinchas Hersh, to whom we're sending you, was called 'Pinchas-Hersh-with-the-pickle.' Mrs. Shore started to laugh and wanted to say something, but Mr. Shamut wouldn't let her speak. He kept on talking and laughing. "He was once caught dancing in the storeroom with a pickle. That's all Lublin needed . . ."

Once again Mrs. Shore wanted to say something, but Mr. Shamut still wouldn't let her and continued. "There was a pretty girl in Lublin named Chanke Mostovlianski, who was the daughter of a hat maker, and a real beauty. She loved to dance the polka-mazurka. And Pinchas Hersh was crazy about her, so he wanted to learn how to dance it too. One Friday evening, before dinner, Pinchas Hersh was sent to the storeroom to get a pickle to serve with the meat. His father, Shimon Dovid, and his mother—I've forgotten her name, Hinde? Yeah, Hinde was her name—were sitting at the table. So there they were, waiting for the pickle. The meat was getting cold, and Shimon Dovid was hungry. And still no Pinchas Hersh and no pickle.

So his sister, Tsipke, jumped up and went into the storeroom and saw . . . what do you think she saw? There was Pinchas Hersh, holding a pickle in his hand and dancing the polka-mazurka with it. At the very moment that Tsipke entered the room, Pinchas Hersh was most delicately holding the pickle and dancing around the barrel. Tsipke broadcast the story far and wide, describing how Pinchas Hersh danced the polka-mazurka with a pickle. Afterward, Chanke Mostovlianski wouldn't even look at him, and the whole town started calling him Pinchas-Hersh-with-the-pickle. The young man had to flee to America, and here, my oh my, he became filthy rich, he's called Mr. Rubin, and he owns a glove factory."

It took my breath away. I was being sent back to the very same Mr. Rubin who had sent me here! Mr. Shamut called in the girl with the fiery-red lips and said a few words to her in English. I heard my name and Mr. Rubin's name. My head was spinning: Rabbi Finkl, Mr. Shamut, Pinchas-Hersh-with-the-pickle . . .

I was lost in thought when Mrs. Shore touched my shoulder, and I saw that Mr. Shamut was already on his feet. He said that the girl would give us the letter for Mr. Rubin. He showed us out and called out, "*Nekst!*" In came a Jew with a long beard and unforgettable, pitiful eyes. Who knows? Maybe I, too, had such pitiful eyes when I left the office? The girl with the red lips handed us the letter, and Mrs. Shore said *tenk yu*. I was all confused. I had, thank goodness, a letter to take with me, this time from the vice president to Mr. Rubin instead of the other way around. There I was turning this way and that and going nowhere. Still, there's no choice but to go Mr. Rubin tomorrow with the letter. Why else does a refugee need feet?

Dreams

March 2

The letter to Mr. Rubin is in my purse, and I don't know what to do with it. Mrs. Shore and my aunt said that I might as well take that letter and throw it out and then go look for work somewhere else. And my uncle said, "Let her go; you never know, maybe it will actually help." He smiled oddly. I don't know if he was laughing at me because of my letter or at something else. Still, tomorrow I'll take my letter and go see Mr. Rubin. The truth is that nothing I do matters to me anyway. Today, I read in the newspaper about what is being done to Jews in Lublin. Even though I already knew about it earlier, it was upsetting. Yesterday I dreamed that I saw my brother Mikhl standing deathly pale, and suddenly he jumped wildly as if he was in great pain. My heart broke, and I woke up with a start. My tears fell so fast that I couldn't stop them, and when I opened my purse to get my handkerchief, I saw Mr. Shamut's letter.

"Go to hell!" I yelled at the letter.

I wasn't angry, but at that moment the letter seemed so beside the point that I thought I might as well throw it out. It seems that there is no such thing as quiet tears. My aunt heard me crying (even though I thought that I was crying silently), and I heard her sigh quietly in her room. "Sleep, Rivke, sleep," she said. "There's nothing you can do about it. Sleep." When my aunt said that, it seemed to me as if my mother, may she rest in peace, was talking to me. And later when I fell asleep, I saw my mother sitting near my bed and saying, "Sleep, Rivkele, sleep. There's nothing you can do about it. Sleep." It was good to see my mother, if only in a dream. It's such a terrible shame that dreams end.

The Good Luck Flower

Sunday, March 3

Today, Selma stood in front of the mirror for two and a half hours. (We were going to my uncle's brother's daughter's wedding.) My aunt stood in front of the mirror for only half an hour. Selma likes to try out different hairstyles. First she parted her hair in the middle, until Mrs. Shore came in and said that the part made her look about five years older than she is. So Selma put the part to one side, and my aunt said that she looked like a Brownsville rabbi's wife. Then Selma threw down the comb and went to the beauty parlor again (even though she had sat there for two hours in the morning.) She came back with three stiff curls, one on top of the other, and a rose sticking out of the third one. Everyone finally said, "*Very niys.*" Selma and I both started to dress, and I pinned my braids around my head. (I've kept my braids; I don't like short hair.) Mrs. Shore said, "Believe me, Rivke doesn't need a beauty parlor." Selma was furious. She said something in English, and Mrs. Shore tried to make up for her words. "*Stylish eet izn't,*" she said.

Selma and Marvin left first, and she told me to go with her father. My aunt explained that Selma doesn't like to go anywhere with a *bontch* of people.

My uncle said, "She doesn't know what she wants. How are parents a *bontch*?" My aunt said something in English, probably defending Selma.

Mrs. Shore went home and brought me a velvet lily. "It's a lucky flower," she explained. "One girl even got married because of this flower." Mrs. Shore really is good to me, and the flower she gave me really was a good luck charm. Eddie came to the wedding too, and when Selma was dancing with Marvin, he came over to me and said, "*Iy liyk yu mor . . .*" He cut himself off in the middle and then added, "*Den eneevon.*" My aunt came over as she always does when Eddie talks to me, and Eddie went to dance with Selma. I didn't dance with anyone. How could I? It was hard enough going to a wedding. My mother died less than a year ago, and I'm still in mourning. I was thinking about her the whole evening.

Eddie's friend, Red, barely left my side. He wanted us to drink from the same glass. I drank a little of his wine, and he said something to me in English. My aunt translated, saying that now that I had drunk from his glass, I must obey him in all things. I remembered the actress in the movie and how she deceived all the men, and when my aunt left to congratulate the new in-laws, I told Red the same thing Eddie had said to me: "I like you more than anyone." Red was very happy, and I saw how Eddie was looking at us even though he was dancing with Selma. Selma's chin dropped down again. I went over to the mirror and saw Mrs. Shore's good luck flower, because of which a girl can become a bride. When my uncle brought me a sandwich and some wine, he said, "Don't hesitate. Eat. I've made them a present of fifteen dollars." My uncle is a good man. He doesn't talk much, but I know that he thinks about me even though it's my aunt who is my mother's (may she rest in peace) sister. Red said that he would teach me English. I know this is all thanks to Mrs. Shore's good luck flower.

English

Tuesday, March 4

I never expected what happened today. Mr. Rubin read the letter from Vice President Mr. Shamut very carefully. He told me that Rabbi Finkel had also called him up, and Mr. Rubin had promised him that he would do something for me. "I have no clue what I'll do, but a promise is a promise," Mr. Rubin repeated several times. "Rabbi Finkel insisted that I make him a promise. So what could I do? A promise is a promise. In two weeks' time, the girl who collects the *peeses* in the factory is getting married. She earns ten dollars a week. But you have to know English. If a seamstress says, '*Kom ove' heyer*' (come here), you have to know what it means; and if another one says, '*Tayk eet avey*' (take it away), you have to know what that means. And if one of them is *noyvus* (nervous) and starts yelling, 'I'm sick and tired of this dust,' you must also understand what she means." In the end, we agreed that I had to concentrate on my English studies and to wait until the girl who collects the pieces gets married, God willing, and that nothing, God forbid, delays the wedding.

Mr. Rubin didn't smoke his cigar at all. It had gone out, and only a thin gray bit of ash was on its tip, but no glow at all. He couldn't contain himself and blurted out, "Just so you know, this business has already cost me twenty-five dollars before I even turn around. Rabbi Finkel called me up to talk about you, but meanwhile he also threw in a word about the yeshiva that now has to support a new rabbi. The rabbi is also a refugee, the son of the Novoteplitser rebbe. So, I told him to send me his assistant and I'd give him twenty-five dollars. Do you think, God forbid, that his assistant put it off for even one day? Not at all. He flew right over, as if he had come by airplane. So I wrote him a check. A promise is a promise."

Today, Mrs. Rubin was walking around again with those little machine-like things that curl her hair. She was busy washing all the glassware and was pleased about something. Every now and then, she would say, "Why shouldn't they take it from you? Where else should they get it? From someone who doesn't have it?" And to me Mrs. Rubin said, "Rivke, I've got some *soper* for you. You'll eat with us." When she served rice pudding, she laughed and said, "In Lublin we never ate rice pudding. And certainly not rice pudding with Jello."

It seems that Mr. Rubin was reminded of something, because he said, "It's true that we didn't eat rice pudding with Jello in Lublin, but there sure were some beautiful girls in Lublin . . ."

I was reminded of Chanke Mostovlianski, because of whom Pinchas Hersh—that is to say, Mr. Rubin—danced the polka-mazurka with a pickle. I could hardly keep from laughing. But to my great surprise, Mr. Rubin himself mentioned Chanke Mostovlianski. "A girl like the hat maker's daughter, Chanke, can't be found in all of New York."

Before I left, Mrs. Rubin said, "Listen, you should really look for a job in the meantime, because it's no great prize to be collecting piecework in my husband's factory."

At home, I found an English book on my bed. Red must have come by to teach me English, but no one told me about it and I didn't want to ask. They might think that I'm chasing after him. But who else could have left that book on my bed if not Red?

My First Dollar

Wednesday, March 5

The fact that I cry at every turn is such a misfortune. My uncle brought me a box of stockings today. He had gone to one of his customers where there was a great sale on stockings, so he bought three boxes: one for my aunt, one for Selma, and one for me. What is there to cry about? Selma glanced at the socks and said, "*Tanks, Pa!*" My aunt clutched her head because he had spent so much money on stockings. "A stocking-fair," she yelled. "Three boxes! Thank goodness there wasn't a sale on wives. *Abetche* (I bet) you would have brought half a dozen women home with you." When my uncle gave me my box of stockings and I wanted to thank him, I got all choked up, and tears came into my eyes.

"If I'd known that you would cry over these," my uncle said, laughing, "I would have bought you twice as many. At least then it might have been worth making such a to-do."

My aunt started to laugh, and in the middle of my tears, I also laughed so that, in the end, I was both laughing and crying. How mortifying!

In the evening, Red came, and my aunt told him that I already have a *dzshob* collecting pieces in Rubin's factory but that I need to know English. Red immediately started teaching me what I need to know for my job. "*Kom ove' heyer*"—"Come here," he said in a combination of English and his weak Yiddish. "*Don' bee layzee,*" he continued. "*Tayk eet eezee,*" and so on. In the middle of the "lesson," Eddie came in. They both started to teach me how to spell. I sat with a piece of paper and a pencil and each of my rabbis on either side of me. "A real cheder," my aunt joked. But Selma was out of sorts. "*Dat's fooleesh,*" she said. I know that when Selma says something is foolish it means that she's angry. But what can I do if they both really want to teach me how to spell? I was glad when Mendl Pushcart came in. He entered quickly and with great energy, announcing that he had found me a *dzshob*. "A *dzshob*?" everyone shouted at once. "Yeah, a *dzshob*. For now, for just one night. The laundryman caught a cold in his back, and he's in bed. His wife needs to send laundry to the customers tomorrow and the packages need to be bundled up. Come, Greenhorn! I'll take you to her, and you'll earn a dollar and a half. Here, as soon as you earn your first dollar, you're an American; you're practically a *seeteezen.*" I grabbed my coat and went with Mendl Pushcart to the laundress to earn my first dollar in America and become a citizen. "Here's the greenhorn," Mendl said, introducing me. The minute we got to the door, he left to go back and play pinochle with my aunt and Mrs. Shore.

The laundress taught me how to tie up the packages and what to write on them. Count the *sheertz* and write down a *figer.* Count the *tawvelz* and write a *figer.* Overnight I learned the meaning of shirts, towels, sheets, and more. The laundress ironed, and I tied the packages and wrote numbers on them. At first, she was silent, showing me how to fold the shirts around cardboard so they remained starched, without wrinkles. "Don't make creases," she said. "A crease is worse than anything for these people. A crease is a black mark in the laundry business." After a few hours, when it was already the middle of the night, she began to talk. At home in Europe she had studied to be a dentist and was already "practicing" as a student in Shimonovski's School of Dentistry in Warsaw. And here in America she had become a *lawndreelaydee,* ironing underwear and wasting her life. She ended her story of the past thirty years and quietly sang a familiar Russian song about a fast-moving troika. I'd heard the song before and even knew the melody. When my uncle Zaydl in Lublin used to come now and then and take us for a ride on his sleigh, he would sing the very same song. And now, sitting at night with the laundress, I imagined that I was hearing both of them singing together.

I came home at dawn. My aunt opened the door and asked, "So, have you become a citizen?" I showed her the three silver half dollars that the laundress had given me. "Set aside one coin," my aunt said. "People say that the first silver coin you earn is a good luck charm." When I went to sleep, I remembered Mendl Pushcart and thought that he wasn't so bad after all. He was right. I really did feel like a "citizen" this morning when I earned my first American dollar.

The Laundress

March 7

At night things look a certain way, and by day they look different. It's like people say: it's as different as night and day. And so is the laundress.

During the day, she orders everyone around. She stands in the laundromat and issues orders: she sends the *boyes* to collect bags of laundry; she sends them to deliver clean laundry; she collects money and gives change; she irons and in the middle of ironing, she yells at the maid not to waste time; every now and then she looks my way to check if I'm writing the numbers correctly. In short, she's a general. She seems to have entirely forgotten that at night she told me about being a dentist and practicing in Shimanovski's School of Dentistry. She forgot the song about the racing troika. At night, she was a different laundress, and by day there was no sign of that woman. In the evening, she gave me a dollar and invited me upstairs for a cup of coffee. She lives in the same building as the laundry, one flight higher. Upstairs, with the lights on, she was again the nighttime woman. She showed me a picture of Lev Tolstoy that hung on her wall in a silver frame with a green twig on top of it. "He was the greatest man in the world," she said.

She opened several drawers one after the other and finally took out a brown portfolio full of photographs and showed me a photo of a group of young men and women.

"That's me," she said, pointing to one of the girls. "And that one," she said, pointing at a young bearded man, "spoke to Lev Tolstoy personally."

She put the photo back in the portfolio and the portfolio back in a drawer and then closed all the drawers, covered the cupboard with a cloth, and put a model of the *Mayflower* on top of it.

Her husband was asleep. We drank a few cups of coffee, and I ate the *sendvitch* she offered me. I'm not so fond of eating sandwiches. As soon as I try to take a bite, either cheese or salami or some other filling falls out. Americans make a big deal of a *sendvitch*, but I think of it as three separate things that should remain separate. When we had eaten the sandwiches, the laundress said, "Mr. Pushcart told me that you finished high school back home. That's why I showed you all these things."

When I got home, I was too embarrassed to tell my aunt that I had eaten a sandwich. I don't even know why I was embarrassed, but I didn't tell her. Somehow, I thought it wasn't right to eat bread baked in too many ovens.

At home, I found Mendl Pushcart and, for the first time since my arrival, his wife was with him. Eddie and Red were also there. Mendl Pushcart asked me how I liked my new *dzshob*. "Are you a Rockefeller yet?" he said, and he reminded me that the laundryman's back problems would pass and I'd still have to wait for Mr. Rubin's factory and its piecework.

Red came to teach me English. He even brought a picture book that showed the English words for the things shown in each picture. But instead of teaching me, Red, Eddie, and Selma started to talk among themselves, quarreling over who was the biggest star in America. Selma said it was Clark Gable, Red said Eddie Cantor, and Eddie said that he was sure it was Glen Miller, the *jereebug*. I kept hearing them say *jereebug* and I thought that Mrs. Shore was right all along and that Eddie must be a jerrybug and it's a pity for Selma. I could barely understand a word of what they were saying, but I saw that everyone was getting red in the face, everyone was angry, all in a rage. I thought that they must have been arguing over other things than Eddie Cantor and Glenn Miller, things that lay deeper in their hearts. Who knows? And maybe it's true that Glen Miller really is so deeply rooted in their souls. Since they're speaking English, it's hard to tell. It's a miracle that at least the older ones can speak some Yiddish and I can understand them.

Mendl Pushcart's wife told my aunt all about her doctors. I noticed that, here, people talk a lot about their *diyet*. According to Mrs. Pushcart, if a person wants to be healthy, he must have his *diyet*. Just as every person must have his own clothing and shoes, he must also have his own diet. Mendl Pushcart, who had in the meantime managed to get himself a glass of tea, interrupted his wife to say, "If I'm hungry, I can eat what's on my diet and on her diet, and it never hurts me a bit."

In the middle of these quarrels, Red said to me: "*Kom on. Iy vil teetch yu English.*" He said it in a way that made it clear he had only come for that. My heart felt lighter knowing that I had such a good friend in America: Red.

My Uncle Tells Stories

March 8

"You can keep the apple, and you can keep the worm inside it too," my mother (may she rest in peace) used to say. And that's how it is with Mendl Pushcart. Every Friday evening he comes over to play pinochle, to tell his stories, and to get me to fetch his tea. But today he was so beside himself that I barely recognized him. He kept calling me "greenie." Greenhorn, it seems, is not enough for him. "More tea," he said at least eight times. He couldn't even drink the last one, and it got cold sitting on the table. I thought he was so full of himself because he took me to the laundress to get a job. In the end, it turned out that he did something even greater: he brought Miss

Paulie home to us in order to have my uncle write her insurance policy. Miss Paulie played pinochle too, and my uncle played slowly and carefully. Mendl Pushcart winked to let him know that she was a *kostomer*.

Today, for the first time, I heard how well my uncle can tell stories. He told Miss Paulie lots of stories, all about insurance and insurance agents. My uncle went into his briefcase and took out lots of pads of paper, notes, printed and handwritten, books with different accounts. "Let's take a look at this Talmud," he said, bringing a book that had long columns of accounts showing how much a person would have to pay as insurance against, God forbid, an *eksident*.

"In this Talmud it is written that all you have to pay is thirty-six dollars a year. In case, God forbid, of an accident, you get one thousand dollars immediately and then another forty dollars a month until you are well again. In this little prayer book, it says another thing." And then my uncle told her what was written in his "little prayer book." Miss Paulie is a *noys* in a hospital. She spent a year in Palestine, and she really liked that my uncle called his accounting books "Talmud" and "prayer book." He asked her all about the Western Wall and Mount Carmel and said that, as soon as he could free himself from *biznes*, he would also travel to Palestine for a year.

"Everyone," said my uncle, "must spend at least one year in the Land of Israel." He told her how important it was to have insurance not, God forbid, in case of an accident but precisely the opposite: so no accident happened. And the best guarantee of that was the rich insurance company's good luck. He also told a story about one of his clients, Mr. Melamed, who was richer than the biblical Korach. "He owned houses and a farm and a hotel and other businesses. And he didn't want to insure himself. What did he need it for, he said. He thought he had his own insurance policy. In addition to all his possessions, Mr. Melamed had an old aunt. This old aunt had a habit of scrunching up her nose. She'd say a few words and wrinkle her nose. Another few words and again wrinkle her nose. Mr. Melamed loved her as if she was his own mother, but he couldn't stand how she scrunched her nose. He would have given anything to get her to stop. Once she came to him and said—no more and no less—that he should immediately go and insure himself for at least ten thousand dollars because she had a dream that showed all his houses melting as though they had been, God forbid, made of snow. They didn't burn in a fire; they simply melted like snow. First the roofs, then the doors and windows, and then the walls and even the thresholds. His aunt told him all this and never once stopped scrunching up her nose.

And the more she got heated up about her story, the more often and more strongly she wrinkled that nose. Mr. Melamed couldn't take it anymore, and he sent for an agent—for my uncle, in fact—and wrote up a policy for ten thousand dollars, just as his aunt had wanted. And guess what? One of Mr. Melamed's houses burned to the ground. He was still quite rich anyway. So he joked with his aunt, 'You said that the houses would melt and, instead, they're burning,' reminding her about her dream. 'I wish you no ill fortune, God forbid,' his aunt said, 'but they'll melt too.' In the end, they really did melt away. The crash came, the hotel went bankrupt, the houses went to hell because of the mortgages, and Mr. Melamed was left with the ten thousand dollars, let it not befall any poor man. And that's why everyone must be insured so that no *eksident* happens." And that's how he ended his story, although his words made no logical sense at all.

I had thought that my uncle was only lively when he played pinochle, but then I saw how well he told Miss Paulie his stories. Miss Paulie really enjoyed them. She laughed over the "Talmud" and the "prayer book" and the clients, and she asked him to come to her in three days' time to write up an insurance policy. She couldn't do it right there because she refused to tell everyone her age. Everyone laughed, and Mendl Pushcart assured her that she would not find an agent anywhere as good as my uncle. Miss Paulie won seventy cents playing cards. Mendl Pushcart drank seven glasses of tea, leaving the cold eighth one sitting on the table. When I heard how well my uncle told stories, I thought it was really a shame that whenever he came home he took a vacation by being silent.

When I was going to sleep, I was surprised to find a note under my pillow: "I like you more than anyone. E." My heart skipped a beat. I don't know what Eddie wants from me. He went to the movies with Selma, so what does he want from me? It looks like he wants to force me to run away from here and flee straight to Lublin. I have nowhere else to go now.

A Letter from Layzer

March 9

"One joy sweetens all sorrows," my mother of blessed memory used to say. I received a letter from Layzer today. Layzer is in Palestine! Layzer is alive! It happened so strangely. I was just going down to see if there was any mail, and that's exactly when the mailman came. I told him my name—Zilberg—and he handed me a letter right away, as though he had been holding it for me all along. I was so overwhelmed with the letter that I didn't want to go upstairs to read it; I went out to the street and opened it. "My golden Rivkele," he wrote. Layzer would sometimes call me that. He's in Palestine! He came there with a Greek ship. How did he wind up on a Greek ship? How did he manage to leave Lublin? Who knows? "Miracles," he writes, "miracles happened." He writes that he will bring me to Palestine. "That's why I went," he writes, so he could bring me to Palestine. I didn't notice that as I was reading the letter, I wandered over to another street. I turned back. The letter and even the blue envelope in which it had come were such a miracle to me. When I looked around and noticed where I was, all of a sudden there was Mrs. Shore. "*Hallo,*" she said, "where are you wandering off to?" That Mrs. Shore sees absolutely everything. She saw that I was lost, but it's good that she didn't notice the letter. I folded it and put it away before going to our building with her.

"You know what, Rivkele? Red has started to come over to your house very often. He never used to come," she said.

My heart was light, and with Layzer's letter in my pocket, I was even able to joke.

"That's because of the velvet lily you gave me when I went to the wedding," I said. "It looks like it really is a lucky flower."

"No, I think it's because of your braids. The *boyez* are sick and tired of the way the girls here get done up." As always, Mrs. Shore winked.

All day, I wandered around in a daze. I kept feeling Layzer's letter in my pocket. Layzer is alive, and he's not in Lublin! Now, who needs the pinewood forest where we used to walk? The forest was meaningless now. Layzer is in Palestine. What's it like there? He writes that he lives alone. I'm in New York, living with my aunt. My mother (may she rest in peace) is not living anywhere at all. My father is in Lublin. I have no idea where my brother Mikhl is. I just know that he's alive. "Dispersed and scattered," my mother, of blessed memory, used to say. I couldn't stop thinking about the Greek ship. What does a Greek ship look like? Lots of things were spinning in my head, and I didn't know what to make of any of them.

I didn't tell my aunt about the letter even though I really wanted to tell somebody. I thought it was better for my aunt not to know. I won't tell Red either. What would he understand about Layzer?

I decided to go see my teacher, Sheinfeld, and tell him about the letter. He had been Layzer's teacher and knows him. Sheinfeld had talked to me as he would to his own sister. He told me that his nails were black because of the chemicals with which he washed the old spoons in the factory where he worked. I'll talk to him and on Monday, after work, I'll go *opsteyrz* to the laundress's apartment and I'll answer Layzer's letter. He's so far away! Lublin is so far away. Everything is far, far away!

I Was Helped Because of the Merit of My Ancestors

March 10

Since Red started coming to us, Ruth has called twice. I saw her at the wedding. She's Selma's friend, a tall girl who my aunt says is a *mowdel*. My aunt says that in order to become a model, you have to be beautiful. This is the very first time in my whole life that I've heard of such a job. In Lublin there wasn't a single girl who became a model. It's an odd sort of work: wearing strangers' new clothes all day long so that others can see them. I mean, see the clothes, not the people. That kind of work is ten times worse than wrapping up packages of laundry.

Ruth called again today to talk to Selma. Eddie called too. So did Abe, Marvin's friend. All day long people were calling on the phone. I learned that Glenn Miller, who Eddie thinks is the greatest *star* in America, has come to New York with his *bend*. They're giving a concert today. They're all going: Selma, Eddie, Ruth, Marvin, Abe. My uncle said, "They're going to their rabbi." Selma didn't say a word to me about the band.

Who does Selma think she is? If I had been born in New York, I'd be able to speak English too. And if she had been born in Lublin, she wouldn't have known English either. And, really, what's wrong with being born in Lublin? It was a good thing that I knew that Layzer's letter was in my pocket. Layzer was also born in Lublin.

Today, Selma stood in front of the mirror again for a long time. She did the same thing to her hair that she had done before the wedding: three rows of curls, one on top of the other and on top of the third, a rose. I don't know why I felt as if I were being shamed. Everyone is going to hear the band. And I? It's as if I weren't even in the house. As if I weren't even in the world. In the evening, the phone kept on ringing again. They were talking about the band. Eddie came. He acted as if he had never left the note under my pillow. He walked around the apartment and saw that Selma was dressed up and I wasn't. I saw him noticing that. He wanted to say something to me, but Selma kept on talking to him. I pretended to ignore the whole thing and started to copy the English words from the picture book that Red had brought me. I sat with my back to the room and thought, Who the hell cares? Go to your band. Fine people are born in Lublin too, even though you're embarrassed to take me along to hear your band.

All of a sudden, my heart started beating faster, and I stopped seeing the English words that I was copying. I heard Red's voice. "Hello, Rivke," he called out. And then he said something to me in English that I didn't understand. He showed me two tickets: "*For yu end mee. Kvik, kvik.*" I know that *kvik* means fast. At that moment, such a silly thought came into my head: I was helped because of the merit of my ancestors. That's why Red came with those tickets. He refused to see me shamed in front of Selma and the others. I'm going to hear the band! I'm going. That's all I thought about as we left. I don't know why it made me so happy.

In the end, I didn't like the concert. Such thrashing around, as if demons were dancing. The only thing I liked was the fact that I had been able to go. After the concert, Ruth came over, and Red introduced us. "*How du yu doo?*" she sang out. The last "do" came out with a kind of screech, and I thought that she was angry. There are lots of ways to say "How do you do?" When Eddie says it to me, it's as if he wants to say more but stops himself. On the radio, I've heard someone say it putting his whole heart into that first *do* and it sounded like "How do-o-o you do?" Red simply says, "How are you?" He speaks Yiddish to me, although it's not really Yiddish but Yiddish-like. He told me that he had once studied in a Talmud Torah and, without my having to ask twice, he told me the things he knows: King David, Solomon the Wise, and Joseph the Righteous. He remembered Solomon the Wise better than anything else, and he told me the story of the *tu vimen un di kid.* Layzer certainly knows a lot more than Red. "I like the Jewish stories," Red said. I believe him, even though at home people used to say that a redhead is a swindler. But when I look at Red, I think that he isn't that at all; he wouldn't make a fool of anyone. When he brought the tickets for the concert, I wanted to kiss him, but that's all I need! If Layzer were to know what I'm writing now, he'd certainly think that I'm an awful person.

During the concert, when it was dark, Red kissed me. I think Mrs. Shore was right and the *boyez* like my braids because Red first kissed my throat and then my hair. I don't think anybody saw it. That's all I need! I used to think you could always tell the truth, but now I see that that's not so. I won't write to Layzer about Red. I can't. And I won't tell Red about

Layzer's letter either. I guess I learned something from that actress. This is exactly what she does.

Before going to sleep, Selma asked me how I liked the concert. "I really liked it. I'll go all the time," I lied. My head hurt from all the noise but I didn't want Selma to think that the whole world was created just for her.

Under the *Mayflower*

March 11

The laundryman is still sick. He's staying with his sister (who lives two blocks away from the laundromat) so she can take care of him since his wife is so busy. Mendl Pushcart says that my good fortune comes from his misfortune. The laundress gives me a dollar every day and calls me to come *opsteyrz* for *a kup koffee* and a *sendvitch*. It's as if she counts that as part of my *vages* because she doesn't hand it to me as if I were a guest but as if I had earned it. I've stopped eating at home in the evening. I just thank my aunt for offering and tell her that I've already eaten. It makes me feel good to say that. In addition to the sandwich and cup of coffee, the laundress hands me photographs to look at. The drawers of the dresser on which the *Mayflower* stands are chock-full of photos. If she wants to show me something, she opens one drawer after another until she's opened them all. The dresser stands completely opened until she finds what she's looking for. Today, she took out a photo of a young man in a student's cap with a ribbon in front and buttons on his blazer.

"This is Abrasha," she said. "Abrasha." She went out with him for eight years. She was in dental school, and he was in technical school. He was a great singer, and when he started singing the troika song, everyone stopped to listen. She thought her whole life had been laid out before her and that things would always continue as they were then. Who was then her equal, the equal of Bashke Licht?

"One summer, Abrasha and I came home to Vladeve. When he started singing in our house, everyone on the street opened their windows: 'Bashke Licht's fiancé, the student, is singing.' My mother, who is no longer alive, begged him to stop singing. People will talk . . . the evil eye. . . . A year later, Abrasha came down with a lung disease. He left for Otvotsk. Within a year he was unrecognizable. He was thin and coughed uncontrollably. My mother was afraid I would catch his illness, and so she 'pulled me out of the fire,' as she put it, and sent me away to her sister in America. Abrasha didn't write me a single letter. I must have sent him hundreds of letters, but he never answered a single one. I heard that he lived for several more years and even worked in his brother's pharmacy. My mother thought she was making things better for me, but for my entire life, I've regretted going away. You don't always have to obey your parents. I got married here; I have a fine home, a fine daughter, a good husband, may he live and be well. But Bashke Licht is no more. Birdie Shlivke lives. And I'm telling you that one day of Bashke Licht's life was worth more than all the years of Birdie Shlivke's."

That's what the laundress said after she had shut all the drawers of the dresser and placed the *Mayflower* back on top. And I thought that beneath that *Mayflower* lay disturbing stories. While she spoke, I thought about Layzer and me. Let the story of Bashke Licht not be my fate! Who knows what will be? Now people are telling me to change my name to Ruth. "Ruth is a good name," they say. Maybe Rivke Zilberg will disappear and Ruth will take her place? Ruth and what else? I thought of Red's last name—Levitt—Ruth Levitt. And my heart beat faster. What if Layzer doesn't answer any of my letters? I looked to see if Layzer's letter was still in my pocket. I saw the blue envelope and calmed down.

Red came today too. He started to teach me how to spell, and within a few minutes, Ruth called up on the phone. She spoke to Selma. Red said, "*Greetings*" and once again showed me how to write *father*. My aunt joked, "Look who's become a teacher!" But I see that Red has taken it upon himself to teach me English, and I think that's exactly what Layzer would have done. I think it's not true that a redhead is a swindler, as they say at home. It can't be that Red wants to deceive me. He's no jerrybug. Is he?

Three Mazel Tovs

March 12

Today is a day full of congratulations. First of all, Mrs. Rabkin decided to insure her children. Before the meeting of my aunt's *Laydees' Sosayetee*, Mrs. Rabkin took her aside and asked her advice. "I can't decide," she said, "if I should insure my children or not." My aunt's whole face glowed with delight when she told us the story. "My mother didn't raise a fool," said my aunt. "I learned more from my mother than just to chew my cud. So I said to her, 'Let it go for now, Mrs. Rabkin. We'll have more time to talk after the meeting.' And then I nominated her for the vice presidency. I told the other women that Mrs. Rabkin had been a member for twelve years, and it was high time to make her our vice president. Some of them wouldn't hear of it, but then they saw how late it was. They really wanted to be done and get home and, in the end, they agreed to make Mrs. Rabkin our vice president. She was so thrilled that she came over to me and said, '*Ay neveh new yu'r sutch a niys vumen.*'"

My uncle smiled. "'You too are a nice woman,' you should have said to her." And my aunt ended her story, saying, "In short, she decided to insure the children."

When my uncle smiles, I never know whether he's mocking or he's serious. He doesn't laugh, but he does smile. That's what happened today when Marvin came home all excited. He's going to take charge of the *gaymz* in his club, Happy Hour, and he'll get five dollars a week for it. My uncle smiled and said, "Ida, we've taken care of our Kaddish; we don't have to worry about his future anymore." My aunt was annoyed at him and said, "So why shouldn't he do that? Everything is a business in America."

Marvin was so excited that he finished eating before everyone and went to the movies, saying that he couldn't just sit still at home.

The third mazel tov is because the laundryman is well again. He'll be the one to wrap the packages and write the figures now. I'll have to go to Mr. Rubin to see when the girl who collects the piecework in his factory is getting married. "Don't put it off," Mrs. Shore advised. "Go over to Mr. Rubin's, because if the girl has a *dzshob*, she may not want to get married at all." She said this with that odd wink she has. Mrs. Shore is right. I'll go see Mr. Rubin tomorrow.

When I was leaving, the laundress said, "Believe me, you're like a sister to me, but thank God my husband is well and can work." She suggested I go to the Council of Jewish Charity Women. They're doing a lot of work with refugees, and she was *shur* (certain) that with their help, I would be able to find work. She gave me their address and encouraged me, saying, "If you seek, you will find."

Lately, because of my work at the laundry, I haven't been going to school, but tomorrow I'll begin studying again. I'll see that nice Mrs. Schwartz who used to look at my writing every now and then and give me a friendly smile that lightened my heart. "*Yur yung,*" she'd say. And I'll stop thinking about Red. He came to pick me up from work today. When I left the laundry, I saw him waiting for me, looking like he wanted to tell me something. He kept putting it off, and then, when we were already near the house, he said he wanted to take me for a walk and show me the East River. A little later, he asked, "Rivke, do you ever tell a lie?"

"Why not?" I said suddenly, and started to laugh. Red also started laughing, and it was clear that he hadn't asked me what he had meant to ask. I really regretted answering him like that, but there was nothing I could do about it. Maybe it's better that he didn't ask me whatever he had intended. Maybe he knows something about Layzer.

There were lots of lights burning brightly around the East River. It reminded me of Lublin, and I imagined myself there, in its illuminated pine forests.

At home, we found Eddie, and a little later Ruth suddenly appeared, all dressed up in a blue jacket with eight silver buttons. Mrs. Shore came in too and said to my aunt, winking toward Ruth, "The greenhorn has stirred up the girls." But then she stopped herself. She must have remembered that Selma was there. Ruth kept smiling at my aunt, at Selma, at Eddie, at Red, and even at me. Her smiles in my direction were stiff. I don't understand why everyone is mad at me. Selma keeps a close eye on Eddie, and Ruth seems really put out because of Red. Mrs. Shore told me that Ruth is *krayzee* for him. I know now what this *krayzee* thing is. In Lublin they might have said that I was *krayzee* for Layzer and he was *krayzee* for me. But in Lublin they don't speak English. Instead, in Lublin, the expression is *going with*. "Rivke is going with Layzer," people used to say. "She'll go with him until she goes to the marriage canopy with him." I wonder where you go if you're *krayzee*. I have no idea. I'll ask Red.

It looked like Red wanted to get away from Ruth, and he left very early. "*Iy'm bizee*," he said and left. And maybe he just plain wanted to leave? And maybe he was unhappy that I had laughed like that? The problem is that I saw that actress in the movies and learned how to behave like her. I would never have done that in Lublin. It would be so good if I could tell all this to Layzer and hear what he had to say.

Mr. Rubin Looks for an Enemy

March 13

It was really good that I earned some money in the laundromat. Today I was able to buy a new pair of shoes. The shoes that my brother bought for me in Antwerp were all worn out. And, anyway, they have long pointy toes, and that's no longer stylish here. My new ones have a pattern of little cutouts, and they look really good on my feet.

"On a young foot, everything looks good," Mrs. Shore said. "Everything is pretty, and everything fits. The only problem is getting those young feet." I thought that something was bothering Mrs. Shore when she said that because she didn't even wink once, as she usually did.

When I brought the shoes home, Selma glanced at them and muttered that they were *tcheep*. She shouldn't have said that because she knows I have no money. My aunt got mad at her: "Cheap, cheap. What do you think, she follows all your craziness? A shoe is a shoe, as long as it's whole." I put on one of the new pairs of stockings that my uncle bought for me and the new shoes, and I went off to ask Mr. Rubin if the girl who collects piecework in his factory was getting ready for her wedding.

Mr. Rubin seemed like a completely different person today. I had never before heard anyone talk the way that he did to the young man who was at his house. When I came in, Mr. Rubin said hello to me and just kept on screaming—really screaming—at the young man: "So, you want to save the world? Look at what you've accomplished. You brought on wars and lots of trouble. They're persecuting Jews, all because of your work. Who asked you to save the world? What business is it of yours?" The young man who brought wars and trouble to the world wanted to answer him, but Mr. Rubin wouldn't let him. "Forget all this nonsense," he said angrily. "Forget about trying to save the world. As it is written: 'There is nothing new under the sun.' The world is eternal, and you and your stories, your rich and poor, your equal-shmequal have brought only tragedy and led to the one whose name should be erased."

The young man, a slender, short man with thin arms, tried to argue with him: "I'm the one who's brought on the war? What are you talking about, Mr. Rubin? We only want to improve things for people." Mr. Rubin got so mad, he jumped up and said, "That's it. That's the whole problem. Don't tell me such stories. Who's asking you to make a new world? Anyone with any sense is able to make a way for himself just as things are now, and only a fool keeps chasing after the cart until its wheels run over his feet."

The young man jumped up, too, but he couldn't do a thing except cry out, "Who told you that?" Fortunately, Mrs. Rubin came in from the kitchen with a plate of potato pancakes, and Mr. Rubin relaxed. He took a fork and sat down at the table. The young man barely ate anything. Apparently, he still had lots of answers to give, and his unspoken answers took away his appetite. While he was eating, Mr. Rubin told me that the girl who collects piecework in his factory would get married soon. "You do understand," he said, "I can't just throw her out, but she's getting ready to be married soon, and then you'll have the job." I really wanted to ask him what "soon" meant, but I just couldn't do it. After they ate their potato pancakes, Mr. Rubin and the young man who is bringing wars into the world left, and I stayed with Mrs. Rubin for a while.

"When my Harry gets a little crazy, it doesn't matter to him who he fights with. He just has to find an *enemee*. He fights with whoever he finds. And if no one is there, he fights with me. If not for me and my advice, he says, he would have been a Rockefeller by now. But I'm the one who keeps him from getting rich." Mrs. Rubin started to laugh. "Do you know what I do then? I make potato pancakes! My Harry really likes them. No matter how angry he is, if I bring in a plate of potato pancakes, he makes up with his *enemee* right away. I don't know how we'd live if there were no potato pancakes in the world. That young man is Mr. Rubin's *nefyu*, his brother's son. And he got it into his head that he's an *arteest*. He sculpts people, hands, feet. He can't make a living. He came today, and Harry started arguing with him. But, really, Harry is a good man with a good Jewish heart. But everyone has his own issues."

I listened to Mrs. Rubin and thought that the worst thing I'd heard is that the girl with the piecework job is taking a little too long to get married.

Red didn't come today. I was sorry I had laughed at him. Maybe he was offended? I don't know what happened to me, but I just couldn't do a thing all evening. Red isn't Layzer, so why do I think about him so much?

"What's new with Mrs. Rubin?" my aunt asked.

I guess she wanted to know about my *dzshob*, but she didn't want to ask about it directly.

"Mr. Rubin told me that the girl is getting ready to be married. And then I'll have the *dzshob*," I answered. It turns out that that is exactly what she wanted to know, because she didn't ask anything else. I told her that the laundress had suggested I go to the Council of Jewish Charity Women because they'll do anything to help refugees.

Selma threw in her two cents too: "Yes, they do lots of things."

Eddie was really unhappy today. He barely said a word. I noticed that he and Selma looked at one another with daggers in their eyes. I didn't understand what they were talking about, but I gathered from Eddie's tone and the look on Selma's face that something was not right between them. At least I'm not responsible for that. That's all I need to add to my troubles!

A Little Scared

March 14

Today was my day to get a little scared, but at least it all ended well. The elevator that took me to the Council of Jewish Charity Women office flew so quickly that my heart skipped a beat when it started to go up. In hell, God forbid, people must also fly this quickly. And when I got upstairs, I saw that I must have made a mistake. There were German and English signs on all the walls, and everybody was speaking German and English. I thought that I'd come to the wrong address and ended up in some German office somewhere.

In line behind me, there was a woman with very light eyes, definitely not Jewish eyes, and when I asked her what this office was, she answered, "*Ich vershteye zi nichs*" (I do not understand you). Here we go, I thought: she speaks so oddly—with *ye* and *ch*—that she can't possibly be a Jew. I wanted to leave and go find the right address. Meanwhile, much to my relief, a thin young woman walked by. She had two little blond curls on her forehead, and around her neck I saw a silver star of David, and in the middle of the star there was a Zion and a little jewel. I was so happy! And I went over to her and said, "Please be so kind and tell me where I can ask about finding a job." She glanced at me and said, "*In dee liyn, pleez.*" I went to stand in line, and when I got to the front and started to talk to the woman in Yiddish, she smiled sweetly, opened her lips as though she were playing a fife and said, "*Soree, Iy don' onderstend yu.*" What was I supposed to do? I told her that I wanted to talk to someone who knows Yiddish because I couldn't speak English. She said something to her neighbor at the next table, and that one shrugged her shoulders. They looked at one another, and then she gave me a piece of paper with the name Eichenbaum on it. I went off to find Miss Eichenbaum, who also smiled at me and sent me off to Miss Rabinowitz and Miss Rabinowitz also smiled and sent me off to Miss Kasher and Miss Kasher read all the names that were written on my piece of paper. I saw that she wanted to laugh, but she just settled on a smile instead and said, "*Vayt a minit.*" She went to find someone who spoke Yiddish and then brought me a business card with the name Mrs. Mayofes on it. Mrs. Mayofes asked me lots of questions and took notes: my father's name, my mother's name, how many siblings I have, who were my relatives in New York. She wrote it all down and then asked me my *profeshun*. I didn't know what to tell her. In Lublin, I was a student . . . and here? I thought about it for a minute and said that I had worked in a laundromat for a week. Mrs. Mayofes seemed really pleased and wrote down: "profession—laundry worker." Some profession she crowned me with! She underlined my address in red and told me that they'd *mayl a leter*.

I was really happy to get away from that "Yiddish" lady. I ran into my teacher, Sheinfeld, who was surprised to find me there. He asked if I too had been told that they'd send a letter. He laughed. And I saw how thin his face was. "I've washed all the spoons," he said, "and now there's no work in our factory. It's worse than awful," he added, "and my wife is begging me to bring her over. I've been to every organization. They're good at writing on their typewriters," he said and lowered his head. I wanted to tell him about Layzer's letter, but I saw that he was too worried and I didn't want to add to his concerns by piling on my own.

"What does our fellow Lubliner, Mr. Shamut, say?" I asked him.

"Oh, I forgot to tell you that he said he had given you a *dzshob*. He also said that you had a lovely mother." I answered that I'd only get the *dzshob* when Mr. Rubin's worker got married and that my lovely mother was now in a better world. I took Sheinfeld's address and went down into the subway. There in the subway, I found Eddie, who was really happy to see me.

"Rivke," he said with some kind of weird speech that made him sound like Pan Stefanovski. "*Rivke, iy liyk yu mor den yur kuzin.*" He didn't even say Selma's name, but I knew what he meant. He said it was too bad that I hadn't come sooner. Eddie asked me to go to a movie with him, but I remembered Selma's drooping chin, and my aunt, and how my uncle smiled silently when something displeased him, and I said, "Eddie, let it go. Just let it go." What I actually said was, "Hak nit keyn tchaynik"—that's one of Eddie's few Yiddish expressions. He knows it means I don't want him to bother me. When he understands a little Yiddish, he no longer seems like Pan Stefanovski but rather like other Jews in Lublin and New York. Eddie laughed and said, "*Yu'r a gud girl, Rivke. Iy liyk yu so mutch.*"

Eddie didn't want to go home with me. He went one subway stop further, saying that he needed to do something there. He said, "*Iy'l see yu layter,*" and waved to me through the window. He didn't lower his hand until

I was out of sight. What if Selma were to find out about this? What if my aunt found out? Or my uncle? And what about Layzer? And Red? Would it bother Red or not? I'd really like to know that.

Red, Ruth, and I

March 15

Ruth has started coming nearly every day. She comes in, smiles, walks around, and dances with Marvin. As a result, Red has stopped coming. He hasn't been here for several days. Mrs. Shore calls Ruth "the bride." "The bride's here," she says whenever Ruth comes in. Ruth's cheeks turn all red, and her eyes flash fire. Mrs. Shore also says that she's a nice-looking girl, but the *boyez* don't take to her. From the way she talks, I can see that Mrs. Shore really has my best interests at heart and, mostly, that she wants me to find a *boy*. She keeps reminding me that I'm already twenty years old. "And once you've passed twenty," she says, "you don't even notice that you're becoming an old maid." Who knows? Maybe she's right.

Today, Red came during the day instead of the evening. He wasn't wearing a coat, just a warm sweater. I like that Red makes no secret of the fact that he's coming to see me. My heart started beating faster when he came in. Crossing the room, he took a chair and sat down next to me and asked if I was going to school today. I told him that I had missed a lot of school and that I was planning to go, and he said he would come see me there. He said it all so quickly that my aunt didn't even have time to overhear us, and when she came over to us, Red said he was in the neighborhood so he stopped by to say hello.

Red stayed a little while, chatting in English with my aunt. When he left, his chair was still near me, and I felt as if he were still in the room.

When I was going to school in the evening, I met Ruth on the stairs. She was wearing a small red hat with a tall feather.

"Where are you going?" she asked.

"To look for a job," I answered, and caught myself once again telling a lie. It's odd how these lies just seem to pile up. I don't understand it. Why didn't I tell her the truth? Why did I need to lie to her? Still, I thought it was better for Ruth not to know where I was going.

Red waited for me at school and wanted me to take a walk with him, saying that he had something to ask me. It occurred to me that Red wanted to ask me the same thing he hadn't asked before when I had started to laugh. We walked to the East River, where we saw ships sailing all lit up, and it looked to me as if they were buildings swimming around with lights shining through the windows. Happy people lived in those houses. They never left the ship. And Red and I would soon also come to such a bright house. I was glad to be taking a walk with Red. I thought of Layzer. If he were to know, he would be unhappy.

"Tell me the truth, Rivke. Did you make a date with Eddie?"

"Ridiculous," I said. "Eddie is Selma's fiancé. And, anyway, he's a jerrybug."

That made Red laugh. He laughed very loudly and every now and then would repeat, "Eddie is a jerrybug." He must have found it hilarious because he kept saying how funny it was. Later, Red said to me, "You know, Rivke, Eddie told me that you made a date with him in the subway and that he kissed you."

I was really upset that Red had been talking to Eddie about me, and I was even more upset with Red than with Eddie.

"So what did you say to him?" I asked.

"*Iy told him* that it was a lie."

It all made me very sad. I thought that Layzer would never have interrogated me like that. It made me feel like crying. I regretted going to the East River when I should have stayed in school to study. It would have been better if I hadn't come. Red noticed that I was unhappy and tried to explain himself. "*Iy no dat's a liy. Ay no.* But I wanted to ask you."

I wondered whether I should tell Red how much I regretted the walk we were taking. Would Layzer have asked me such questions? Never! . . . Should I tell him or not? Yes or no?

Red saw that I wanted to say something, but I was silent. "*Rivke, vot abowt du yu tink?*" (What are you thinking about?)

I said that I wanted to ask something of him. "I don't want you to ever ask me such questions again."

"*Viy*, Rivkele?"

"I don't know why, but just don't do it again."

"And *eef* I want to ask?"

"Then still don't ask."

"And *eef* I want to know something?"

"Even then, don't ask. And even *eef* you're about to pass out, don't ask, and even *eef* you dance like a jerrybug, you should still not ask."

Red laughed, and so did I. My disappointment in him passed, but something still gnawed at me: Layzer wouldn't have done this.

Red didn't want to come into the house, and I went upstairs on my own. I met Ruth and Eddie on the stairs.

"Did you get a *dzshob*?" she asked, smiling.

"I wasn't looking for a *dzshob*," I answered, also smiling. Let her hear the truth at least once. Why should I lie now?

"*Gud niyt!*" she sang out, still smiling. I guess smiling is a custom here, and you need to smile whether you want to or not. I'll have to get used to that too.

I didn't say a word to Eddie, but I know he felt that I was angry with him.

"Good night, Rivke," he said, without looking at me.

"Good night."

I thought of how I had just recently arrived in New York. I had no home, no work. I don't know the language. I have hardly a penny to my name. So why is everybody mad at me? Selma and my aunt and Red and Ruth. Mrs. Shore says that it's all because of my braids. Of all the things in this great big city, how can it be my braids that bother them? It really is an odd city, this New York.

Mrs. Koshes

March 17

May there be no more days like this one! A few more like this, and I'll be ready to meet the Master of the World even though I'm still a young woman. My father writes that he's living at Krasulye's and Krasulye is no more. I received the letter this morning and read it aloud to my aunt and uncle.

My aunt said, "So, thank God, at least they have a roof over their heads!" She thought that Krasulye was someone's name, but when I told her that it was the name of our cow and that my father and brother were now living in Krasulye's shed, she stopped thanking God. She even stopped fussing with the poppy seeds that she was preparing for Purim. Sighing, my uncle said, "It's worse than Pharaoh's Egypt. . . to be living in a cowshed . . . winter."

I wept uncontrollably. The letter was mailed in January, in the coldest weather. Where are they living now? And what's happened to our home? Has it burned down? Did the Germans take it away? Who knows? Every hair on my head seemed like needles stabbing me, and I thought that, if only I could walk all the way to my home right now, I'd go. But how long can a person cry? And what about me? I needed to find a roof over my head too. And all the roofs in New York suddenly seemed to open, and through each one the outside world came in, bringing the evil tidings that pursue the forlorn. But, really, how long can a person cry? I put on my new stockings and shoes and went downstairs. First of all, I went to chase away my gloom. And, second of all . . . who knows what is second of all? Maybe something will come second.

I went off to my teacher, Sheinfeld, to see if perhaps he could give me some advice about what to do with myself and how to help my father. I thought I'd go from Sheinfeld to Mr. Shamut in case he could do something for me. What's the use of sitting in the house? And how long can I stay here at my aunt's?

Fortunately, there was such lovely weather today that it seemed like spring. However awful things are, it's all a little easier when the sun shines and warms your cheeks. I really was more cheered up on the street. I saw so many people living their lives, and I realized that I, too, have hands and feet and eyes, and I'll no doubt be able to live my life too. I didn't even notice that I had walked along Grand Street all the way to Broadway or that I had stopped in front of a display window. *Display window* is one way of putting it! It was just a plain window, and inside of it there were crocheted tablecloths, towels, handkerchiefs, and collars. The window had a sign that said "Handmade." I thought to myself, Maybe? Maybe I should go in? I'm an excellent seamstress. My mother, may she rest in peace, was an excellent seamstress, and I learned it from her. Maybe I can find work here? Why not? How is this any worse than a laundromat or polishing old spoons like my teacher, Sheinfeld, or collecting piecework in Mr. Rubin's factory? There was a sign on the door with the name "Betty Koshes." Koshes is certainly a Jewish name, and Betty is the name of a woman, so I thought I should go in and try. I opened the door and a bell rang so loudly you would have thought a gang of thieves was about to be caught red-handed. An old, gray-haired woman came out of a door, and I saw three steps leading up. She was leaning a bit on a cane. Probably because it was so dark there, I scared myself with the thought that she was a witch.

"How do you do?" she said, looking at me and smiling. And I saw that she was no witch. She had clever Jewish eyes. Very Jewish. And she moved calmly, without hurrying. I could tell she was someone who would wait to hear what a person wanted.

"I'd like to see Mrs. Koshes," I said, not really knowing what to say.

"Why do you want to see her?" the old woman asked, still standing calmly, waiting for my answer.

I didn't know what to tell her.

And then she said, "I'm Mrs. Koshes."

"I know how to do this work," I said, pointing at the towels, collars, and pillowcases lying in the window. "I know how to embroider. I'm a refugee, and I'm looking for work." I said it all in one breath, and then I waited. Mrs. Koshes hobbled over to the wall, and I noticed that she wasn't just leaning on the cane as I had thought before; she had a real limp. She moved a chair for me to sit on and sat down too.

"What can you do?" she asked. "Can you sew with colors, or only white?"

"Both," I said. "I'm a good embroiderer." From my purse, I took out a handkerchief that I brought with me from Lublin. My name was embroidered on it, and under my name there was a twig with leaves and over my name, a crown.

"This is my handiwork," I said, showing her the handkerchief.

"This is European style," she said. "It's no good for America. Here, we work quickly. Everything is *horry op*."

But she didn't let go of the handkerchief. The glimmer in her eyes told me that she liked the work even though she said that it was no good here but only in the old country. She hobbled away on her cane, went up the stairs, and closed the door, leaving me there alone.

So that's how it is, I thought. But why did she leave? What am I supposed to do here?

A few minutes later, she came back with a tablecloth covered with drawings of poppies.

"Can you do this?" She handed me a box full of shiny silk thread, needles, and thimbles. Delicately, I embroidered one poppy, then another and another with tiny stitches. The old woman ran her fingers over the stitches and said, "Come tomorrow morning, and bring a five-dollar deposit with you."

"What for?"

"In case you spoil something."

Should I go tomorrow or not? I don't know. I don't know what to do with myself.

When I got home, I found my aunt pickling herring. The smell of vinegar and cloves was all over the apartment. It smelled like Purim. At home, my mother, may she rest in peace, used to prepare a feast for twelve people on Purim. It was for our family, for Uncle Zaydl and my aunt, for Bayltche and Nakhumtche, and for one or two guests. The noisemakers would joyfully bury Haman. The thought of it made me even sadder today. Look at what can happen in just one year.

Today, before Purim, I went to Mrs. Koshes. My father is living in Krasulye's stall. In his letter, he asks me to send him some warm things. I'll go to Mr. Shamut. Maybe something can be done. If only I could walk all the way back to Lublin.

And on top of everything else, I was upset with Red. When he came, I told him about my father's letter.

"You're here, not there," he answered. I could see in his face that he wasn't the least bit concerned. Red saw that it upset me, and so he added, "What can you do?"

I don't know if Americans are really heartless or they just pretend to be. I have no idea. They're probably pretending. Take the laundress, for example, who looks at her photographs at night.

A *Dzshob*

March 19

I dreamt about my father last night. He was lying in Krasulye's stall, on the ground, with his back against the wall, and I saw how cold he was, how he held his hands under a mound of straw. It tugged at my heart, and I jumped up wide awake. My mother, may she rest in peace, used to say that after a bad dream comes a good day. But this time my mother's words proved untrue because no good day followed this bad night. On top of Mrs. Koshes, I had to deal with Eddie and his notes. She was bad enough. I have to put up with her since, after all, it's a *dzshob*. But what does Eddie want from me? I have no idea.

I went to Mrs. Koshes in the morning without the five dollars. Where was I supposed to get five dollars? She was in no hurry. She brought the tablecloth, once again examined the poppies that I had sewn yesterday, once again took the handkerchief that had my name on it with the twig and crown, and when she finished looking at all of it, she said, "All right, you can give me the five dollars . . ."

There goes my job, I thought to myself. I told her that I didn't have the money but I assured her that I wouldn't spoil the cloth and that I had already embroidered about five hundred tablecloths. When I erupted with "five hundred tablecloths," I scared myself. I never expected to tell such a lie. At home, I sewed handkerchiefs or pillows for everyone. I sewed Bay-ltshe's (Uncle Zaydle's daughter's) wedding dress. I really can sew. But five hundred tablecloths! Well, the old woman was thinking as calmly as she did everything else, apparently still wondering whether or not she should let me work on the cloth.

"No one sews here," she said. "You take it home, and even if you don't spoil it . . ."

I was thinking that I had a good job with the laundress. Meanwhile, Mrs. Koshes was still thinking about what to do with me. She showed me a stool and brought over the box of silk thread. She sat there until I had sewn another poppy. Then she went up the stairs and closed the door. It was uncomfortably quiet in the house. What was Mrs. Koshes doing there? Was she sleeping? Or sewing? There was no sound at all on the other side of the door. Only the cloth on my knee and the box of thread remained as a sign that the old woman had been there. It was really eerie. If not for the window and the nearby front door, I would probably have left the tablecloth and the *dzshob* and fled. But I saw people walking by the window, the door was just ten steps away, and Grand Street was as busy as ever. What was there to be afraid of? Still, I went over to the door just to make sure I could open it. Yes, it opened! I started sewing the flowers, but Mrs. Koshes had heard me open the door, and it made her uneasy. She came slowly down the three steps, looked at the tablecloth, and went back up the stairs. And everything in the house was as silent as before. All of a sudden, I heard a phone ringing. It was as surprising as if I had seen the old woman turn into a young one or seen her hair turn black. If she had a telephone, she must talk to people, I thought. And people must come to visit too. And she also probably went out now and then. That changed things.

In the evening, Mrs. Koshes gave me a quarter. "I don't have more now," she said. "Tomorrow, God willing, I'll give you another half dollar. Meanwhile, this will be enough." I remembered that yesterday she had told me that here in America, everything is *horry op* and, looking at her, I felt like laughing. When I left her place, I thought that she must be so calm because she didn't remember that time was passing by. That telephone was the only thing out of place in the whole house.

I stopped at Mrs. Shore's instead of going straight home. I worried Ruth would be there, and I didn't want her to know about my *dzshob*. I wanted to show Mrs. Shore my quarter and to tell her about Mrs. Koshes. I also wanted to ask her if she thought I should go back to work there tomorrow.

"She gave you a quarter after a day's work?" Mrs. Shore asked, clutching her face. "Listen, Rivkele, I'm afraid your old lady is, God forbid, either crazy or that she's Fenye the rebbetsin. That's what we call Fenye here on Grand Street. She, too, had an embroidery shop, and on Fridays, when she needed to pay her girls, there would be such battles that the neighbors had to stop up their ears. Her neighbors couldn't stand all the screaming, and they felt sorry for the girls. You may have fallen into the hands of Fenye the rebbetsin. She'll eventually pay you, but it will be harder for you to see a single cent than to find yourself a husband."

I went home after talking to Mrs. Shore. I really wanted Red to come and ask me to go with him to the East River. I wanted to do away with the quiet that had taken hold of me at Mrs. Koshes's house, a quiet that seemed possessed, God forbid, by a quiet dybbuk. But Red wasn't there. Just Eddie, wandering around the apartment. I told my aunt about my "bargain" at Mrs. Koshes's. Eddie also came over to listen, and when my aunt went to answer the phone, he put a note into my hand and vanished. He went off to talk to Selma. Just my luck! As if Mrs. Koshes wasn't enough, now I had to figure out what Eddie wanted from me. Was he telling Red more stories? I put the note into my pocket without reading it, and began copying the English words that Mrs. Schwartz had given us as homework. "How's your English coming along?" Eddie asked loudly enough for everyone to hear, looking at me and waiting for an answer.

"All right," I said without even looking at him. I sat and wrote, hearing Eddie pacing the room. Selma was looking at the pictures in her *megezeen* and was saying something to Eddie. He answered her, still pacing the room and occasionally walking near me.

You can pace from now to next New Year, I thought. I still won't read your note now. I'll read it tomorrow. Eddie said good night to me from the other room as he was leaving.

"Good night," I answered, thinking that I didn't need this mess with Eddie and his notes.

I couldn't sleep. I was afraid that I'd once again dream about my father freezing in Lublin.

People Then and Now

March 21

Mrs. Koshes really did pay me the half dollar she owed me from yesterday. And how! She handed me five dimes, laid out one by one on the table so that there would be no mistake about the sum. I guess she's not Fenye the rebbetsin, because she didn't argue with me at all. Just the opposite. She was friendly and said that she was once young, too, just like me. But people grow old. Looking at Mrs. Koshes with her cane, the thought didn't exactly thrill me, but what could I say? That it's a lie?

Because she had paid me the half dollar from yesterday, she didn't pay me today. "I'll pay you tomorrow," she said again, like the day before. "It's enough for today."

To my great surprise, Mrs. Koshes didn't take the three steps up to her room. Instead, she put her cane on the table and asked: "Where are you from?"

"From Lublin," I answered.

"So, what's going on there? War, right?"

"Yeah. Things are not good there."

"It's good in paradise," she said dismissively. "And how do you like it here?"

"New York is certainly a nice city."

"Nice? What's nice about it? It's so loud and busy it can make you, God forbid, crazy, *dat's awl*. Who are you staying with here?"

"With relatives. My mother's (may she rest in peace) sister."

"What are relatives nowadays? Once upon a time an aunt was an aunt. I brought every one of my nieces and nephews to America. So now they make an appearance only if they need something. That's when they remember I exist. *Dat's awl*. When do they come? They come to say, 'Auntie, maybe you have a tablecloth? Auntie, maybe you have a pillowcase? Auntie, maybe you have silver candlesticks?' And you think that I don't give them things? I give and give and *dat's awl*. It's lucky for them that I'm still an old-fashioned aunt; nowadays, aunts give nothing. It's all 'How-du-yu-du?' and 'How-du-yu-du?' and *dat's awl*. Different times and different relatives. So, do you eat at their house too?"

"Of course I do."

"That's wonderful. There are still such people in the world? I never meet them." She shrugged as if to say, "I don't believe such things, even if you tell me it's true." She looked at me and said, "Now it's everyone for himself and *dat's awl*." With that, she went up the three steps that lead to her room. I left and was happy to see that Grand Street was as noisy and busy as ever.

Mrs. Shore came over to ask if I was really working for Fenye the rebbetsin.

"No," I said, "it's not her. It's Mrs. Koshes, the one with a limp."

"Did she pay you the half dollar?"

"She paid for yesterday, but not for today."

"I still think it's Fenye the rebbetsin," said Mrs. Shore. "We need to find out if she broke her foot." And, with that, Mrs. Shore winked, just like always.

Ruth came this evening. It looked like she was waiting for Red to come. He came later, and Ruth told him that she had gotten two complimentary tickets to see a Greta Garbo movie. "*Kom an*," she said, "*kom an*, Red!"

"Come on!" Red said, and he stood up. Ruth's face lit up. I've never seen her look prettier than at that moment. She seemed to glide over to Selma, as lightly as a bird.

"*Gud biy*, Selma," she said, and she kissed her good-bye.

Strange things happen to people. When Red got up to go to the movies, I suddenly thought that the room we were sitting in was becoming very large and I was sitting in a distant, faraway corner. I wasn't sorry about it, but I felt a great distance between me and everyone else in the room. It was a distance that seemed to stretch all the way to Lublin.

Red came over to me and said, "*Kom on, Rivke*—we'll go see Greta Garbo." When he approached me, I felt a tightness in my heart. What's happened to me? Why on earth should I be thinking about Red? Why should it bother me whether Red goes to the movies with Ruth or not? I debated whether to go with them, when my aunt said, "Go ahead, Rivke, you'll see Greta Garbo. She's a *vonderful* actress." Red didn't wait for my answer but just brought me my coat.

"I have two tickets," Ruth muttered.

Red said something to her in English. He must have said that they would get a third one. Ruth became hoarse all of a sudden and couldn't make a sound. She was the first to go downstairs, and I saw that her shoulders seemed to have shrunk. I don't know; maybe I shouldn't have gone? But, then again, maybe Ruth shouldn't have come over with tickets for her and Red. But, anyway, I went. Maybe, after all, it's better that I did.

I didn't like Greta Garbo in the movie, and I wouldn't have liked her in person if I had met her. She was too arrogant and traded too much on her beauty. I don't understand Ruth. In Lublin, a girl would never have brought a boy tickets, especially not in someone else's house. What a strange city is this New York. A strange city with strange girls.

The Ball

March 22

All of New York called us up on the phone because of the Purim ball. My aunt heads the table committee, so the phone never stopped ringing. Mrs. Rabkin, the new vice president, called up to say that she had a *kayk*, and what a *kayk*. She didn't say what she meant by "what a cake." All she said was, "You have to see it."

Mrs. Erlich called to say that she was bringing fifty hamantaschen and a poppy seed cake to the ball. She also reported that Mrs. Rubin had gotten a hundred bottles of Coca-Cola. Mrs. Sunshine called to say that she had twelve bottles of Carmel wine and Mrs. Rotshteyn had a hundred and fifty noisemakers. There were calls from the vice president, Mrs. Shapiro, the treasurer, and who knows how many more. The telephone was working as though it were a living being, not a phone. In the end, even the president, Mrs. Tkatsh, called to say that the vice president of the Refugee Aid Society, Mr. Shamut himself, would come to address the gathering.

"Your Mr. Shamut is coming to the ball," my aunt told me. And then she put on her coat and went to set up the tables in the hall. Selma went with her in order to make the decorations and prepare the young people's table. My aunt told me to come help too since it was all for Lublin.

At the hall, we met several women, all of them wearing blue, red, or green aprons. Mrs. Rabkin wrapped her head in a kerchief and ordered everyone around, just like a real vice president. In the ballroom, we learned that Rabbi Finkel was also coming and that there might be an even more important person, but whoever that was remained a secret. Later, Mrs. Tkatsh called up and said that Mr. Edelshtein, their wealthy compatriot from Lublin who now lived on Long Island, would be coming to the ball. He'd come late, but he'd *shur* come.

A *speshl* table was set for Mr. Edelshtein, Rabbi Finkel, and Vice President Mr. Shamut. And Mrs. Rabkin's "what a cake" was put on that table along with two bottles of Carmel wine. On both sides of the "what a cake," Selma placed two fir branches, and on each branch she hung a noisemaker, one green and one red. The Weintraub Company sent a case of grapefruit, and the janitor came in carrying a crate of hot dogs on his back. There was a mountain of green branches on the floor. We spread the tablecloths and decorated them with the green branches. The plates and saucers, the forks and knives looked like blossoms peeking out from the branches.

In the evening, the women left to get dressed. On the way home, Selma went to the beauty parlor. We found my uncle and Eddie at home.

"Where's Selma?" Eddie asked.

"No doubt, she stopped off at the beys-medresh, her House of Study," my uncle said, smiling. He calls the beauty parlor a beys-medresh.

Eddie said, "Oh, yeah," and laughed too. His laughter struck me as odd, and I think the laughter bothered my aunt too because she got mad at her husband and said, "So, and you do go to the beys-medresh? Why are you sending Selma there?"

"Who's sending?" he answered. "And if I were to send, would anyone go?"

My aunt got even angrier. "I think you suddenly have a desire to be a rabbi."

The phone rang, and when my aunt answered it, she said it was Red letting them know that he would come to the ball too. Eddie went over to the mirror and I thought he was turning pale. Or maybe it was just that the mirror made him seem so.

Selma came back from the beauty parlor, done up with seven curls around her throat. It was a lot nicer than the three-story curls with the rose on top.

"*Iz eet niys?*" she asked, twirling in front of Eddie. I felt sorry for Selma at that moment. Eddie barely touched one of the curls and told her it was *veree niys*, but it was clear from his voice that he was thinking of something else.

Mrs. Shore brought me the velvet lily. She really is a good woman.

"I won't let you go without this flower," she said. "Without it, your luck may end, God forbid."

"What kind of luck?"

"The way the *boyez* are attracted to you," she said, winking and pinning the lily in my hair.

Red came to the ball, acting very strangely.

"Rivke, I have to ask you something! Really, I need to ask you . . ."

"Again with the asking?" I laughed.

"Don't laugh, Rivke. I want to ask you something."

"After the ball," I said to Red.

"No, before the ball."

I made a knot in one end of my handkerchief to draw lots. Red pulled out the smooth end, and I was left with the knotted one.

"You're *lukee*," he said.

"What does *lukee* mean?"

"It means you've got good luck. You win."

Mr. Shamut arrived, and the whole crowd started applauding when Mrs. Tkatsh led him over to the *speshl* table and helped him to his chair. Mr. Shamut smiled, and I saw, clear as day, that he has a womanly face that makes him look like the wife of the Lubliner cantor. Rabbi Finkel came soon after that and sat down between Mr. Shamut on his right and an empty chair on his left that was waiting for Mr. Edelshtein, the wealthy man from Long Island. Rabbi Finkel sat without moving a limb, just as though the entire assembly had come to ask his advice about something and he was sitting and thinking about what to tell them.

Red asked me to dance.

"You know that I can't. My mother, may she rest in peace . . ."

"Oh, yeah," Red said, and he danced with Selma instead.

While she was dancing with Red, Eddie came over to me.

"You know, Rivke, Ruth is angry with you."

"Why?"

"She says that Red is a *lowfer*."

"A what?"

"A *bum*."

"What?"

"Well . . . a *lowfer*."

I didn't understand what he meant about Red, but I knew that it wasn't anything good.

"Ruth has already been going out with Red for the past three years and four months."

"And four months?"

I was angry. I wanted to give him what for, and I asked, "And how long have you been going out with my cousin, Selma?"

"You're mean, Rivke, really mean."

My aunt came over to us as she always does when I talk to Eddie. This time, she said she was hot and asked Eddie to bring her something to drink. And Eddie left.

Mr. Edelshtein came into the hall, and it was as if a great chill had entered the room, freezing everything in its place. The dancers stopped dancing. The speakers stopped speaking. And everyone was so awestruck that they forgot to applaud. Only when Mr. Edelshtein sat down in the empty chair near Rabbi Finkel did people come to themselves and then they started clapping like mad. I'd never heard anything like that in my whole life. Mrs. Rabkin went by hurriedly. She was carrying a tray with a bottle of Coca-Cola for Mr. Edelshtein and she wanted to be the one to deliver it. But it didn't work out. She tripped on a chair, and the tray fell out of her hands, spun around three times, and stopped. And the bottle of Coca-Cola rolled on its side all the way to Mr. Edelshtein's table. Everyone applauded.

"OK, good," said Mrs. Rabkin.

The president herself (Mrs. Tkatsh) picked up the bottle of Coca-Cola and gave it to Mr. Edelshtein. But the greatest surprise was Mr. Edelshtein himself. On the very same blue tray on which the soda had stood, he put down a hundred dollars. Everyone applauded and yelled *bravo*, and even Rabbi Finkel moved from his spot and looked at the hundred-dollar bill.

Even though Mr. Shamut wasn't the master of ceremonies, he made himself right at home, signaling with a knife against a bottle and announcing: "We invite everyone from Lublin to sit, and everyone who isn't from Lublin should behave as if they were!" The Lubliners were pleased and sat themselves down. Rabbi Finkel said the blessing over bread and split the huge hamantasch into ten pieces. Mr. Shamut pointed to the pieces and announced that they equaled a hundred dollars and that anyone who wanted to taste this wonderful hamantasch had to buy a piece from him.

Mr. Rubin gave him ten dollars and bought the first piece. And the audience clapped and shouted *bravo*. Mrs. Tkatsh, the president, bought the second piece, Mrs. Erlich the third, and that was it. There were no more takers, and then Mr. Shamut held a *speetch*.

"Dear ladies and gentlemen, all those gathered here! On every Purim of every year, we may eat hamantaschen or not eat them. That's nobody's business. But this year, my dear fellow Lubliners, this year we *must* eat hamantaschen because there are people in Lublin who also want to eat." He pointed at his back with his right thumb and added, "And they've got a Haman there too."

A woman sighed, and the "table of youths" immediately bought a piece of the hamantasch. Selma brought over the ten dollars, and the audience clapped and shouted *bravo*. Then Mrs. Rabkin's "what a cake" was raffled off. Noisemakers were sold for a dime apiece. Dances were sold, and the ladies were put on *sayl;* every man had to pay a quarter for a dance. Mr. Shamut "bought" the president, Mrs. Tkatsh. Mr. Rubin bought his own wife. Mr. Edelshtein looked around over the entire hall, and I saw him look at the lily in my hair and then say something to Mr. Shamut.

"Our dear guest, Mr. Edelshtein, is giving one hundred quarters for the lady with the lily."

Mr. Shamut looked me up and down and recognized me. "Oh, the greenhorn from Lublin! She's earned as many quarters as all the rest of the ladies put together."

Mr. Shamut motioned me to come over and said to Mr. Rubin, who was sitting near him, "So, what did you do for the greenhorn?"

"A promise is a promise," Mr. Rubin answered. "The girl who collects piecework in my factory is getting ready to be married."

Mr. Shamut interrupted him to say, "Make sure she doesn't take too long getting ready."

"A promise is a promise," Mr. Rubin insisted.

"Well, we thank you very much," said Mr. Shamut, earnestly stretching out his hand. The two shook hands very warmly, obviously pleased with one another.

When the dance started and every lady had to go to her "customer," I said to Mr. Edelshtein, "I can't dance. . . . my mother, may she rest in peace . . . it hasn't even been a year since her death."

Mr. Edelshtein looked at me with his gray, clear eyes, and I didn't know whether he was laughing at me or had pity on me, but it looked like both at once.

"Where did your mother die?"

"In Lublin.

"How long have you been away from there?"

"Eight months."

"So, if you can't dance, then at least help me count out the quarters."

I helped him count out twenty-five dollars in quarters.

"Call me up if you need anything," Mr. Edelshtein said to me, and once again looked at me the way he had before. More than anything, his eyes seemed to be laughing. He stood up, shook hands with Rabbi Finkel and Mr. Shamut, and said to me, "*Gud biy, miy yung laydee.*"

Mr. Shamut announced that the ball had brought in $350, and everyone applauded happily. They applaud everything here.

The dance was lively. Everybody seemed to want to get their money's worth out of their quarter. As they were stomping their feet, I thought of my father lying in Krasulye's stall, with his back leaning against the wall. He was very cold, and he kept his hands under a mound of straw, just as I had seen him in my dream. I felt faint and sat down.

Red came over and asked what was wrong. I didn't want to tell him about my dream, and so I just said that I was cold.

"You're tired," he said, and he brought me a hot cup of coffee.

"Tell me, Red, what's a *bum* and a *lowfer*?" I asked him.

Red thought about it and smiled. Then he said, "A loafer? Well, Eddie's a loafer." I started to laugh, and so did Red. We understood one another very well.

I don't think Red can possibly be a *bum*.

The Beautiful Peacock

March 24

I've never seen Mrs. Koshes in a better mood than today. Maybe it was because of the weather. It really was an exceptionally nice day. It was warm and sunny and everyone on Grand Street opened their windows and you could hear radios everywhere. It was a mild day, just as it's supposed to be on Purim. Maybe Mrs. Koshes was happy because of her *aydzshentkes*. (That's what she calls her sales agents.) Four women came to pick up their merchandise today, and from them I learned that Mrs. Koshes was once called "the golden needle." She was the best craftswoman in New York.

One *aydzshentke*, who had great big brown eyes that looked as if she cried too much, said, "You're really an exception, working here for her. She can't stand to see how the other girls ruin the work they're doing, so they have to do everything in their own homes and bring the finished product to her here. It's not easy to make a living working for her since she cares only about how the flowers look and not about anyone's need to make a dollar. Who can afford that?" Pointing at the three steps and the woman behind them, she said, "She once embroidered a peacock that was so extraordinary, it was part of an exhibition. It won a prize from an art society, and then she got a letter from the mayor. My goodness, what went on then!"

Later, another agent came, this time a pale, round woman with freckles all over, even though it was March and not yet summer. "Is anybody there?" she asked me, pointing at the three steps.

She looked at my handiwork for a while and then started to tell me how she had worked for "her" for nine years. "She's golden now compared to then," she said. "She used to bow down to the needle as if to a god. I'm better off as a selling agent. I take what I can, and I can make a dollar."

Mrs. Koshes called the freckled woman Zisele. I really liked that. The name means that she's sweet, and it fits her so well she could have been born with it.

The third agent sat down next to me and pointed out flaws. "You can't do it like that. She's an expert," she said, gesturing toward the three steps, "but that's all she cares about. There's nothing else in her head," she said, pointing at her forehead.

The fourth agent was a young woman who said something to me in English, but I didn't understand any of it. "*Yur a refyugee?*" she said, pointing at me and not saying another word.

When they had all gone, Mrs. Koshes came back downstairs. "They all came into this business through me," she said. "That Zisele didn't know how to thread a needle when she first came to me. She learned to do good work, but what's important to all of them is *horry op*. She spent the day working, got her dollar, and *dat's awl*. They all worked well, but with no feeling. Forty-one years ago, when I came here and was as young as you are now, I produced the finest work in all of New York." She went to her room and brought back a blue woolen cloth. It had a golden peacock sewn onto it, with its tail spread open, looking like a rainbow. The cloth seemed to radiate light, and the peacock's feathers appeared to be rustled by a breeze. It really was a beautiful fabric and a gorgeous peacock.

"In those days, I was as pretty as this is," she said. "I don't want to sell this cloth because I was married in it and I looked as pretty as a peacock. I was offered two hundred dollars for this piece of cloth. Mr. Warburg's daughter-in-law wanted to buy it for herself, but I didn't want to sell it. It's worth it to me to keep it so I can look at it now and then. What can I say? Later, my husband died. My eyes went bad. I broke a leg. The years passed. I don't want to be parted from this peacock." The old woman folded the cloth carefully, put it into a white bedsheet, and pinned it with safety pins to keep it from getting dusty.

When I left Mrs. Koshes's house, Grand Street was already lit up with red, yellow, and blue lights. It looked to me as if the beautiful peacock was flying around. It stole out of Mrs. Koshes's quiet room and flew all over Grand Street, shining like a rainbow throughout the long night.

Mrs. Shore came by to ask, once again, if I was working for Fenye the rebbetsin.

"No," I said, "she's not Fenye the rebbetsin. She's the beautiful peacock who broke a leg and lost her husband and ruined her eyes and grew old."

"OK. And did that beautiful peacock pay you the dollar she owed you?"

I didn't want to say anything bad about Mrs. Koshes. She had only given me half a dollar, but I said, "Yeah, she paid me."

Mr. Shore

March 25

Somehow, it never occurred to me to wonder where Mr. Shore was. If there's a Mrs. Shore, then there must be a Mr. Shore too. Today, though, Mr. Shore came back from California. He has a wholesale fruit business there. Mrs. Shore invited us all for a fish supper in honor of the guest, as she called her husband. Mr. Shore put some liquor on the table. Mendl Pushcart came too, and he tasted every one of the bottles. "Somebody has to make an *inspekshun*," he said. "You have to drink in order to see what's good and what's not."

Mrs. Shore spoke cheerfully, referring to her husband as "he" even though he was right there. "I don't know how everyone finds out that *he* is coming. I don't think I'm sending out telegrams . . ." And Mrs. Shore brought out a fistful of envelopes. "When these envelopes start to arrive, I know that *he's* en route." And she called off the names of them all: "A bill from the Jewish National Fund. A bill from the Workmen's Circle. A bill from the Rebbe Yitzhak Elhanan School. A bill from the Old Ladies' Shelter Society. A bill. . . . I ask him, 'How many memberships do you have?'"

Mr. Shore cut her off abruptly. "What does it matter where I'm a member? The bills must be paid." And then he made his own accounting for Mrs. Shore: "Do we need Palestine? What will we have without the Holy Land?"

Mendl Pushcart put in his two cents. "I agree entirely about Palestine. Let's just hope that good-for-nothing leader they have there doesn't spoil things."

Mr. Shore went back to his accounting. "Also, you can't go around without—you should excuse me—pants. The *boyez* need to study at the Rebbe Yitzhak Elhanan School. Otherwise, they'll just be gentiles."

Mendl Pushcart mixed in again. "You're throwing away your money. You think they can learn anything?"

But Mr. Shore wouldn't give in: "So, whatever they learn, they learn. I forgot how to pray too. So what?" He went on. "And the Workmen's Circle? Its schools—they read Sholem Aleichem's books. So don't tell me you don't like to hear Sholem Aleichem's stories."

"You're throwing away your money," Mendl Pushcart said again. "You think they can read? My neighbor's son, some *boychikl*. He mumbles and he stumbles and he trips himself up, God protect us all, like a blind horse."

But Mr. Shore stuck to the same line. "So what? What they do, they do. You can't get it all at once. I'm also not such an *ay-ay-ay* reader. Still, I'm OK. Once, you see, people collected good deeds, and nowadays all we have to take to the next world are receipts for these few bills. Still, it's better than nothing." With that, he turned to Mrs. Shore and said gruffly, "You hear me, Bashe-Gitl? Don't lose the receipts. Put them into a drawer. God willing, we'll use them one day. I'll get some for you too, don't worry."

Everyone laughed, and my uncle said, "It would be good if they can read the English on these papers in the next world."

"They're in the drawer. They're already there," Mrs. Shore said, winking with one eye as usual. "I don't care about all these pieces of paper. But, tell me, what do you have to do with the Old Ladies' Society?"

Mr. Shore laughed. "That's for you. On your behalf."

"*Tenks a lot,*" said his wife. "He's packing me off to the Old Ladies."

We went to our house to drink coffee because my aunt needed to get rid of all the hamantaschen that had been left over from the ball and divided among the committee members. "You've got to eat them up. I'll even make coffee for you."

Selma and Eddie came by too. It would have been better if we had just stayed at Mrs. Shore's all evening, listening to Mr. Shore pile up receipts for the next world. Maybe we would have avoided the fight and there would have been one less problem.

All of a sudden, Mendl Pushcart said, "It's a good thing, these haman-taschen. May we live to see the day when we eat the moustache of the evil one, may his name be erased." Selma said something in English, and Eddie threw in something too. All I could make out was *hyuman, hyuman, hyu-manitee.* Somebody said something about the *bend.* I saw that Selma was becoming furious and again talked about *human* and *humanity.* I had no idea that they were arguing because of me, but still, the whole thing made me very sad. Later, Mrs. Shore said, "Rivke, you know, Eddie was mad at Selma because she hadn't wanted to take you along to hear the band, and it was only because Red came that you were able to go. He said that there's a bit of Haman in everybody, and that's why there are Hamans all over the world."

"That's why they were fighting?"

"Yeah, that's it." Mrs. Shore shrugged her shoulders and said, "Eddie makes it his job to stick up for you and say that it's right that you live here. He's quite the genius, that Eddie." My heart sank. What does Eddie want from me? He's really a pain added onto all my troubles.

Red Can Guess

March 27

When I got home from work today, I found two letters on my bed. I was happy to see them even before I knew who they were from. For me, letters are a sign that people are still thinking about me, that I am not a fallen leaf that can wither away without anybody noticing. I recognized the letter in the blue envelope right away. It was from Layzer, whose first letter had also come in such a blue envelope. The second letter was from the Council of Jewish Charity Women. I wanted to read them both at once, but I opened the council's letter first. It was in English. I only understood one word in the letter—"laundry"—and I figured out that it must be about work. My aunt read the letter for me and said that they wanted me to come see them about a job in a laundromat. I remembered that they had written down that I was a "laundry worker." I'll go see. Maybe it's a better job than the one I have now, where I earn seventy-five cents a day.

Layzer's letter had a photograph of him and several young people who had come with him to Palestine on the Greek ship. Layzer was in the middle, without a hat. I recognized the checkered suit that he had worn in Lublin, and tears sprang to my eyes. If I hadn't been embarrassed in front of my aunt, I would have wept aloud. But I swallowed my tears and wiped my eyes. As I was reading Layzer's letter, Red came in. What wind blew him here just then? Couldn't he have come half an hour later?

I've learned at least one thing in America. Whether things are good or bad, the first thing you have to do is smile. And maybe these Americans are right after all. If you smile, everyone sees that the world hasn't turned topsy-turvy overnight. You're still smiling. So what if there's some *trubl*, as they say, "it will all even out." I really like the expression "It will all even out."

"You've got a letter from home? What does it say?" Red asked me.

Should I tell him about Layzer? Who he is? Or should I just say the letter is from home. But my aunt certainly noticed that the letter was from Palestine, and she'd know I was lying if I said it was from Lublin. That's all I need. It turns out that lying must be a real shame, because you're ashamed when you're found out.

"No, this letter is from a neighbor," I answered Red. I saw that Red was looking at the photograph that was lying in my lap. I showed it to him, and he looked at all the faces in the photo and then asked who had written to me.

"Guess!" I said, pleased that the photograph was of several people and not just of Layzer.

Red examined the photograph again, and I felt strange when he pointed at Layzer. "This one?"

"How did you know?"

Red laughed and pointed at his heart. "This told me," he said.

I quickly finished reading the letter and put it in my pocket together with the photo.

"What are they writing?" asked my aunt.

"They're describing how they fled to Palestine on a Greek ship."

"They're fleeing as if from fire," she sighed. "At least it's possible to find some kind of a boat somewhere."

I saw that Red was out of sorts, and I wanted to get him out of his bad mood, so I asked him to give me an English lesson.

"Look. I can't even read the letter that came from the Council of Jewish Charity Women."

Red shook his head from side to side. "Tomorrow," he said, and then he asked my aunt where Selma was.

"She went with Eddie to see a movie picture."

"Come on, Rivke; we'll go too."

The movie was about some detectives who were chasing a criminal. There was shooting and running over roofs and climbing up ropes. It was awful. The best detective was a woman, and she was the one who finally found the crook.

In the middle of the movie, Red took my hand and said, "Rivke, *yu liyk dis boy?*"

"What boy?" I asked, as my heart started beating faster and louder.

"The one in the picture?"

"I told you not to ask me any questions," I said and slapped his hand playfully.

I was lucky enough to have the people sitting near us start shushing us. "Sh, sh. We're bothering them."

And even though lately I've taken to telling a lot of lies—to my aunt, to Mrs. Shore, to Mrs. Koshes, to Ruth, and to others—I feel as if the greatest lie I ever told was the one I told Red. It bothered me a lot.

It's All about the Here and Now

March 28

Since that strange argument between Selma and Eddie, my heart has been heavy, even though I don't feel at all responsible for it. How could it have been my fault? I always flee from Eddie. When Eddie asked me to go to the movies with him, I didn't go. I didn't answer his notes. Still, my heart is heavy. And today I realized it was not for nothing that I felt this way. Very early in the morning, when everyone was still asleep, my uncle got up, and I heard him wandering around the house, shuffling papers, looking into a religious book. He kept pacing around. I didn't want to sleep anymore, so I took out Layzer's letter and read it again. He writes that I should not forget that I have yet to reach my destination. I must come to him, to Palestine. He said he was a little angry with me. His heart feels that I've strayed from him. He gets no letters from me, and while it may be that they're simply not reaching him, "if your letters were lost somewhere trying to get to me, I would feel it." That's what he writes. Maybe he's right? I don't know. I'm too taken up with Red. But if I could go to Layzer today, I'd do it. I would go back to my home, to those happy times that are now gone forever. My uncle heard that I was awake; he must have heard me rustling the pages of Layzer's letter. I was surprised when he stuck his head into my room.

"You're not sleeping, Rivke? Why not? It's still so early."

"I'm reading a letter. I can't sleep." My uncle came nearer and sat down on a chair near my bed. He had a strange look on his face, at the same time kind and uneasy. I felt my love for him, and it hurt me to see him so unhappy. He was quiet for a while and then he said: "Rivke, I think you're a smart girl, a good girl. And I love you as much as my own daughter. I want you to know that. I feel the same way about you and about Selma."

That's what he said, and he grew silent again. So, what can I say?

God has cursed me with tears. Before I could say or do anything, my eyes welled up, and I knew just what my uncle wanted to tell me. I could see how hard it was for him.

"I want to talk things over with you," he said. "But don't tell your aunt. You can see what America is like. It's hard to make a living. It's like parting the Red Sea. Believe me, Rivke, when I start going to my customers, I have to agree with every one of them. If someone is religious, I have to pretend to be too; if he's an ignoramus, I have to behave like one too; if he's just plain nuts, I still have to say OK. It's hard to slave away like that. But you have to make a living, so you clench your teeth and go on living. I often think it might have been better if I had stayed a rabbi in Novogrudek rather than become an insurance agent on Grand Street. I'm not talking about nowadays. Now there's a war, there's destruction everywhere. Thank God we're here in America. I'm just thinking out loud. Up to now . . . but you can't go back. A person can escape a lion's den or a fire, but once he's made his way into a livelihood, he can't escape it. That's all there is to it. There's nothing to be done about it once you're making a living. You just carry on. My biggest worry now is Selma. Selma needs to get married. You know these American children with their *beutee parlers*, their *bends*, and all the clothes that must *metch*. It's all a devil's game. You think I'm so pleased with Eddie? He's hardly even Jewish, barely knows a word of Yiddish, and doesn't know how to pray. I don't know how anyone can live with someone like that. But I can't change America. And Selma is an American. She wants what others want. And what about Eddie? When he first saw Selma, he only had eyes for her. Now that you've come, it's you he looks at. What difference does it make to them? All they're interested in is this world. It's all about this world, never the world to come. What can you expect from someone who only cares about the here and now? Yesterday, or the day before, I saw how Eddie took a handwritten note out of his pocket and put it under your pillow. He did it so that no one would notice. I wouldn't have noticed it either, but I saw him pacing around your bed when you weren't here. When he left with Selma, I went over to your bed. I don't know why, but something drew me there. After all, Selma is my child. I found the note. What's written there doesn't matter. There's a lot to read. A great deal. It's not enough to make you happy, but it is enough to make Selma miserable."

"Uncle, believe me, I'm not at all . . ."

"I know. You don't need to tell me. You have a heart of gold. You're just like your grandfather, Reb Mottele. You're cut from the same cloth. You wouldn't hurt a fly. I know that. But Eddie . . . Eddie isn't you. For him—I mean for all of them—it wouldn't matter if he had to give up his mother and his father and Selma too if it meant he'd have what he wanted right now. Listen to me, Rivke. I want you to know that it's a great joy for me to have you here, to have such a child, a good child in the house. But there's the story of Eddie. Eddie! Eddie! Eddie. What can we do? It would be better if he didn't see you. People like him see only what's in front of their noses. When he sees you, he wants to spend time with you. And if he won't see you? He won't. Wouldn't it be better that way, Rivke?"

"Yes, Uncle, you're right. I was thinking the same thing."

"Well, don't think that I'm throwing you out of the house, God forbid. I'll help you out with money, and you're already earning some. It will be better like this."

"Good, Uncle, I'll rent a room somewhere."

"But I beg one thing of you: don't think that you're in the way here, or that your aunt thinks so. It has nothing to do with that. It's worrying about Selma. I've grown old and gray because of her."

He spoke those last few words all in one breath, and I could see on his face that every single word was the truth.

Meanwhile, my aunt called him. "What are you doing in there? What is this business of getting up in the middle of the night? Aren't there enough hours in the day for you?" And then she got out of bed too. My uncle put his finger to his lips, asking me not to say a word, and left. When I went downstairs to go to work, he called me back, closed the door, came down a few stairs, and handed me fifteen dollars.

"Here. Take this, Rivke. But don't rush. There's no need to rush into anything. Take as long as you need."

I took the money with a light heart, as if my own father had given it to me.

All Alone

March 31

When I was in Antwerp and learned that my mother, may she rest in peace, was no longer alive, I felt as if I was all alone in the world and that no one cared what happened to me. Thursday morning, after the conversation with my uncle, I felt the same way. I felt all alone on Grand Street. I have to leave my uncle's house because it's better for Selma if I go. As I was walking to work, it seemed as if Grand Street was running after me, throwing me off the sidewalk, chasing me from my uncle's house. But where should I go? Who knows? I'm on my own. Whatever will be, will be, I said to myself. And I imagined that when I got to Mrs. Koshes's house, she would be standing on the threshold and would say, "I don't need you. Others will sew the flowers on tablecloths." That's what I was thinking. As luck would have it, Mrs. Koshes didn't leave me alone for a minute. Every now and then she would come down the stairs and take a look at my handiwork. I was sewing a heart onto a dress. It was delicate work, and Mrs. Koshes bent over the needle once again, just as the sales agents had described. When I saw that she was going up and down the stairs with her cane and that she did it more lightly than usual, I knew that she wanted to say something to me. What could it be?

It turns out that no one in the world has only bad luck. On the very day when everything seemed awful, Mrs. Koshes sat down next to me and said, "What's your name?"

I was surprised that she didn't already know my name.

"Rivke," I answered.

"Rivke isn't any kind of name here. You need to call yourself Ray. My niece's name is Ray too, also from Rivke."

Afterward, when she had changed my name so that it would fit "here," she said, "You've got a feeling for this work, Ray, you really do." She took a pointer out of her box of silk thread and moved it back and forth over the petals that I was sewing and said, "This curve in the leaf is what others can't do. It comes out just as it should when you do it. I like that a lot. Others have no idea what a stitch means. One stitch can bring a leaf to life or make it seem wooden, stiff. They don't understand that. And when I talked to them about it, they thought I was crazy or a witch. That's what they called me. 'She,' 'she' is how those girls referred to me. You, on the other hand, understand these things. If I still had the eyesight I once had, I would teach you how to work with colors. That's a special skill. Listen, Ray," she said, smacking her lips as if she had eaten something very tasty, "if you know how to work with colors, you can do anything. You can make the sky, a bird, a forest. There isn't a thing in the world that can't be made with colors. It's a powerful, moving thing. You'd be able to learn all that, but I don't have the eyes with which to teach you."

As she spoke, Mrs. Koshes looked at the leaf I had sewn and was obviously pleased with it. Slowly, my fear of being all alone on Grand Street left me. Mrs. Koshes kept sitting there, with her pointer in her hand. And I was reminded of our Lubliner teacher, Reb Berish Tartakover. I once came to him in school because my mother, may she rest in peace, sent me with a pear for my brother Mikhl.

"Take pity on the child," she had said. "The pear will give him new energy." When I came to Reb Berish Tartakover with the pear in hand, my brother was in the middle of reciting his lessons, so I stood and waited. Just then, a fire engine was passing by with firemen in brass helmets. They weren't running to a fire but walking in a parade. Their orchestra was playing and the trumpets blew so loudly it was deafening and the brass hats were shining in the sun and lighting up the windows. The boys stared and listened. My brother Mikhl stopped his recitation. Suddenly, Yankele the scoundrel—that's what we called him because he had a lot of chutzpah—sprang up and called out, "Come on, guys, look at the fire! Let's go!" And he leapt up from the table. All ten boys followed him, some running out from under the table, some from under the bench. They looked like goats jumping around. And Reb Berish Tartakover was left with only the bony pointer in his hand.

"Look at them. Just look. If there was at least a fire!"

And then he turned to me. "What do you want?"

"I've brought a pear for Mikhl."

"Take it back," he said angrily. "He'll be fine without the pear." I saw that he was furious but even more sad than angry. I went back home with the pear, and he was left there all alone, but he never let go of the pointer. That's just how Mrs. Koshes was sitting now with the bony pointer in her hand, disappointed with the girls who had no feeling for a stitch.

I didn't want to go home. Maybe I should have asked Mrs. Koshes if I could spend the night. But I remembered what she had said about relatives nowadays: "You eat there, too? They are good people."

She wouldn't know what my uncle said about his worries over Selma, and she would think that I'd been thrown out of the house. No, it was better to say nothing and ask nothing of her. But I still didn't feel like going home, so I stopped off to see the laundress. She was in one of her commanding moods. She commanded the *boy* to go quickly because he needed to deliver a bundle of laundry to the barbershop. And she told the colored girl to hang all the bundles in the yard overnight so that they would dry out. And she yelled upstairs to her husband, telling him to take an aspirin. "Why should you go around with a *hedayk*?" Even though she was ordering everyone around, she glanced at me and smiled as if to say, "Don't bother me now because now I only have eyes for the laundry."

"Wait," she said, "soon we'll go *opsteyrz*."

Upstairs she was, as always, a different person.

"It's good that you came," she said, and she went off to make coffee. It was good to sit there. In her house, I no longer felt like I had in the morning, that I was all alone on Grand Street.

After the *kup koffee*, I told her that my aunt was expecting guests, and the apartment would be too cramped. I needed to find a room.

"I'll set things up for you here in the meantime," she answered right away. And if I had not been too embarrassed, I would have embraced and kissed her.

I hadn't known that the laundress had a story for everything. The stories were about days gone by, when she was still Bashke Licht and not Bertie Shlivke. She had a story about my staying over with her and about how things were getting cramped at my aunt's. "Nowadays," she said, "people live in four or five rooms, and there's no place for anyone to sleep. But things used to be different. When I was in dental school, I lived in a room that was about as big as an egg peel. And all my girlfriends used to spend the night with me. What's the use of a bed? A bed was unnecessary. We would take 'the big bear'—that was my old coat with wide sleeves. That's why we called it 'the big bear.' We'd lay that big bear down on the floor and spread a sheet over it and put down a pillow and that's how we'd sleep. If there were two of us, then two slept there; if there were three, then three. The big bear was as big as we needed it to be. What? Do you think it was a problem to sleep like that? We slept better than now. A lot better. And believe me, I'd be happy to pay twenty-five dollars if I could sleep on that big bear on Krokhmalna Street again."

She shook her head as if to say, "Gone. Finished!"

I didn't want to spend the night there because I didn't want to upset my uncle. And, anyway, I wanted to see Red. Maybe he had stopped by. I arranged to come sleep at her house tomorrow night.

There's No One to Say Good-bye To

April 3

I couldn't sleep last night. I kept thinking of how I would move away from my aunt. What would I say to her? What would I say to Selma? To Mrs. Shore? To Red? I couldn't tell him what my uncle said to me about Eddie. I thought about it for so long that I finally fell asleep. And in the morning, I decided not to say anything but just to move. At first, I'd go for only one night and then for another night. And beyond that, who knows? Maybe I'd think up a good excuse. But the truth is that I didn't need to think about it so much. No one asked me so many questions. What's the expression? No one put a stumbling block in my way. When my aunt saw me putting my nightgown, towel, and toothbrush into a suitcase, she said, "What's the matter, Rivke? Is it too crowded for you here?" And before I could answer her, she added, "Well, maybe you'll be more comfortable." And she went off to a *sayl* of lamps. There's a separate sale for everything here. A sale on clothing and a sale on shoes, a sale on furniture, on lamps, on every single thing. I wouldn't be at all surprised if there were a sale on brides and grooms here. Maybe there would be customers for that too. Everybody would go take a look at the sale, as they say, *djost for fun*.

There was no one at home when I left. There wasn't anyone to say good-bye to.

The laundress showed me where to put my things, and then she disappeared. She only had eyes for the laundry now.

When I left school today, I wound up at my uncle's house. At the entrance to the house, I remembered that I was spending the night at the laundress's.

I've wandered off, I thought, and my throat tightened. Despite everything, this had been a home for me. If not for Eddie . . .

Meanwhile, Mrs. Shore came out. "I was just going to see you!" she said. "There's a postcard for you. And, anyway, I wanted to see where you'd run off to."

"Run off?"

"Of course run off. You didn't even say good-bye."

I tried to explain that I was planning on coming by, and often.

"I know," she said, winking. "I know that you're running away from Eddie. You did the right thing, the smart thing." And Mrs. Shore laughed.

"All my cards are on the table," I thought. "We may think that nobody knows what's going on, but people know. Everybody knows." That's what I thought.

The postcard was from Sheinfeld. He's sick. "Come visit," he wrote. "I've been sick for four days already, and I don't have too many friends here." That's how he put it: not too many friends. He may be in worse shape than I am. Who knows how bad things are with him? I'll go see him tomorrow. I'll leave work a little early and go see him.

The Silent Housewife

April 4

I can't get out of my mind the thought of Sheinfeld lying all alone in the little room he rents from his silent landlady. His bed is low, and when I came in, he looked like he was lying on the ground, and I thought my heart would break at the sight of it. He smiled and said, "Rivke, please, first of all buy me some rubbing alcohol because I haven't been able to wash myself for the past three days, and it feels as if I'm growing moss." He waited, squinting at me as if his eyes really were overgrown with moss. I saw that he was swallowing his own saliva because he was so thirsty. So, before I went down to buy him the alcohol, I went into the kitchen to make a glass of tea for him. In the *kitshn*, a woman was sitting and knitting.

"I want to make some tea for Mr. Sheinfeld," I said to her.

She didn't say a word but silently handed me a teakettle that must have been a hundred years old. I once saw exactly the same thing in my grandfather Reb Mottele's attic in Lublin. The teakettle's cover was attached to its handle with a small chain so that it wouldn't fall off and get lost. Silently, she turned on the gas burner for me. Silently, she handed me a glass and a saucer and a spoon, and silently she sat down and started knitting again. She was knitting a sleeve that had a little bit of gray, a little bit of brown, and a little bit of only God knows what kind of color. I gave Sheinfeld his tea, and he drank it in one gulp.

"I always drink it hot," he said apologetically.

He looked awful. Maybe he looked so bad because his bed was so low to the ground.

I asked him if his landlady was a mute or just didn't like to talk. She hadn't said a single word to me.

Sheinfeld licked his lips and said, "Some days she's mute. If I'm late with the rent, she turns silent. Others use words to ask; she uses silence, and that's much harder to take. I'm already four days late with my rent, and she's been as silent as that wall for the past three days. I have to give her fifteen dollars, but until I'm well . . ."

I went downstairs, bought Sheinfeld rubbing alcohol and something to eat. When I came back, he said, "It's hard to live like this. I wouldn't mind giving up the whole thing, but my wife and child—my child is only six years old. Maybe there's still a chance that I'll see them and be able to help them. But still, why does my landlady begrudge me even one word? Why does she turn silent?"

I told Sheinfeld about my father's letter and how he's living in Krasu-lye's stall.

"Both things are no good," he said, pointing to his room with its narrow table against the wall. "Both are no good."

I went home, leaving Sheinfeld with a glass of cold tea, two oranges, the bottle of rubbing alcohol, and the mute landlady.

I'll go see Mr. Shamut tomorrow. He's the vice president of the Aid Society for refugees. He has to find fifteen dollars so that Mr. Sheinfeld can pay for his apartment and the landlady can get her voice back. I practiced what I would say to Mr. Shamut and what I'd answer if he didn't want to give the money. Lost in thought, I came to the laundromat.

Someone grabbed my arm. "Stop!"

It was Red. "You left your aunt's house?"

That's all I need now, I thought. All night I wondered what to tell everyone, and in the end I still didn't know what to say. But, luckily, Red hadn't waited for me to answer.

"Very good," he said. "I'm very happy. I'm *gled*."

Why was he so glad? Maybe he wanted to be rid of Eddie too? Or did he want to be rid of Ruth? Who knows? At least I didn't have to explain to him why I left my aunt's.

It was too late to go to the movies, so we walked over to the East River. Red seems to like the East River as much as Layzer liked the pinewood forest. He would always say, "Let's go to the pinewood forest," and Red always says, "*Kom an*, let's go to the East River." But walking with him to the East River, I felt as if I was in the pinewood forest too, as if I was walking both here and there. Is it possible to be in two places at once? I guess it is.

Red is good at guessing things. The other day, he guessed which of the people in the photograph was Layzer. And at the East River, he guessed what I was thinking.

"*Du yu tink abawt Lublin?*"

"Why do you ask?"

"I see . . ."

"No, Red, I'm thinking about my teacher, Sheinfeld. He's sick, and his landlady has grown mute worrying about the rent."

"*Reelee?*" Red asked, and once again I thought that nothing ever bothered him. And, since Red can always guess what people are thinking, he said, "You're a good person, Rivke, *Iy liyk yu*. But Eddie told me that you have a fiancé in Lublin."

"What do you care?" I said, laughing. "Do you pay *tekses* for him?"

"Yeah, I pay taxes for him," Red said. He thought for a bit and then went on. "Rivke, *yu no*, there are *gerls* who cry and *gerls* who laugh. Everything's a joke for them. For you, there's only laughter."

"Laughter," I repeated mockingly.

"You can't laugh over *evryting*, Rivke."

"*Evryting*," I repeated.

"It's impossible to talk to you," said Red, and gestured with his hand, "because . . ."

For a while, Red thought about how to end that sentence. I helped him out with "Because I'm from Lublin."

"*Dat's de trubl*," he agreed. "Because you are too much of a Lubliner."

Red got over his anger quickly. He started to laugh and forgot about whatever had made him mad. Eddie must have wanted us to quarrel. Why would he tell Red a story about me and a fiancé? Eddie wants to have both Selma and me. My uncle was right.

I Meet the Messiah

April 5

It's not for nothing that people believe in the Messiah. He exists. And I met him today. He came to me in my hour of greatest need. He didn't come because of me but rather because of Sheinfeld. Sheinfeld and his illness. I left Mrs. Koshes's an hour earlier than usual and ran to Mr. Shamut to ask for the fifteen dollars that Sheinfeld needed in order to pay his rent. Mr. Shamut greeted me warmly and said, "So, things are still bad, even though Mr. Edelshtein paid one hundred quarters for you. What else can I do?"

I told him that Sheinfeld was sick and needed fifteen dollars so that his landlady would stop being mute and angry because his rent was late.

"She'll have to stay mute," he said. "We can't do a thing. We have no funds with which to pay rent. Every single penny is spoken for."

I asked Mr. Shamut to make an exception. I told him that Sheinfeld was all alone and his landlady was making him miserable.

"Women always make you miserable," Mr. Shamut joked. "Don't you understand? We can help someone find a job, or we can give advice—and that's very important. We can find him somewhere to sleep for a while, but we can't pay his rent."

"Make an exception for him," I said again. "Sheinfeld isn't the kind of man to come begging."

"Exceptions are only made for a *sheyn-meydl* (a pretty girl) but not for a *Sheyn-feld*." Mr. Shamut smiled, enjoying his own joke.

"What is to become of him?" I asked, speaking more to myself than to Mr. Shamut.

"Maybe the Lublin Society will help you. I can write a letter to them for you. But we can't do anything else," he said, spreading his hands out as if to show how empty they were. "We, my dear, can't do a thing."

I saw that Mr. Shamut's hand was moving toward the clock that was lying on his table, and so I left the office. What next? What was to become of Sheinfeld? I kept thinking of how he had said that he would give it all up if not for his wife and child.

I buried my face in my hands, lost in thought about where I should go to get fifteen dollars for Sheinfeld. Maybe Mrs. Tkatsh? And as I was thinking, standing there in the middle of the waiting room, Elijah the Prophet, or the Messiah or who knows who, came over to me. Who cares who it was? He came to help!

"What are you thinking about so much?"

I was surprised to hear him address me in the polite *ir* instead of the familiar *du*. Everyone here uses *du* when they talk to me. Who could this be? A very old and tall man was standing opposite me. I had never seen hair as white as his.

"What are you thinking about?" he asked again and, without waiting for an answer, he said, "I've been a director here for forty years. I built this institution. You can tell me what you need."

He took out a business card:

Yitzhak Fish
Director, Aid Society
1900

"Forty years ago, we built this institution for humanitarian reasons, in order to help people." And he pulled another business card out of his pocket:

Yitzhak Fishman
President, Aid Society
1906

"I sat here day and night. I made these chairs myself. I painted the walls myself. I underwrote the Association's *tsharter* myself."

I told him about Sheinfeld. He was a teacher, a good, gentle man. Now he was a sick man, a refugee, all alone here. He needed fifteen dollars for rent. He was working in a *fektoree* of secondhand spoons, but now he was sick, without family . . .

"What a pity," the old man said. "Truly a pity. Whatever happened to humaneness? What are you to him? A relative?"

"No, I was his student. He taught me math."

"Come," he said. "Come with me." He went up to the second floor. I wasn't sure that he would do anything for me, but I went upstairs with him. What did I have to lose?

The old man walked into every door without knocking. "Where is Mr. Kahn?" he asked.

We came to Mr. Kahn, the president. At a nearby table, two secretaries sat working at their typewriters. When they saw the old man, they looked at one another as if to say, "Here he comes again; there's bound to be some to-do now."

Mr. Kahn gave him a friendly greeting. "*Halo, halo, halo*, Mr. Fish! *Vat nyus?*"

"*Trubl, trubl.* We need to give her fifteen dollars."

"It's not for me," I explained. "It's for a sick man, for Mr. Sheinfeld."

"Fifteen dollars. A sick man. A refugee. All alone. Oy, oy, oy. A little humanity."

"Mr. Fish," said Mr. Kahn, interrupting him. "I don't need to tell you how things are. You were here when we decided that we wouldn't pay anyone's household expenses. We don't have enough for that. You know that, Mr. Fish."

"Decided. Decided. Vey, vey, vey. Humanity. A man sick in bed. All alone. Not everyone comes to us. But, look, she came. What if someone were to fall down in the middle of the street? People would help."

Mr. Kahn stood up and said, "But we can't overturn a decision. We just can't."

The old man waved him away as if he were a fly: "Vey, vey, vey. What are you telling me? I built this *institushun*. I carried the boards myself. I painted it myself. Why? For humanitarian reasons. Vey, vey. . . . Where is the table? I don't see it here. It was a strong table, made of oak, with nails to make it last a hundred years. Why do we need *fornitsher* here? Who needs that? We need mentshlekhkeyt—kindness, common decency. We must give her fifteen dollars."

When Mr. Kahn heard about the oak table, he put his hand on his forehead and said, "But, Mr. Fish, I don't have it. I'm not the one in charge here. *Dat's imposibl.*"

"Possible. Impossible," the old man mocked. With a loud, shaking voice he said, "I'm the one in charge. I painted every wall. I'll give two dollars out of my pocket." And he reached for his wallet.

Mr. Kahn got up and went one flight down with the old man. I wanted to follow them, but the old man told me to stay where I was. "Who knows you here? Who knows who you are?"

"Mr. Shamut knows me. He's from the same city."

"Good. Sit here."

I stayed seated. The two secretaries laughed and whispered to one another. I heard them say *krayzee*.

To be in love is *krayzee*, and it looks like everything the old man had said was also *krayzee*. English is certainly a strange language. I think that *krayzee* means anything emotional. I'll have to ask Mrs. Schwartz or Red.

The old man came back, followed by Mr. Kahn looking like a wet dish-rag. The old man was holding a check, and his hand and the check were both trembling. He walked over to a table where one of the secretaries was sitting and waved her away. He sat down to sign the check, which was made out to Yitzhak Fishman.

"Once I could sign anything standing up, but now I can't do that. I have to sit down." The pen shook until three big blots of ink fell on the check. Very carefully, laboring over every letter, he signed his name in English. The letters were as shaky as his hand, far apart from one another as if to make each letter clearer. His signature took up two lines and then he underlined it all with a third line.

"This *institushun* was built for mentshlekhkeyt," he said, handing me the check. I went downstairs with him, and he showed me four more cards.

"I say *mentshlekhkeyt* to them . . . So, wha-a-a-at," he said scornfully, stretching out the *what*. He left, but then turned around to wish a speedy and full recovery to Sheinfeld.

I ran out to the street and looked around. The old man was no longer there. He must have turned at the corner. I really did think I'd met the Messiah. People say that he disguises himself in order to help people when they need it most. And once again I had to deal with my troublesome eyes; I started to cry in the middle of the street, and everybody stared at me. What did I care? At last, I had the check for Sheinfeld and his landlady, so there would be an end to her muteness.

Mr. Karelin's "Materials"

April 6

Red came with me to see Sheinfeld, who is feeling better. He said that the rubbing alcohol helped him, and I think that what really helped was actually the speedy recovery that the "Messiah" sent. Whatever it was, I was just glad he was feeling stronger and that he'd be able to return to work in a few days.

"I wanted to do it on my own, without having to ask for anything," said Sheinfeld. "But then I got sick. . . . Where did you get this check?"

"I met the Messiah."

"No, I'm serious."

"I'm telling you, Mr. Sheinfeld, I met the Messiah. He brought me the check and signed it himself, and you never asked anyone for anything."

Sheinfeld looked at the signature. "It's an odd signature. It really does look as if it's not of this world."

I was so happy. I hadn't sung for a long time. What was there to sing about? But now, when Sheinfeld asked me to give the Messiah's check to his landlady, I couldn't help myself and started singing the song:

Landlady dearest,
Dearest, dearest landlady,
Landlady dearest,
Dearest landlady . . .

Sheinfeld noticed that Red was staring at his nails, and he tried to explain it away, just as he had the first time he saw me. "My nails stay black. It won't wash off because of the chemicals used to wash the old spoons so they can be sold *sekondhend*." Sheinfeld raised himself a little from his bed. "I could have had clean nails and also a *dzshob*, but I would have had to sign my name and I didn't want to. So, now I'm left with black nails."

Red was curious, and to be honest, I also wanted to know the story of the "signing." I wouldn't have asked, but Red did.

"That's all? What's that about?"

Sheinfeld had had enough silence with his mute landlady, and so he told us the whole story.

"You know, of course," he said, "that my wife is from Lublin and I come from Lodz. Even though I come from there, I don't like Lodz. Because of all the commerce, Lodz is a busy city with all kinds of brokers, connivers, moneylenders, and swindlers. All sorts of riffraff came running to Lodz, and they started sending their wares all over the world. You can't call a whole city. . . . There was a Reb Shmulke Katavitser in Lodz, who had always given a tithe of his income to charity. He used to say, 'I don't want to earn money from the destruction of the Holy Temple.' That's the kind of man he was."

Poor Red had no idea what Sheinfeld was talking about and started asking him what he meant by "tithe" and "the destruction of the Holy Temple." In short, we had to work hard before Red understood what the story of Reb Shmulke Katovitser was all about. But we still wanted to hear the story of the signature.

"Yeah," said Sheinfeld, "It's all about Lodz. I found someone from home, from Lodz here. He was all dressed up, a big shot in New York. We had gone to school together, and he was really happy to see me. He started bragging that he could 'make' someone in New York and 'unmake' them too. He was the chairman of the East-West Loan Society.

"'And what became of you?' he asked. 'I heard you were a professor?'

"'Yes, a teacher, a lecturer,' I answered.

"He took my address, and I thought it would be *gud bay un gud luk*, as they say in America, but a few days later, he showed up with a whole packet of papers. He said that the East-West Loan Society was making a banquet in honor of his fiftieth birthday, and they were issuing a biography of him. So, since we're both from Lodz and I know him and his father and his mother well, and I know his friends, and on top of all that, I'm a professor, he wanted me to write his biography. I wanted to get out of it and told him that I just couldn't focus on such a project now.

"'I have all the materials,' he said to me, handing me a package. 'You just need to add some of your own memories and sign it as an old friend, a classmate, Professor Dr. Sheinfeld. You won't regret it. It's good to be on good terms with the East-West Loan Society.'

"I took the materials, looked at them, and decided I couldn't sign off on them. I was too embarrassed. My father—may he live to be a hundred and twenty—is still alive. I didn't want to sign our family name to this nonsense. His father was a con artist in Lodz . . . . He came to Lodz with a reputation he had earned in Benzin. They called him 'the windmill.' But in the materials I was given, it says that his father worked for the community, was elected to the Jewish community council, and helped orphans. And he—the East-West Loan Society man—had been recognized as a brilliant Talmud student when he was only nine years old. Believe me, it was nauseating. I didn't sign. And as you see, I have blackened nails. That's how it goes."

And Sheinfeld added, "Please don't tell anyone this story. I don't want to have issues with the East-West Loan Society. He can ruin this job for me too."

"*Dat's fulish,*" said Red. "You should have signed the book. *Vat iz dee diferens?* What do you care whether his father was a *vint mil* or a *niys man*?"

"Yes," Sheinfeld said in agreement, "maybe you're right. But I just couldn't. People have to have *mentshlekhkeyt*, some common decency."

His words resonated in my head. He used the word *mentshlekhkeyt*, just as the "Messiah" had. How could that be? Sheinfeld hadn't seen him or heard him speak. How is it that he came upon the very same word just then? How strange that they should both talk in the same way about humanitarianism, common decency, and proper behavior.

When we left Sheinfeld, I asked Red if he would have signed his name to those materials.

"I don't know, Rivke. I don't want to lie about it. He's *awlriyt*, that Sheinfeld."

The best thing was what happened with Sheinfeld's landlady. When I went into the kitchen to make him a glass of tea after she had the check, she spoke nonstop. I had always heard the expression "money talks," but I never really understood what that meant. Now I understand! It talks nonstop.

"Maybe you want some tea leaves? Do you need a strainer? I like to drink tea that way."

"Where are you from?" I asked her.

"From Lodz," she answered, as sweetly as if she wanted a kiss. "Maybe you'd like a nice piece of lemon?" she asked.

Thank goodness that I'm from Lublin and that Red is from New York!

I Look for Work

April 7

It's good that Mrs. Koshes had to go to a *partee* at her nephew's house on Sunday. On Friday she said, "You'd be lucky to earn every day what this birthday party is going to cost me. First of all, his mother will expect a present for the boychick, and the boychick will expect me to bring him candy; that's what's most important to him."

Because of the party, I didn't have to go to work today. I'll have seventy-five cents less this week, but at least I had time to stop off at the office of the Jewish Charity Women to ask about the letter they had sent me. Maybe they had a job for me. I won't be able to make it for long on what I'm earning at Mrs. Koshes's. It's hard to make do with four and a half dollars a week. It's a good thing that she lives on Grand Street and I can walk there and back without spending money on carfare.

If I had been in a lighter mood, it would have been fun at the Jewish Charity Women's office. They almost turned me into a boy! I went straight to Mrs. Mayofes because she speaks Yiddish. I thought I'd come, talk to her, and be done; I'd know what's what. It turns out that you have to wait on a *liyn* to get to the information desk. And then they send you wherever you need to go. I really didn't want to wait on the line, and I tried to sneak into Miss Mayofes's room, but someone stopped me and said I had to wait.

I waited a long time and then, just like the last time, I was sent first to Miss Eichenbaum and then to Miss Rabinowitz and then to Miss Kasher and then to Miss Mayofes. I liked Miss Kasher best of all these "misses." She recognized me and laughingly said: "*O, yu speek dzshewish.*"

The worst was Miss Eichenbaum. When I showed her the letter, she started talking to me and got caught up in the word *reliyabl. Reliyabl* this and *reliyabl* that, and I had no idea what she wanted from me. Fortunately, she got tired of it and sent me on to Miss Kasher, who has at least one virtue: she knows that we don't understand one another. She laughed and gestured with her hand, and at least she wasn't some English record player; this was a human being whom I didn't understand, but still—a human being. She had a good idea and gave me the address of a laundromat and said, "*Go dher, yu'll see.*"

The laundromat was somewhere in the Bronx, and I took the subway and then the elevated train to get there. It turned out that they needed a boy to deliver the bundles. They didn't want a woman. The only good thing was that they spoke to me in Yiddish, and I could understand what was going on. The owner barely spoke. She grumbled, "*Vee* need a boy," and that's all. She didn't look at me or say another word. Her husband was completely different. He asked me who I was and what I could do and where I came from. He took my address just in case something came up.

He must be a good man, and I felt sorry for him because he had such a grouchy wife. People say that there's no such thing in the world as a well-matched couple, and today I saw clear proof.

I had no alternative but to spend another nickel and go home. It doesn't feel natural to say *home*. What kind of home is it? My bed is not my own. It's upstairs in a room at the laundress's house where bundles of laundry lie. The bundles lie on shelves against a wall, and my bed lies near the opposite wall. The laundress gave me a table and chair for the room. Can this be called a home? Still, it was better than living in Krasulye's stall. If only my father and brother were here. Then it would be the best home in the world, and I would want nothing more. There's no point in thinking about my mother, though I think about her all the time.

I have a headache whenever I get out of the subway. I can't get used to the air there, and I always have to think about whether I need to go *uptown* or *downtown* and to be careful not to get lost. It's hard, and my head starts to ache. That's what happened today too. I brought a bad headache home with me and lay down to think about what to do next. Maybe I should call up Mr. Edelshtein and ask him for a job? Even if I continued to live in this room, I'd still have to pay something. Could it all come from four and a half dollars a week? For now, I have the fifteen dollars that my uncle gave me. But what will happen later? Later, after, next . . . Why did I need to think so much about that? I saw with my own eyes that the Messiah is in New York too, and he comes to help people when they need it. He came to me once; maybe he'll come again.

Roses are Blooming for You

April 9

My coat is threadbare. It's not very old, but it's not so nice to walk around in. I don't want to show up at Mr. Edelshtein's looking like that. It's embarrassing. My mother, may she rest in peace, used to say, "If you're going to ask a favor of someone, go in a silk dress." Maybe I should borrow one of Selma's coats? She has at least four of them. I could borrow one and go see Mr. Edelshtein. I just wanted to talk to my aunt and Mrs. Shore, but I had no idea that Red would also have something to say about what I should do.

When I came home today, I found red roses on the table. Red had been there and left a note that said, "I'll see you later."

The laundress said, "Rivke, do you at least know how good you have it?"

"No, I don't know at all."

"Yeah, you've got it good. Roses are blooming for you."

"Red went a little crazy, so he brought me roses."

"It's a good kind of craziness, Rivke."

I thought that she was a little sad. Was it possible that she envied me? Who knows? But I didn't need to think about it for too long because she said it herself, "Rivke, I envy you. But what can I do? You can't live such a time twice."

When Red came, I showed him the bundles of laundry against the opposite wall and said, "What good are the flowers?"

"I brought the flowers for you and not for the room," he said. And he put one of the flowers in my hair.

"It's nice," he said. "The *foyst tiym* I saw you, you also had a flower in your hair."

I told Red that I wanted to go to Mr. Edelshtein to see about a job. He was a very wealthy man, and if he wanted to do something for me, he could certainly get it done. People say that he has lots of businesses, and it would be no big deal for him to take care of someone.

Red shook his head. "*Yu haf not to go dher.* You don't have to go to him for a job."

"Why not?"

"Because you don't need to."

I told Red that I needed a coat and couldn't live on four and a half dollars a week. Red answered me jokingly. "No, Rivke, don't go. I'll be mad at you if you go."

I was angry at Red for talking as if he was in charge of me. I didn't see why he should care if I went to Mr. Edelshtein looking for work. I thought I'd talk it over with my aunt and Mrs. Shore. But really, what was there to think about? I didn't have a coat to wear anyway. It's a good thing that it's almost summer. In a month, it will be warm, and I'll be able to go out without a coat.

In addition to Red, Mendl Pushcart came over today.

"Was it getting too cramped for you at your aunt's?" he asked, and he looked over at Red.

"My aunt is expecting guests. There won't be enough room, so I'm staying here with Mrs. Shlivke for now," I answered.

More and more I see that a person just can't make do with the truth. I never had to lie in Lublin, but here I do it often. Why is that? Who knows? Maybe in Lublin my parents lied for me? Is that possible? I have to think hard about that.

The laundress was in the other room. She wanted to cheer me up after Mendl Pushcart's question, and so she said loud enough for us to hear her, "She's no burden here at all. I've got four rooms. Once, when I was young . . ." and with that she came into the room and told everyone the story of the great bear in her small room on Krokhmalna Street.

"Once we were young," she said.

Gifts

April 11

As of today, I'm rich. Mrs. Koshes gave me a twenty-five-cent raise. It won't be permanent, but only for the few days during which I embroidered the heart. In return for the quarter, she talked to me, unburdening herself.

"Mrs. Freeman was very pleased with the work. So pleased that she placed another *awder*. So I thought that you should get something out of it too. People these days don't do that. Now, there's no such thing as thinking about someone else. They need the whole world for themselves and *dat's awl*. To each his own. *Miynd yur awn biznes*. But I'm still old-fashioned. I still want someone else to have a bit of the Leviathan too. So I thought to myself: let Ray have another quarter a day. Six quarters is a dollar and a half. I'm still old-fashioned."

So today I'm really rich. Maybe I should start saving money for a coat.

I've noticed that when it's a lucky day, everything goes well, but when things start turning topsy-turvy, everything goes badly. On that kind of day, it's better to go to bed and just sleep until you've slept away your bad luck. But why am I thinking about bad days today of all days?

Mrs. Shore also felt like giving me a raise today, for no good reason. It's just a sign of her goodness. Mrs. Koshes would have said that she's also one of the old-fashioned ones.

Mrs. Shore brought me a large package. First, I took out a bedspread and then some gefilte fish, and finally a whole bag of California apples. The beauty of each of those apples was worth all the riches of the world.

"This is what *he* sent you. My *misteh*," she said, winking an eye as usual. "Rivkele, with my *misteh*, just don't be overly friendly. Look, he's sent you the nicest apples in the world."

I promised her that I wouldn't be too friendly with her mister.

"Eat them in good health. He'll send more too, as long as your braids keep growing," she said and tugged at both my braids.

"You want to know why there's gefilte fish in the middle of the week, on a Wednesday? There's a story in that. A Jew with a cart brings me fish. He's been doing it for around eight or nine years. Today he came by, and I asked him why he was coming in the middle of the week all of a sudden.

"'Don't ask,' he said. 'They're good and they're cheap or else I wouldn't have brought them to you. It's from my own fish farm.'

"He owns a fish farm like I own the Empire State building. He's just a big talker. 'What do I need such a huge fish for?' I asked him.

"'You'll give some of it away,' he said, as if he were the boss of my purse. And off he went. So I thought to myself that he must mean you, Rivke, so here you are—gefilte fish!"

I immediately thought of the Messiah. I thought that someone must be watching out for me in New York so that I won't be hungry, won't be all alone, won't lose face. I remembered how Red had come with tickets to take me to hear the band. I remembered the fifteen-dollar check that Mr. Fishman—or as he's now called, Mr. Fish—brought me for Shein-feld. And I really did believe that someone was watching over me. Who knows? Maybe it was my mother. It's said that souls can fly far distances and crossing the ocean is nothing compared to crossing over from this world to the next.

I put the red apples out on the table, near the red flowers. They made the table look festive.

"Mrs. Shlivke, come eat some apples," I called out.

She came in. She was her upstairs self. Her hand flew up to her forehead, and she said, "What gorgeous apples. Yesterday, roses were blooming for you, and today it's apples. Rivke, you should know how good you have it."

Red came later, and I felt as if I had a family. The laundress, Mrs. Shore, Red, and I. Maybe this really is a family? Since no other one exists, at least let this be one. After all, I'm not all alone when I'm with them.

Red tattled to Mrs. Shore about me saying that I wanted to go to Mr. Edelshtein to ask for work. "*Eet iz fulish,*" he said. "*Ay dawn't liyk dis kiynd of vork.*" Mrs. Shore thought it over and said, "If Mr. Edelshtein hadn't given a hundred quarters in order to dance with Rivke. . . . Maybe it's not a bad idea to go to him for a job, but because he gave a hundred quarters, maybe Red is right. Forget him and his jobs."

It looks like I won't be going to Mr. Edelshtein. What's the saying? If two people say you're drunk, then you'd better go sleep it off.

My mother, may she rest in peace, had a habit of crying when she was unhappy. But when she was happy . . . well, that's when she would really cry. I think I've inherited the same flaw. All in all, today wasn't a bad day. I got a raise from Mrs. Koshes. I got apples from Mr. Shore. And after everything, when everyone left and I went to bed, I had a good, long cry.

Marvin

April 12

Mendl Pushcart has stirred things up. First, he went and told my aunt and uncle that I'm living in a "stall" together with bundles of laundry, and that it's a pity. And then he told them that I said there were guests coming to my aunt and it would get too crowded, so I left.

My aunt looked shocked. "Who's crowded? What guests?" And before you knew it, she started crying. That's my family's way. No matter what happens, we cry. My mother, may she rest in peace, was like that. I'm like that. And it turns out that my aunt is too. Mendl Pushcart realized that he had gotten into a mess, so he tried to turn things around: "If only all the Jews could live in America like Rivke. What's the point of crying? Is she lacking anything? Someone brought her flowers and apples, and she looks, may no evil eye befall her, like a *milyon doler.*"

It was Mendl Pushcart himself who told me this whole story. He really is a strange one. I just don't understand what he can be thinking. When he told me the story, he was looking at me so cheerfully you would have thought he had me a big favor instead of making a big mess. In the end, he said, "Come, your aunt has excellent *kookees* today. You'll eat *soper* at your aunt's, and you'll get to taste the *kookees.*"

"Did my aunt ask you to invite me?"

"Nobody needs to ask Mendl Pushcart. Mendl Pushcart already knows what to do. And if I say come, then you don't need to give it a second thought. Just come!"

I really and truly don't begin to understand him. He's like a carousel: spinning around and making noise all at once. Still, I went with him to my aunt's.

He was right about the cookies being very good. My uncle didn't make a big deal of my coming. When he was reading the newspaper, he called out, "Rivke, come here. Sit down near me. I want to show you something in the newspaper." I suppose he didn't want anyone to ask me too many questions. And he read aloud: "Poles are secretly helping Jews by bringing them food."

"Some honorable people they've become, those Poles," said Mendl Pushcart sarcastically. "If only they had been such righteous people when they held the reins! That's when they locked up all their righteousness in a box. But now they've dragged it out?"

My aunt greeted me like a true guest. She gave me an apple and then brought tea and cookies. But Mendl Pushcart stuck to his ways. He sent me to pour him a glass of tea.

"Rivke," he said, "when you give me a glass of *tee*, I enjoy it more. As I'm a Jew . . ."

Today, it didn't bother me at all. On the contrary, I thought that that's the way it should be. They didn't get to play pinochle tonight because Marvin came in with his friend, Abe, and both of them were holding newspapers and yelling, "*Heer it eez!*"

It turns out that Marvin's photo was in the paper, and there was an article praising his *gaymz* and his dancing and his club, Happy Hour. Marvin was so happy that he didn't even want to eat anything. He turned on the radio, found some music, and danced cheerfully with Abe. Mrs. Shore came in and clapped to the music. Later, Selma, Eddie, and Ruth also came in carrying newspapers. In honor of Marvin's photo, they started dancing too. The radio played, and everybody danced. You would have thought we were celebrating a wedding.

My uncle smiled. "Ida, we should build a religious study house for Marvin."

My aunt got really angry. "*Vot heppend tu yu?*" she asked. "What's with you? Thank God, the *boy* is a *sukses*. What difference does it make how he makes a living? A study house, of all things."

And Marvin added, "Benny Goodman *mayks munee*."

"Benny Goodman is a composer," my aunt said, proving that she, too, knows what's what. "You can make money with games too. You'll see."

And, because he was so happy thinking that he would earn money like Benny Goodman, Marvin started dancing again. He really is a good dancer. Eddie can't compete with him, even though Eddie says that Marvin doesn't follow *de rulz*.

Much later in the evening, Red came, and he too brought a newspaper with Marvin's picture.

"*Kongratulayshuns!*" he said. And Marvin danced for him too.

When Red came in, Ruth got all excited. She was beside herself. She started dancing with Marvin and then Eddie and then she called Red over to dance with her too.

Red spun her around a couple of times and then sat down.

"*Yu'r tiyerd*," he muttered to her.

"*Don't voree abot mee*," she said bitterly. She was clearly annoyed. Red said something to her in English. I didn't understand what he said, but I saw that Ruth put her hand to her forehead and, with an ironic smirk, she thanked him.

Eddie asked me for my address. "I'll come visit you, Rivke," he said. I didn't know what to tell him. Should I tell him to come? In that case, what was the point of leaving my aunt's house? Should I tell him not to come? How can you embarrass someone like that? In the end, I answered, "Sure, Eddie. Come with Selma."

"*Awlriyt*," Eddie said, and he walked away.

Awlriyt is the kind of word that always comes in handy. *Awlriyt* means good. But if you say it twice—*awlriyt, awlriyt*—it means leave me alone! Enough already! *Awlriyt* also means I understand you fully. And that must have been what Eddie's *awlriyt* meant.

Red walked me home. I asked him what Ruth had wanted.

"*Don' tink abowt eet*, Rivke," he said. "Ruth means nothing to me."

Did Eddie tell me the truth when he said that Red had gone out with Ruth for three years and four months? And now Red says she means nothing to him. I didn't want to ask him too many questions. It seemed wrong. And what would I do if Red didn't want to answer?

"They"

April 14

Eddie didn't make me wait long. He came yesterday, on Shabbos, right in the middle of the day.

After my talk with my uncle, I was really careful to avoid Eddie. I no longer even stop off at my uncle's house after work. When he spoke to me the other morning, even though he wasn't crying, it seemed to me that he was swallowing his tears. People say that men can't cry; it turns out they're wrong. I never saw my father—may he live and be well—cry. (But who knows how things stand now that he's sleeping in Krasulye's stall?)

I got scared when Eddie came in because he was on his own, without Selma, even though I had clearly asked him to bring her. I also saw that he didn't know what to say to me, and I felt sorry for him.

I asked him to sit down and gave him a chair, and I sat on my bed. Then I gave him an apple, and I asked him why Selma hadn't come with him.

Eddie didn't answer my question. He took the apple and played with it a bit and then looked at the flowers.

"Who brought you roses?"

"Red brought them."

"Why is it, Rivke, that you don't want me to come see you?"

"Eddie, I want you to come with Selma. You know that she's my cousin . . ."

"Rivke, why don't you come to your aunt's house? *Iy'm longing tu see yu.*"

I wanted to say something to cheer him up. "Tell me, Eddie, have you liked a lot of girls?"

"Not too many, Rivke, but anyway, I like you more."

"I'm not here in New York, Eddie. I'm in Lublin. . . . And now, eat your apple. Let's see who can eat it up faster." And I took my own challenge and started eating the apple quickly. Eddie did the same, and we both ate and laughed. And just my luck: at that moment, the laundress came in. She stuck her head in the door and said, "Look at the two of them eating. Such a rush. It makes me want one too."

I handed her an apple, and she sat down on my bed to eat it. I was really glad that she had come.

"*Vel*, Rivke, you'll come to your aunt's . . ."

"Of course, Eddie, of course. Give Selma my regards."

"*Tenks*," he said, and he left.

It looks like the laundress really did have a love affair once upon a time, because she recognized that things weren't quite right with Eddie.

"He's like glue—won't let go," I said.

"Rivke, it should never bother you that a young man sighs a bit."

I started to laugh, because I really liked how she said "sighs a bit."

"They enjoy it," she continued, "and it's better that they're sighing and you're not. It's all a game to them. They couldn't care less. Once they shut the door, all is forgotten."

If so, I thought, then that actress in the movies was right. She made everybody sigh after her, and she sighed after no one. Can it be that Red is like that too? Is Layzer? And I said to the laundress, "In that case, the world is no world at all."

She didn't answer too quickly. It seemed that it wasn't so easy for her to decide if the world is no world at all.

She paced the room for a while, looking for someplace to put the apple core that was still in her hand, and then she finally said, "Of course, there are exceptions. But very few. Abrasha was such an exception. And if you let such a chance go by, it's a real shame."

She left to go get dressed. On Shabbos she always goes to the movies, and she didn't want to be late.

Two Wonderful Guests

April 18

Last night, I dreamed of my mother, may she rest in peace. She came to me in my room here. "A nuisance?" she asked jokingly. She pushed the chair next to my bed and put a pitcher of water on it. "This will refresh you, and you'll lack for nothing." And with that, she left.

The dream was so clear that when I woke up, I wondered why the pitcher wasn't next to me.

Tonight, after work, my aunt came to visit. It was the first time she had come to me. I had wondered why she hadn't come earlier to see where I was and how I was. But I see that an aunt is not a mother. It was my mother who came first, if only in my dream.

"I was so *bizee* with meetings and sales and *evryting* this week that I couldn't come earlier even though I wanted to." She brought me a tablecloth that she had bought at a sale.

"Mrs. Shore told me that she brought you a *kover*. Where is it? Show me."

I showed her the bedspread, but I thought that she had come for some other reason. Or else why hadn't she come before?

"What are you doing? Who comes to visit?" she asked.

"My mother was here yesterday. She brought me a pitcher of water and told me it would refresh me," I answered.

"Don't be childish, Rivke. A dream is a dream. Who's talking about dreams? Does Red come here sometimes?" she asked. "He's a nice *boy*. I'm glad he comes to you."

I was afraid that she would ask me about Eddie, and I didn't know what I'd say if she did. I would certainly have told my uncle the truth, but it's different with my aunt. And just then, as if I had read her thoughts, she asked me if I had seen Eddie lately.

There we have it, I thought, as my heart started to pound.

"I've seen him lately," I said, avoiding looking in her direction. It bothered me to have her examine me like that.

"You have to get a new *dres*. We're getting ready for Selma's engagement," she said.

For my aunt, everything is about Selma! I need a new dress because of Selma's engagement. Because of Selma, I'm not supposed to see Eddie. Because of Selma, I had to move out. That's all my aunt thinks about. It's a good thing that my mother—may she rest in peace—came to me in my dream and brought me a pitcher of water so I could be refreshed.

Maybe my aunt told me about Selma's upcoming engagement so I'd know that there's no point in seeing Eddie.

It was good that Red came to visit later. My heart ached after my aunt left and, once again, I felt abandoned on Grand Street. The main thing is that I'm not supposed to do anything that can affect Selma.

I told Red about the engagement.

"Eddie didn't say a word about it. *Iy'm surpriyzd*," he said.

"My aunt was here today. She told me that I should get a new *dres*."

Red seemed not to hear a word of what I was saying. He stared at a saucer that was on my table. In it, was the butt of a Camel cigarette.

"Do you smoke, Rivke?" he asked.

"No. Eddie was here yesterday."

"*Vot abot?*"

"He just came to see my room."

Red was lost in thought.

"Look at this, Red," I said, showing him his dried roses in the pages of a book. "They were so beautiful that I wanted to keep them."

"You're an odd one, Rivke. Eddie told me that you have a fiancé in Lublin. He told me this twice already. Eddie comes to see your room, and you preserve the roses that I gave you . . ." Red combed his fingers through his hair.

"So you don't want me to dry them out?"

"No, I want to *awlvays* bring you fresh roses."

I had two wonderful guests today: my mother, who told me that the water would refresh me, and Red, who promised that he would always bring me fresh roses.

That's How Things Are Done in Lublin

April 19

The girl who collects piecework in Mr. Rubin's factory is finally getting married! Mrs. Rubin called my aunt, and Selma came to tell me the good news.

"The *goyl* with the *peeses* in Mr. Rubin's factory is getting married," Selma said. "Mrs. Rubin called up."

Selma didn't come alone. Ruth was with her, and she was all dressed up, wearing a short fur jacket over a red dress and with a red feather in her fur hat. To me, she looked like she had put on a Purim costume. Ruth and Selma sat down on my bed. Ruth took out a small mirror and looked into it for a long time.

"*Yu no*," she said to Selma, "*miy pawder iz tu dark*." And then, both of them, holding their mirrors, chatted away in English. They spoke so quickly that I didn't understand a word. Selma tucked her feet under her, and the sharp heels of her shoes stuck out. Selma and Ruth were completely absorbed in showing one another their makeup cases.

I didn't know what to do with myself. I couldn't treat them like guests. They were sitting there as if they were in a railway station, as if there was no sign that somebody lived here. It began to bother me. Is my bed some public bench? In Lublin, no one ever sat on my bed. "A bed should always be white," my mother, may she rest in peace, used to say.

I gave them apples. That made them realize that they were guests, and then they tried to talk to me too.

"Do you sleep here?" Selma asked, pointing to where they were sitting on my bed. I nodded. When I'm upset, I can't talk. And by then I was very angry, especially at Ruth. Why had she come? Who invited her?

All of a sudden, she started talking about the flowers that were on the table. Red's roses.

"*Niys rozes*," she said, and tapping with her red nails, she asked, "*Vehr du yu get sutch niys rozes?*"

My mother, may she rest in peace, always used to complain that I didn't answer the questions I was asked but somehow managed to turn them all upside down. "Your answers stick to the issue at hand about as well as peas stick to a wall," she would say. And now I also felt like answering Ruth in a contrary way, so I said, "They grow on my table."

I should have answered differently. It wouldn't have hurt her to know that no one invited her to come here and that, even with a greenhorn, it's possible to be politer than she was. I could have said a lot more, but I didn't say a word. I always think of the right thing to say when it's too late. Ruth and Selma showed no sign of leaving—quite the opposite; they just sat there, looking into their mirrors and babbling so quickly in English that I couldn't understand a word. I finally figured out what to do. I put on my hat and coat and gloves. If they're the kind of guests who don't care about me, then I don't have to care about them. That's how it's done in Lublin, and that's what I decided to do in New York.

"What time is it?" I asked Selma.

"*Yu hev a dayt?*" Ruth asked me sarcastically.

"No, I'm going to my wedding."

The girls looked at one another. They were offended. But when I start talking like that, it's just impossible for me to stop. No matter what anybody asks me, I answer in that contrary way. My mother, may she rest in peace, used to whack me with a towel for talking like that when I was a child. Selma and Ruth got up from the bed. I straightened out the bedspread, fluffed up the pillows, and put the whole bed back in order.

"*Eksqueez mee.* I ruined your cover," Selma said, sensing that things were not quite right.

"As long as that's the worst ruin there is," I said to reassure her. And all three of us went downstairs.

Thank goodness we were outside. I was at least rid of Ruth with her red feather and mirror!

"Good-bye!" they both sang out. How strange that whether people leave one another as good friends or as bitter enemies, they all smile and sing out the same good-bye. I wanted to sing out my good-bye too, and at that very moment, Red showed up. He was wearing a sweater without a coat. That's how he dresses these days. He was obviously surprised to see all of us together. He looked at each of us, first at Selma, then at Ruth, and then at me.

"*Vehr ar yu gowing?*" he asked us.

"*Shee hez a dayt,*" Ruth told him.

I was silent, but my heart was pounding. Red looked at me, and he saw that something was wrong. We all stood and waited as if we were waiting to see where everybody was going. Selma was smiling.

"*Gud bay,*" I said, wanting to go somewhere, anywhere.

"*Vehr ar yu gowing?*" Ruth asked Red, looking daggers at him.

"*Vee haf dee dayt togeter,*" Red said, sticking up for me.

Ruth turned red. She said something to Red in English, but I didn't understand it.

"OK," he answered, and he left with me.

I can't forget Ruth's face. She blushed right through her makeup, and even her forehead and her throat turned red. Once, in Lublin, a woman poured acid all over a girl because the girl was going around with the woman's husband. I was pretty sure that Ruth would have poured acid over me if she had any. That's what her face told me.

I was glad that Red was with me, even though we were both silent. My heart was still pounding. If Red hadn't been there, I would have burst into tears.

I don't know what Red was thinking because he didn't say anything until later, when we were near the East River. Then he took my shoulders in his hands and said, "*Evryting iz awlriyt,* Rivke."

I wanted to tell him that Ruth had come uninvited and she and Selma sat on my bed and made a mess of it, but I didn't know where to begin. And so I told him nothing but just repeated his words. "*Evryting iz awlriyt,* Red."

We both laughed, and Red, once again, said that I made a joke out of everything.

"You think it's a joke?"

"Yeah, a joke."

There were ships floating on the East River, as big as houses and all lit up. But I thought that if I went onto a ship with Red, Ruth would come with her red feather and polished nails and sit on my bed.

Strange girls in New York. How is it that she wasn't embarrassed to come to me uninvited? I guess that it's no shame here.

Seders

April 22

My aunt and uncle sent Marvin to tell me to come to the Seder. Marvin was already dressed up. When there's a holiday, my aunt looks very much like my mother, may she rest in peace. When she lights the Shabbos candles on Friday night, she also looks like my mother. And tonight, at the Seder, she again looked like her.

There were matzos, wine, cups, and Haggados on the table, and the house was all lit up. It looked almost like Lublin, but it was still not a home for me. At the slightest issue, you can be asked to leave. Last year, at our Seder in Lublin, there wasn't much of a celebration. We had company, but just as the blessing over the first cup of wine was said, Nahumtshe, Uncle Zaydle's son, came running. His eyes were red, and he said, "The evil ones have caught my father. He was coming home from the synagogue, and they grabbed him and beat him on his back with a stick. Why? For nothing. They complained about his short beard. 'A Jew can't walk around like that. The rabbi forbids it,' they yelled in Polish, and they kept beating him until he fell. Then they left, joking that by next year his beard should be as long as it's supposed to be."

Uncle Zaydl hailed a Jewish coach driver who was passing by. The man brought him home and wouldn't take any money for it.

"For this kind of trip, you don't take money," he said. "What Jew is safe from such a journey? May God punish them; let them get a taste of our lives," he added, and then left. By "them" he of course meant the hooligans who had beaten my uncle.

We left the Seder then and there, and we all went to see how Uncle Zaydl was feeling. He had compresses on his back, and he was a little better. We ended the Seder very late at night, and when it came to the part about asking God to "pour out His wrath against the nations that know Thee not," my father told us to stand up. We all wept, and I saw that there were no tears in my father's eyes, but his lips trembled so much that we could barely hear the words.

That's how "joyful" our Seder was last year, even before the war came to Lublin.

I never knew that Marvin knew so much. He asked the Four Questions and translated them into English. It's true that by the time he got to the second question, my uncle had to help him and he was drenched in sweat and he sighed loudly when he finished asking all four. It was as if he himself had just left Egypt. My uncle read the Haggadah, my aunt muttered a bit, and Marvin went through it all in a flash, pretending that he could read the Hebrew quickly.

In honor of Passover, Selma spoke a little Yiddish, saying, "I'll bet you ten dollars that he doesn't know any of the words."

I wanted to read the Haggadah too, but I just couldn't. I could only think about where my Uncle Zaydl was and about the Seder my father must be having in Lublin, in Krasulye's stall. They all passed before my eyes; even my mother—may she rest in peace—was there with the pitcher of water, exactly as I had seen her in my dream. New York became Lublin, and Lublin made its way into New York.

We were interrupted by a phone call. "Mr. Edelshtein? From Long Island?" my aunt asked.

It was as if an earthquake had hit. It was as extraordinary as last year's Seder when we had learned that the hooligans had beaten Uncle Zaydl. My uncle went over to the telephone. It wasn't Mr. Edelshtein himself who was speaking, but one of his employees. When my uncle told him that it was the first Seder night of Passover celebrating the Jews' liberation from Egypt, the man must have asked him something. My uncle said: "*Yes, djost tooday.*"

My uncle came back to the table, and we finished eating and reading the Haggadah as quickly as we could. My uncle went to prepare the necessary paper for tomorrow's early morning meeting with Mr. Edelshtein about an insurance policy for his niece who had just come from Bessarabia. We all talked about it at the table.

"What's that about all of a sudden?"

My aunt looked at me and said, "Maybe because after the ball . . . a Lubliner . . ."

"Maybe."

Marvin, who's a simple being, even though his picture is in the newspapers, said what everyone—including me—was thinking: "*Dat's beecauz hee gayv hundert kvawders* in order to dance with Rivke."

"The things he comes up with!" my aunt said, interrupting him. And I thought that maybe Red had been right all along about not going to Mr. Edelshtein for a job.

We had shortened the Seder anyway. And then Mendl Pushcart and his wife came in, so everybody sat down to play pinochle as though it were any ordinary Friday night. Marvin and Selma left to go to the movies.

I went "home," but I couldn't sleep. Everything was all mixed up in my head: my father with Krasulye, Mister Edelshtein's telephone call, Marvin, Selma, Red, New York, and Lublin. It's hard to sleep when you think about so many things all at once.

The War

April 26

Ever since my father wrote me about living in Krasulye's stall, I'm always worried about what's going on with him. I want to know what's happening in Lublin. What's happening with my father and brother? The newspapers say that they're sending all the young men away to be slaves in Germany. I went with my aunt to a meeting of the Lublin Ladies' Aid Society to find out if anybody had received letters from Lublin or knew anything more than I did.

It wasn't a meeting but an outright war. It's a good thing that the Lubliners don't have guns or they would have (God forbid) shot one another too. Mrs. Tkatsh resigned the presidency because Mrs. Rabkin, the vice president, wrote all the thank-you notes to those who had come to the ball, and she alone signed them.

Mrs. Tkatsh was so upset that her voice shook. "If not for me, we would never have gotten Mr. Edelshtein to come to the ball. I called him up. He promised me that he would come, and that's just what he did. Who could have accomplished that?" There were tears in her eyes as she spoke. "*Eet iz nat supozd tu bee so*," she said, shaking her head from side to side. Mrs. Rabkin, the vice president, tried to explain that the invitations are supposed to come from the president but the thank-you notes should be written by the vice president. "*Dat's di rul*," she said. "What's the big deal with my getting a reply from Mr. Edelshtein? What's the matter with that? You can always write another thank-you note, *speshl* in the name of the president."

"No, it's not supposed to be like that," Mrs. Tkatsh said again. "Mr. Shamut also sent a reply addressed to Mrs. Rabkin. And so did the musicians."

Mrs. Rabkin was red in the face. You would have thought she had a high fever. She ranted and raved. "So what? Did the letters make me suddenly happy? *Vat's di meter?*"

My aunt tried to make peace. She came up with a plan to have Mr. Edelshtein and Mr. Shamut named honorary members and then Mrs. Tkatsh, as president, would write them a personal invitation to participate. That's how she put it: "Let them be invited to participate."

It almost worked. My aunt's suggestion seemed to please everyone. And then Mrs. Rubin went and ruined the whole thing by saying that you can't invite men to join a Ladies' Society, even as honorary members. They could feel offended, and then we'd have a real mess on our hands.

Everybody agreed with that too, and Mrs. Tkatsh said, "*Vot's di yuz? Iy riziyn, end dat's awl.*" And that was the end of her presidency.

The meeting lasted until late at night. The women had so much *trubl* that I couldn't even find out what kind of letters they were getting and what was going on in Lublin. One woman was able to tell me that her family was sent off somewhere, and they wrote that they don't know where they'll end up. Two large tears fell down her cheeks. She wiped them away and powdered her face.

The women passed a *rezolushn* saying that Mrs. Tkatsh was to be *dreftet* into remaining as president.

"She'll get over it," Mrs. Rabkin quietly said to my aunt. "She'll come back. No one gives up this position so quickly. It'll last another meeting. . . . And what? Didn't thank-you notes need to be sent? What kind of thing would that be?"

Meanwhile, the Ladies' Society remained without a president, and I remained without any information about Lublin.

My First Day in the Shop

May 2

Mr. Rubin was right: you need to know English well to collect the pieces in his factory. The girls—the machine operators—talk so strangely. I've never heard anything like it in my life. They mutter a few words, and you're supposed to know what they mean. Go figure out what they're muttering!

One dark-haired, short, thin girl named Mary—a flat board and not a woman—talks like a windmill. How can anyone speak so quickly? She said something, and all I heard was the word *vawter*. So I was relieved that I understood she wanted some water. (It's only early May, but it's already hot.) I went and brought her a glass of water. She shrugged her shoulders and again mumbled something, and once again I heard the word *vawter*. I stood stock still, not knowing what to do. If she didn't want water, then why did she keep on saying *vawter*? The thin board of a girl stood up and, the devil take her, went to a corner of the room, took a spray can of water and sprayed all around her machine. She was bothered by *dost*, the dust. She put the can down and went back to work, mad as can be. I put the spray can back and understood that *vawter* means the can with water for spraying around the machine. Then someone else asked for water and, needlessly, I schlepped the can and began spraying, but she really wanted a drink. It was shameful to see how I ran around the factory, sweaty and confused, while the girls called me to come here and there. They figured out that I'm a greenhorn, and it led to one request after another. I thought I'd pass out. I was ready to take myself and my things and go back to Mrs. Koshes to embroider flowers, but I remembered what Mrs. Rubin once told me: "Going away is easy. If you have to come back, God forbid, it's much harder."

Luckily, the forelady calmed me down a little. She's an older woman. I think she's Jewish even though she doesn't speak any Yiddish. Still, she has a Jewish nose. She must have noticed how sweaty and confused I was, and she said: "*Tayk eet eezee.*" And she gestured with her hand as if to say, "New York isn't going away."

At one o'clock, the operators went down for *lontsh*, and I went down too. I couldn't eat because I was too hot and my head was spinning. I took a cup of coffee. A girl from our shop sat at my table, and I was really surprised when she started talking to me in Yiddish:

"You just came?"

"Yes, not long ago."

"A refugee?"

"Yes."

"You don't understand English."

"Very little."

"They're making a *dzshok* by calling you over every minute. They do that with every new person. They give them *di hel*."

"What do they give them?"

"Hell. They torture them because they're new. It's a joke. And *dat's awl*."

Here's a new sort of suffering. People are tortured, not for some sin they've committed but just for fun.

Mr. Rubin wasn't in the factory today. Maybe he would have stood up for me, but on the other hand, maybe it's better that he wasn't there. I came home completely exhausted, and the laundress gave me an aspirin and asked if the work was hard.

"No, it's just that the operators are making jokes."

"Take an aspirin," she said. "At first, America has to be taken with aspirin. Afterward, it gets easier."

Mendl Pushcart showed up just then. He saw how tired I was, lying on my bed, and he started talking. "When I came to America, we used to work fourteen hours a day, and when we were done, we went off to earn some more money. In America, you don't count hours, and you don't measure how much your head aches."

Everybody says something different about America. The laundress says you have to take America with aspirin in the beginning, and Mendl Pushcart says that you can't take the measure of your headache here. Maybe he's right. Should I be upset just because I'm tired? Maybe it's all not so hard. I just thought . . . and then my heart ached again because I saw how alone I was on Grand Street. Will I be able to bear it? What will become of me? I don't know. I don't know. I don't know anything.

Miracles

May 5

Today, Mrs. Shore brought me a letter from Layzer. It came yesterday, but when my aunt saw that it wasn't from Lublin, she thought it wouldn't hurt to wait another day. It was so nice of Mrs. Shore to bring me the letter.

"I know that sometimes a person can wait for a letter that's not from home even more than for a letter from home." That's what Mrs. Shore said, winking as was her habit.

Layzer writes:

It was a miracle that I got to Palestine. My gold watch helped me out—the one about which you used to say that it's gold, but it's not a watch. That's the very watch that Hontche wanted. Remember him, that guy who was the janitor at the post office? Hontche asked if I wanted to leave Lublin. I was afraid to say yes. Who knew what he was up to or what he could do? But he could see that I wanted to leave, so he didn't even wait for my answer but just stood and stared at my gold watch.

"The watch works?" he asked me.

"What do you mean does it work? Of course it works. You wouldn't believe how fast it runs." As you know, that was no lie.

And Hontche told me to give him the watch, and he would take me to Rumania. He could have just taken my watch with no problem. I could hardly have gone to the German general to complain. And that's exactly what Hontche said to me: "I could take your watch anytime I wanted to and you wouldn't be able to do anything about it. But I am an honorable Pole, and I don't do such things. You were a soldier in the Polish army? Take your papers with you, and I'll bring you to Rumania."

In the evening Hontche took me for a walk to Biyale Gnyazdo, and then we went on a wagon. First, we wandered around the woods until dawn, and then he brought me . . . where do you think? Do you think he brought me to Rumania? No! To Ostrodoge.

"Give me your watch," he said.

"But we're not yet in Rumania."

"There are Polish soldiers here; you'll go with them to Rumania. They'll run away, desert the army," he predicted.

I gave him the watch. His prediction was right. There were military units, armed and unarmed, all along the way, and I crossed the border with them. I didn't see a crumb of bread for two days. I could no longer bend my knees, and the mud was so deep that it was almost impossible to move. I fell down at every step and felt that I couldn't go on. I either sprained my leg or hit my knee. The Rumanian who was guiding us apparently didn't think that a Polish soldier was worth much, and he just left me there on the road. He muttered the name of some village or town, and off they went. So there I was sitting in the muck with an injured leg and wondering how I was going to save myself. I have no idea if I sat there for an hour or two or more or less. My watch was gone, and since it was so dark, my watch wouldn't have helped anyway. Suddenly I heard footsteps. It was another group of Polish soldiers who had crossed the border. I yelled and yelled, but they went by. I crawled after them on all fours. One of the Rumanians, it seems, took pity on me and told two of his men to get me. They helped me, and I limped away with them. That was the second miracle that happened to me, because I would certainly have frozen to death that night in the cold mud. We were taken to a barn where we were given hot water, just plain hot water. Never in my life had I liked any food or any drink—even the best Passover wine—as much as that night's cup of hot water. Every limb in my body was happier. Even my injured leg stopped hurting. We lived in that barn for two weeks. One third of the people there became ill and walked around with fever. Two weeks later, a doctor came to the barn. When he arrived, I was lying on the ground, too sick to even hear what was being said to me. I was taken to a hospital where the doctor, a Jew, spoke to me half in Yiddish, half in German. He couldn't believe that I had survived with such injuries.

A representative of the Joint Distribution Committee came to the hospital and—just imagine this—it was a new miracle. He was Abraham Rafalovitsh, Shakhne Rafalovitsh's son, from Lublin. He recognized me when I told him I was from Lublin. He did me lots of favors later.

How did I get to the Greek ship? How did I get to Palestine? Here, too, there were great miracles, just as great as the ones that the Jews experienced when they left Egypt. I'll write you all about it in another letter. Now, I want to ask you to write to me often, Rivke. Whenever the post arrives, I wait eagerly to see if there's a letter from you. Why don't you write, Rivke? Why? Why?

You are often in my dreams. I'm so happy that I'm alive and that I will see you again. You'll come, won't you, Rivke, to Palestine? I eagerly await that day.

That's how Layzer writes. And the laundress says that "they"—by which she means men—"shut the door and forget everything." That's not true, and you don't have to believe everything people say.

Red Wants to Read Layzer's Letter

May 6

It turns out that Layzer's letter was at my aunt's house for a few days, and Selma and Eddie saw it there. I don't know who told Red about it, but when I came home from work today, Red was waiting for me. I noticed right away that he wasn't sitting but just standing there. He stood and waited as if he wanted to say something and then leave. He stood with his face to the window, and when I entered the room, he turned to me.

"Sit down, Red. Why are you standing?"

"I want to stand."

"So stand."

I saw that Red wanted to pick a fight with me, although I still didn't know why. He stood for a long time with his face to the window and didn't say a word. Meanwhile, I took off my coat, combed my hair, and went to the kitchen to make tea. When I came back, Red was still standing at the same spot, looking out the window.

"Are you counting the stars, Red?"

He didn't answer.

"What do you see there in the window, Red? Tell me, and I'll take a look too."

My words made as much of an impression as you'd make throwing peas at the wall. He was standing and looking out the window as if he couldn't tear himself away.

"Come on, Red; drink some tea and tell me why you've become mute."

Red came over to the table and sat down. I drank the tea, but he didn't touch his glass.

"Tell me the truth, Rivke . . ."

He stopped for a while, and I realized that Red must have, once again, heard something from Eddie.

"Tell me, Rivke, have you had a letter from the one who was in the photo?"

"Yeah, Red, I received a letter from him."

"Will you go to him?"

"What do you mean?"

"Rivke, I want to read his letter."

"That's all you want, Red?" I asked him jokingly. "Maybe you'd rather drink your tea?"

The truth is that I didn't want to offend Red, but I didn't want to show him Layzer's letter either. Red was furious. It was the first time that I'd seen him so angry. He took my hand and squeezed it so hard that my fingers hurt.

"Rivke, don't talk like that. *Don' speek tu mee dis vay.*"

My fingers hurt. An angry Red sat opposite me. I looked around and saw the parcels of laundry against the wall, and I really felt like laughing. I tried to force myself not to laugh, but it was no use. I just couldn't control it, and I laughed so hard that tears rolled down my cheeks and my ribs ached. I knew that my laughter made no sense, and I wanted to stop, but I just couldn't. Red looked at me and said, "*Krayzee,*" with no hint of a smile. He waited patiently for me to finish laughing.

"Tell me, Rivke, do you want to go to Palestine?"

"Who told you that?"

"Eddie told me."

"Eddie? How would Eddie know? And you believe him?"

"Yeah, I believe him."

"Why?"

"Because you don't tell me anything."

"What should I tell you? What?"

"Show me the letter."

"Let Eddie show it to you."

Red stood up. He paced up and down the room for a few minutes. He stood by the window for a while, and then he picked up his hat.

"*Gud bay*, Rivke," he said, and then he just stood in the doorway.

"Why are you leaving, Red? It's still early," I said, and I felt my heart grow heavy with sorrow.

Instead of answering, Red again said, "Good-bye, Rivke," and closed the door.

I don't know why, but I was so hurt that I cried when he left. Red was my best friend. Red took me to hear the band when I felt so shamed by everyone—by Selma, by Ruth, by Marvin, and even by my aunt. I know that Red will not come back to me. I am certain of that.

I Think about Yesterday

May 7

As I predicted, Red didn't come today. I've been thinking about everything that happened yesterday. I certainly shouldn't have laughed. My laughter made no sense at all. And I should have answered him differently. I should have said that it wasn't right for him to talk about Layzer's letter. It's not nice to read someone else's letters from friends. That's what I should have said and then I wouldn't have offended him, but it's too late now. And maybe it's better like this. I'll go to Layzer in Palestine. He asked me to remember that I haven't reached my final destination yet. Layzer was right. Still, it hurts to know that Red didn't come. He didn't have to get so mad at me so quickly. He forgot his cigarettes here yesterday. I'll put them away until he comes to get them. If he comes. The laundress says, "They shut the door and forget everything." It's possible that Red has already forgotten. Who knows? It's exactly the things that you really want to know that you don't know. I've noticed this many times. I really want to know what's going on with my father in Lublin, and I don't know. And now, Red . . . maybe Red has gone off to see Ruth today. She'll get all dressed up in her red hat and her red feathers, and she'll take a walk with Red near the East River.

Maybe he'll say to her, "*Don' voree*. Rivke means nothing to me," just as he said to me about Ruth. And if I had shown him Layzer's letter? Would he still have gone away and not come today? That would have been worse. But I would never have shown him Layzer's letter. I'd never do that.

It was hard for me to sit in my room the whole evening, and so I went out to Grand Street and walked all the way to Mrs. Koshes's house. I wanted to go in and ask her, "When you were the beautiful peacock, were you also left alone behind closed doors, as I was today? Did anyone close your door and leave you alone?" But I didn't go in. Who knows if the old woman even remembers anymore what went on when she was the beautiful peacock? So I walked back and forth on Grand Street, back and forth again until my head was spinning. I went up to my room and thought that maybe I'd find Red standing near the window just like yesterday. But Red wasn't there. I thought about how Red had promised to *awlvays* bring me fresh roses, but now I was left with only the ones I had dried. I put them away with the cigarettes. If he comes, I'll give them all to him at once. If he comes, I'll even remind him that he promised to *awlvays* bring me fresh roses but he didn't keep his word. And maybe America is the kind of country where you don't need to keep your promise? You just have to promise. Who knows? I don't know anything now. I wanted to reread Layzer's letter, but I couldn't. I went over to the window to see what Red had been looking at for so long yesterday. It looked as if fires were blazing outside. One fire went out. Maybe that was my fire that was extinguished before my very eyes. Just as I am—I, who can't do anything else now except think about yesterday.

Helped By a *How Du Yu Du*

May 9

One "How do you do?" and "How do you feel?" saved me from the machine operators. They were just having fun at my expense by rushing me back and forth without a minute's rest. Thank God that Mr. Rubin came to the factory today. First, he went into his office and then he came onto the factory floor. He saw me and asked, "*How du yu du?*" and "*How du yu feel?*" He didn't have any more time to talk to me and went back to his office. Still, because of that one "How do you do?" I was saved. The operators see and listen to everything that Mr. Rubin does, and they heard what he said to me. And the dark, thin little operator who looks more like a board than a girl, got even straighter and stiffer. She stopped bothering me and calling me over all the time. Later, she did call me over once, but there was no laughter in her eyes as there had been up to now. She even said *pleez*, and then, when

I brought her the spray can, she said *tenk yu*. That was the first time I had heard such words from her. She became so polite and nice.

Today was the first day that I had time to really look at the pieces and to separate the woolen and silk ones. Today, you could say, I was able to breathe. It really was a miracle from heaven that Mr. Rubin came today and said *"How du yu du?"* and *"How du yu feel?"*

I never imagined that a person could be so different in different places. In the association, he's a compatriot like everybody else. He talks to this one and that one, and his wife, Mrs. Rubin, is down to earth, one of us. She even shed a tear when I saw her for the first time and told her about my mother, may she rest in peace.

In his own home, Mr. Rubin acts like a nobleman. A real nobleman. The few times that I've been to his house, he was dressed in a silk robe; his cigar was almost entirely extinguished, but from time to time, he gave a tug on it and a few smoke rings came out. He's a nobleman who speaks Yiddish.

In the factory, Mr. Rubin is a boss. A boss is a hundred times greater than a nobleman and maybe a thousand times greater than a compatriot. A boss is an important thing. When Mr. Rubin came back from his trip, the factory knew about it in the wink of an eye. And when Mr. Rubin came in, even the machines started humming more quietly. It was still the same *zshu-zshu* but somehow a bit calmer, more restrained. And with one word, he saved me as quickly as you can pull a strand of hair out of milk. In the factory, Mr. Rubin spoke English. He spoke in English to the forelady, and even to me he had said, *"How du yu du?"* and *"How du yu feel?"* in English.

Today, for the first time, I got paid. I got eight dollars from the office and two dollars for the pieces. That's really a lot of money. I will certainly be able to buy a coat now, and maybe I'll even buy a dress for Selma's engagement party. We still don't know when that will be. I'm sure to see Red at Selma's party. He must be coming. I would very much like to see him and ask why he doesn't visit me anymore.

Mrs. Shlivke, the laundress, came to me today and said, "Rivke, you've grown pale. What's the matter?"

"It's hard to work in the factory."

She was silent. I think she was trying to figure out whether I was telling her the truth or not. Everybody wants to be told the truth (or, as Red says, *di trut*) and, still, people tell so many lies that if all those lies were to lift themselves up off the ground, the world would be weightless and simply fly away.

"What happened to Red?" she asked me after she had sat silently for a while. "I don't think I've seen him for several days."

If my aunt had asked me that, I would have answered her in some way that would have put her off. But it's hard for me to lie to Mrs. Shlivke. She has been so good to me. She told me so many stories about her life. I told her the truth. "For some reason, Red is mad at me. He probably won't come anymore."

She laughed. "He'll come. He'll definitely come. They always come back when they like a girl."

It's odd that the laundress refers to all men as "they." It's as if she were talking about people who aren't Jewish: "they." I don't feel like that, and I don't understand why she does.

Still, she thinks that Red will come. Maybe she's right? Maybe he really will come.

I told her that I had received ten dollars at the factory and that I wanted to pay her for the room.

"If you give, we'll take," she said. "There's no such thing as not taking money in America." And she called to her husband. "Sam, we're getting rich."

Mr. Shlivke came to the door. He's a quiet man; you can barely hear a peep out of him at home. Instead of talking, he smiles.

"We're getting rich? Well, that's good."

"Rivke wants to pay. She's become wealthy."

"Well, that's good too."

I'll pay them two dollars a week. I'm happy to be able to pay my way.

Eddie Again

May 11

Thank God, I finally got rid of my winter coat! My eyes opened wide, and I threw poverty off my shoulders. It's warm already, and spring has come to New York just as in Lublin. There's a breeze that comes down and lifts your hair to the sky. It's a shame that my beret hides it. I'm already wearing my dress out on the street. Before this, I would save the dress for company and just wear the clothes I had brought from home, but now, when I'm going around without a coat, it feels good to be wearing the dress. I'd really like to meet Red dressed like that. Maybe if my coat hadn't been so threadbare Red wouldn't have stopped coming. Maybe he couldn't stand to see my coat. Who knows?

It seems that Selma doesn't want to come to me anymore. On Friday, it was Marvin who came to invite me "to eat gefilte fish." He uses the same words all the time, as if he spent the whole week trying to memorize them. In his mixed-up Yiddish, he said something like, "Tatte and Mamma says you come, eat fish." I thought that maybe I'd meet Red there. He knows that my aunt always invites me to eat with them on Friday night, but he didn't come. Selma and Eddie weren't there either. Every Friday they go to the movies, and I go to eat fish.

Mrs. Shore came in. "Rivke, you're all dressed up!" She must have been talking about my dress. I said that I had earned ten dollars this week, and everybody applauded and said bravo. Afterward, my aunt said, "May God grant that you'll have even better news to tell us soon." And her eyes filled with tears. That's because she's in our family, where everybody cries. Maybe she's also sorry that they sent me away from the house. They don't know that Red is mad at me.

When Mendl Pushcart came to play pinochle, my aunt told him that I was already earning ten dollars a week.

"I knew right away that she was no greenhorn. Believe me, there are men—American citizens—who would be thrilled to earn so much. Oy, oy are there such people! More than one."

In honor of my windfall, he sent me to pour him a glass of tea. For Mendl Pushcart, everything ends with a glass of tea. In honor of my ten dollars, Mrs. Shore gave me a scarf that she says *metches ekzektlee* my *dres*. She took me to her apartment to give me the scarf, and there I met my old acquaintance, the Turkish princess with the crown and her attendants who hand her pieces of fruit. I remembered that whenever things become too hard to bear, I see the Turkish princess hanging on Mrs. Shore's wall. And then I remembered that Red was mad at me and wasn't coming anymore. . . . It's a bad habit of mine, to remember Red all the time.

The scarf that Mrs. Shore gave me really does match my dress nicely, and it's good that I'll be well dressed. When I was getting ready to go home, Selma came in, and Eddie came with her for just a few minutes too. I didn't want to leave together with him, and so I stayed a little longer.

When I saw Eddie, my heart started pounding. He and the stories he thinks up to tell about me!

He said hello, and even that was too much for me. It would be better if he didn't say a word to me and left me in peace. But when I came back home later, I saw Eddie pacing around in front of the laundry. I never expected that.

"Eddie?"

He didn't answer but just stood there silently. That's what he's like: at first he doesn't talk. And then he said quietly, as if asking a favor, "*Yu don' understend mee, Rivke.*"

I didn't want to ask him, but it simply erupted from me: "Eddie, how do you know that I'm going to Palestine?"

He was silent again, as if he hadn't even heard what I was asking.

"No, tell me, Eddie. Who told you that I'm going to Palestine?"

But Eddie had only one thing on his mind: "*Yu don' understend mee, Rivke.*"

At first, I was upset with him, but that passed, and I felt warm and took off my beret. Eddie patted my hair all over. "*Don' bee engree, Rivke.*"

I felt a tightness in my chest, and I sat down on the stairs leading to the laundromat. Eddie sat down next to me.

"When is your engagement party, Eddie?"

"*Ay don' know. Don' esk mee abowt, pleez.*"

Eddie leaned against the stoop and looked at the lights on Grand Street. I remembered how Red had also looked out through my window at those lights.

After a long time, Eddie said, "*Ay vud liyk tu go vit yu.*"

"Where would you like to go with me?"

"To Palestine."

"So, come on, Eddie; let's go," I said, and I stood up.

"*Di foyst tiym* that you've said yes to me about *somting.*"

Eddie smiled a bit sadly and looked older than usual.

I went up to my room. Now Eddie will tell Red that I've made a *dayt* with him. Well, all right. Red doesn't come to see me anyway, so why should I worry about that?

I kept thinking about the strange way that Eddie went down the stairs, slowly, as if sliding on an icy street. What would my uncle have thought if he had seen us there?

Ruth Is Going to California

May 14

There's a typhus epidemic in Lublin. There are reports about it in all the newspapers. How will my father protect himself from it if he's lying in Krasulye's stall? When I read about the epidemic, I imagined it as having long legs and walking all around Lublin like some giant heron. If my father, God forbid, is sick, who will take care of him? It's a good thing that I can forget about everything when I get to school. But I don't really forget about everything. I never forget that Red isn't coming. It's been a week since he was here. He's lost somewhere in New York. Where is he? Maybe he's walking around near the East River? I imagine that if I were to go to the East River—there where the glowing ships were floating—I'd meet Red.

Today, when I came home from school, I found four fresh roses on my table. I was so happy that it actually scared me. I thought that Red had been there. Maybe he remembered that he had promised to *awlvays* bring me fresh roses. But there was a note on the table that said "Eddie." He must be crazy to be bringing me roses. I didn't know what to do with them. I didn't want to put them on the table. What did I need Eddie's roses for? Should I throw them out? I didn't have the heart to do that. But the roses seemed to take over my whole room. I left and brought them to Mrs. Shore.

"How come?" she asked. "Have you struck it rich?"

"This is a thank-you for my scarf. It looks so good with my dress."

Mrs. Shore put the roses into a tall vase, and when they were standing on her table, I saw how pretty they were. As pretty as the ones Red had brought me. Yet, at home, I thought they weren't roses at all.

I was glad that I hadn't met anyone on the stairs, not my aunt or my uncle or Selma. Mrs. Shore told me the good news. "You know, Ruth is going away to California. She got a *dzshob* there." And, as was her habit, Mrs. Shore winked.

I was so happy about Mrs. Shore's news. For a while, I thought that everybody was going somewhere. Red went to hide somewhere in New York. Ruth was going to California. Layzer went to Palestine. I was on Grand Street. The whole world was going somewhere, and then they wouldn't be able to find one another. I wanted to go somewhere too. I thought that maybe I should take a walk to the East River.

Mrs. Shore brought a *kup koffee*. "Do you see Red?" she asked. "Since you moved away, he doesn't come to your aunt's anymore. That's probably why his 'bride-to-be' is going to California." Mrs. Shore meant Ruth when she said *his bride-to-be*.

"I haven't seen Red for several days. He must be busy."

Mrs. Shore smiled. "You should know, Rivke, that *boyes* are never too busy when they want to see a girl. If they don't come, it's either because they're being contrary or they just don't want to. There's no such thing as busy. Maybe Red is playing some kind of game with you, because it's clear that he's *krayzee* about you."

I didn't notice that I had finished drinking my coffee but was still holding the cup to my lips. It's a good thing that Mrs. Shore wasn't paying close attention. I would have been really embarrassed.

Grand Street was bustling. I imagined that I heard a train rushing by and that Ruth was taking that train to California.

Sheinfeld Lands on His Feet

May 17

Sheinfeld has landed on his feet. He was wearing a blue suit when he came to see me today. His black nails are almost completely clear now. He's got a *dzshob* in the East-West Loan Society, where Mr. Karelin, who, like him, comes from Lodz, presides. Sheinfeld is an assistant to the bookkeeper, and he earns thirty dollars a week.

"I've become rich," he joked, but I thought he looked sad.

Sheinfeld looked at his nails as he spoke. He really suffered when they became black, and now he was happy that they were turning whiter again.

"Karelin can 'make' a person in New York," he said. "He's buddies with everyone and calls everyone 'a friend of mine.' Since I started working with him, he must have called about fifty people '*a frend of miyn.*' Yes, indeed, Mr. Karelin can 'make' a person in New York!"

Sheinfeld invited me to go with him to the movies. I didn't want to ask him if he had decided to write Karelin's biography. Why should I hurt his feelings? I was happy to see that he was healthy, no longer lying on his low bed that made you think that he was barely off the ground. It had been a shock to see. Why should I ask him too many questions? But, as if he could read my thoughts, Sheinfeld said, "I'm doing his book—Mr. Karelin's biography. That's why he gave me this job in the East-West Loan Society. I want to bring my wife to America. I took this work because of her."

Sheinfeld spoke in a matter-of-fact way, the way you speak about a necessity. He didn't look at me but at the table. I thought that he wasn't really talking to me but to himself. Again and again he repeated to himself the reason for taking on this work.

"Now I can return the fifteen dollars that you brought me when I was sick. You didn't tell me who had given you the money."

"I told you that I got it from the Messiah, and you don't need to repay the Messiah."

"You've got some strange ideas," he said, laughing. "Surely. The Messiah . . ."

Then he asked, "What's the name of that young man you were with when you came to visit me? That young man probably got it right when he asked why it mattered whether or not Mr. Karelin's father was a *vint mil* or a *niys man*? Who cares?"

Now I clearly saw that Sheinfeld was talking to himself, because he didn't wait for any response from me.

"If I had been able to ask my wife's advice, she would no doubt have told me to do it. I'm sure of it. I've already sent her two packages of food. Maybe she'll be able to get them."

Sheinfeld was no longer the same Sheinfeld. "Do you understand, Rivke? Lodz no longer exists. His father, the *vint mil*, no longer exists. Reb Shmuel Katovitser, who never told a lie and couldn't stand it if anyone else told a lie, no longer exists either. So what's the difference if Mr. Karelin's father was this or that? Really, what's the difference?"

At the movies, we saw how one spy betrayed another and they met again in prison and started fighting with one another.

"What a world this has become," said Sheinfeld, wringing his hands like somebody who had just heard of a disaster.

"I won't sign 'Professor' with my name in the book. I'll write 'Doctor,' and that's all. That's my agreement with Mr. Karelin. After all, I do have a doctorate." And Sheinfeld gestured with his hand. "I'd like to see that young man who was with you when you came to visit me. What's his name?" Sheinfeld asked again.

"Levitt," I answered. This time, Sheinfeld was, in fact, waiting for an answer.

"Come see me again with him," he said as he was leaving.

He wanted to see Red. Why did he want to see him? Everybody wanted to see Red, and Ruth went away to California because of him. I imagined Sheinfeld in his room, lying on a bed that was so low it was almost on the floor, and talking to himself. Does it matter to anybody whether Mr. Karelin's father was a *vint mil* or a *niys man* now that Lodz no longer exists?

The Conflagration

May 19

It's just my luck that nothing goes smoothly with me. Mrs. Shore got it into her head to tell everybody at my aunt's house that I had brought her roses. It became a big production. It wasn't enough that she told them; she went and brought them the flowers in their vase in order to show what today's greenhorns are like. And worst of all, Eddie was there too. He must have recognized the roses. If I had known that such a mess would come of it, I would never have brought her the flowers. I always see what a foolish thing I've done when it's too late to undo it.

"You became so rich? All of a sudden to bring four roses?" my aunt asked. I ate supper at her house today. Selma and Eddie had gone on a trip to Atlantic City, so my aunt invited me over. If she only knew where the roses had come from—that's all I need.

Red now knows all about the roses too. He came over to my aunt's on Friday night to bring Marvin a magazine with games. Why did he have to come just then? Maybe because I'm usually there on Friday night? Or did he really come because of Marvin? After all, they're friends, or as Sheinfeld's compatriot says, "*a frend of miyn.*" Who knows? I'm just sorry that on that particular Friday I went to the movies with Sheinfeld. If Sheinfeld hadn't come to me on Friday, I would have seen Red. Maybe the laundress is right when she says that "they" always come back when "they" like a girl.

My uncle seemed really worried today. He paced through all the rooms as if he was looking for something. Finally, he took a pencil and made an accounting of the conflagration. My uncle calls the cost of Selma's wedding a "conflagration." From his accounting, I learned that there wouldn't be an engagement party. It costs too much. The wedding alone will burn everything up. Eddie's mother said she had to invite a hundred couples. And if they're going to invite a hundred couples, then my aunt has to invite at least seventy-five.

"Since she's got the *boy*, she's holding all the cards," my aunt said, "so we have to give in to all her craziness. She wants nothing less than the Raleigh Hotel. Otherwise, she won't bring her Eddie to the wedding canopy. And she has to invite a hundred couples. What is this? A presidential campaign? And she needs a master of ceremonies. And an emcee in the Raleigh Hotel wants to see a check for fifty dollars."

"So, it's a conflagration," said my uncle, "a conflagration and not a wedding. Let's see how much this conflagration will cost. One hundred couples on their side and seventy-five on ours adds up to seven hundred dollars."

My aunt, who seemed more upset about the master of ceremonies than anything else, added to his accounts: "And the master of ceremonies, that curse, will cost fifty dollars."

"The rabbi and the cantor and assistant to the rabbi and the choir and the woman who sings for the bride—that adds up to two hundred dollars."

"If there's a rabbi, why do we need an assistant?"

"We need him," my uncle explained, "because her daughter, Irene, had an assistant to the rabbi, and do you think *shee* will make her son look like less than her daughter?"

Shee meant Eddie's mother, the woman holding all the cards.

My aunt came up with a plan. "Why should we invite seventy-five couples? Maybe fifty will be enough? It'll be a big enough to-do."

"No, Ida," said my uncle in a singsong voice, as if studying Talmud. "If we've got the drummer then we've got to have the cymbalist too. And don't forget that the guests will bring presents, and then we won't be embarrassed to compare all the presents from the groom's side with the presents from the bride's. Maybe we'll even invite a hundred couples too. If things are going up in a conflagration, let it burn brightly.

"Let's not forget liquor, candy, flowers, tips, invitation cards. And the dress for the bride—that's no small thing either—and the wedding pictures, and, anyway, on such an occasion, you have to say to hell with the money. Fifteen hundred dollars won't cover it all."

Eddie appeared before my eyes, leaning on the stoop near the stairs leading to the laundry. And I was reminded of that tune he had been humming.

My uncle saw that I was lost in thought and caught himself. "And what about Rivke in all this reckoning? We have to fit her out for the wedding too. If there's enough money for a door, there's enough for a doorknob."

I saw that my uncle had stopped himself from continuing to talk, and his face turned red. I guess he regretted having added up the cost of the "conflagration" in my hearing.

More than anything, I was bothered by the fact that they were delaying the signing of Selma's engagement contract because it meant that I wouldn't see Red. And the wedding isn't until October. May, June, July, August, September, October. That's too long to wait, much too long.

A Letter from Ruth

May 21

I saw Red today when I was on the streetcar, returning from work. He was walking with a girl. He wasn't wearing a hat, and his red hair was shining.

Who was that girl? Where were they going? I thought about it so much that I missed my stop and went two stops further than I needed to. I walked back because it was better to walk than to sit. If you walk, you can stop whenever you want and go over to whoever you want.

On my table at home, I found a letter in a long yellow envelope. I wanted to see who it was from, but there was no return address. The letter had been delivered to my aunt's house, and it was probably Mrs. Shore who brought it to me. She's the one who does the good deed of always bringing me my mail. I would sooner have expected to see Lublin come to New York or the walls of my room start to talk than to receive a letter from Ruth. Why would Ruth write to me? Ruth's letter consisted of just a few words:

"Don't think you're lucky. Ruth."

What kind of curse is this? Today, of all days, when I saw Red walking with a girl, Ruth sends me her good wishes. Maybe she's right, and Eddie was also right in saying that Red was a *lowfer* and a *bum*. Ruth's short letter was written in printed letters, not in cursive. She must have wanted to be sure that I would be able to read it. Or maybe she didn't want to use her own handwriting in case I showed the letter to Red. Who knows what that's about? The girls here are different. And the males here are *boyez*, and it may be that the laundress is right about them: "they shut the door and forget everything." That's probably what Red is like. Why else would Ruth write "Don't think you're lucky"?

Today I heard the laundress talking to her husband. He wanted to take her to a movie, and she wanted to lie down and read a book.

"You're still living with Tolstoy," he said to her.

"So, how does that concern you?"

"It concerns me a lot," he answered, and went to the movies by himself. Before leaving, he muttered, "It's as good as living alone."

Is it possible that he's jealous of Tolstoy's picture? That's what it looked like to me.

The World Spins Around, and So Does the Lublin Ladies' Society

May 25

It's not for nothing that people say the world spins around. Not only the world, but also the Lublin Ladies' Society is spinning. Mrs. Tkatsh has once again become the president. She was lucky that Mr. Shamut is turning fifty this summer. The Lublin Ladies' Society called a special meeting to decide what to do, and Mrs. Rabkin suggested that Mrs. Tkatsh should be *kepten* of the whole event. (It seems that Mrs. Rabkin wants to get back into

Mrs. Tkatsh's good graces and get over the episode of writing the thank-you notes after the ball.)

Mrs. Tkatsh played hard to get at first. "I'm not rejecting the idea," she said, "but maybe there are better candidates than me."

Mrs. Rabkin made a *speetch* saying that we'd never be able to find anyone better than Mrs. Tkatsh. She reminded everyone that it was because of Mrs. Tkatsh that Mr. Edelshtein had come to the ball. She also mentioned the twelve bottles of Palestine wine that Mrs. Tkatsh had organized for the ball and that it was an honor and a pleasure to work with her. The speech was so successful that all the members applauded loudly, and Mrs. Tkatsh was elected "captain" of Mr. Shamut's birthday celebration and, on top of that, was reelected president of the Lublin Ladies' Society.

"Gloyb mir," Mrs. Rabkin said to my aunt. "Believe me. I didn't sleep for two nights thinking about how to make things right with Mrs. Tkatsh. And finally, I hit on Mr. Shamut! We'll make a birthday party for him, and Mrs. Tkatsh will be the *kepten* and *dat's awl*. I didn't sleep for several nights, but it was not for nothing. And, anyway, it's worth making a party for Mr. Shamut. He made such a beautiful appeal at our ball. Mrs. Rabkin showed her great satisfaction with the plan. Mrs. Tkatsh was also pleased, even deeply moved. She called all the officers of the Lublin Ladies' Society to her home for a glass of tea. It turns out that there are eighteen officers: the president, four vice presidents, a secretary, an assistant, four on the executive committee, four on the social committee, two on the table committee, plus a treasurer. That's eighteen in all.

After the meeting, Mrs. Tkatsh pressed Mrs. Rabkin's hand very warmly and said, "*Reelee, yu'r vonderful.* I never knew that you could speak so well. *Dat's beyutiful.*"

At the meeting I learned that hundreds of young people were taken from Lublin to work as slaves. Where is Mikhl? And what's happening with my father if Mikhl has been taken away?

I left the meeting with a heavy heart and fearful thoughts. I was full of concern for my father and brother. And then, just what I didn't need happened: I found Eddie near the laundromat. I remembered his roses that I had given to Mrs. Shore. I didn't know what I should say to him.

"Eddie, we've got a president . . ." My mother, may she rest in peace, used to say that I turned things topsy-turvy. I felt that I was doing that with Eddie. He seemed to understand that too, but he didn't know how to put a name to it.

"*Veree gud*, Rivke." He didn't even smile. What was wrong with him? Was he angry? So why didn't he show it?

"*Yu don' liyk rozes?*" he asked.

"Why do you think that, Eddie? I dried your roses in the pages of a book."

I have no idea why it occurred to me to say that, but it was hard for me to confess the truth. I don't know if Eddie believed me or not because he didn't say another word. He didn't say anything about Mrs. Shore. A bit later, he added: "*Eneehow*, Rivke, I'm *gled* that I'm seeing you."

I didn't answer him. I was thinking about my uncle calling Selma and Eddie's wedding in the Hotel Raleigh a conflagration, and I asked, "When is your wedding, Eddie?"

"*Don' esk mee, pleez*, Rivke."

Eddie leaned on the railing just like that other time. He quietly whistled a tune.

"Tell me, Eddie, are you a *jereebug*?'"

"Sure, I'm a better jerrybug dancer than Marvin."

"I was told that a jerrybug is never sad."

"*Dat's a liy*," Eddie said, smiling, "*A jereebug* can even die too."

I could see that Eddie doesn't want to get married. He was sad. Maybe my uncle wasn't right about him? When my uncle spoke, he was right, but when Eddie stands at the railing whistling, I think that Eddie is right. Now I see that I don't know who's right.

Layzer

May 26

I received a letter from Layzer today. It looks like one of his letters to me got lost because he wrote: "In my last letter you saw how many miracles had to happen for me to get to get to Palestine, to Erets Yisroel." But I don't know anything about them. I only know about the 'miracles' of his Rumanian travels and hospitalization. In this letter he writes: "I came here without a cent, without shoes, in torn pants, with an injured hand leg, and with great sorrow because I didn't know what had become of you. Today I received your first letter, and I think the pain in my leg has been replaced by great joy. I thought the pain would never go away."

Layzer is a better person than I am. He doesn't go around with Red and with Eddie as I do. Layzer is Layzer. He writes that he'll send me a visa at the very first opportunity. "Rivke, you need to come here. New York has already been built. What will you accomplish there? What will become of you there? Yet another factory girl? Or another storekeeper? It's a shame to waste your life on that." That's how Layzer writes, as though he were with me. What will become of me? "I may go back to my old profession," he writes. "I'll work as an electrical engineer. I met Hershl Zomersheyn here. He's now called Hershl Shimshi. He works in construction, building houses. He says that he'll help me get settled. His Hebrew flows like water, and he's a good man, a good friend. He's helping me a lot. Can you imagine that he remembers your braids! He asked me if you still had such long braids. Rivke, you need to be in Palestine, here in Erets Yisroel, and Erets Yisroel needs to see your braids."

I don't know what's become of me! My mother, may she rest in peace, was right when she said I was all topsy-turvy. Anyone else in my place would behave differently. I'll stop thinking about Red. And I'll forget all about Ruth's "lovely" letter. In Lublin, no one would have written such a letter. They would have been too ashamed to write it, and whoever received it also would have been ashamed. I'll put Ruth's letter with the cigarettes Red left here, and if Red comes I'll give him all of it. Maybe I'll even read him Layzer's letter so that he can see who Layzer is. Layzer is right in saying that I need to go to Erets Yisroel.

Anatomy

May 28

What a good week this is. First there was Layzer's letter. And second, Mrs. Rubin. I wasn't counting on her remembering that she was my mother's friend. All of a sudden, she asked me to come to her. I couldn't understand what she needed me for. I even thought that maybe it was all over with my *dzshob*. Mr. Rubin no longer wanted me in his factory. But I was completely wrong. She was looking out for me.

As usual, Mrs. Rubin was all done up with those little machine-like things that curl your hair. I don't understand why she's always going around with those things. When is it possible for her hair to look good if it's always looking like she has horns growing on her head? Still, because of those machines, her hair never stirs when she comes to a Ladies' Society meeting. It just lies there as if it has sworn not to move, one curl next to another, four on one side and four on the other and a part in the middle. Still, I don't think it's worth going around with horns always on top of your head just to come to a meeting of the Lublin Ladies' Society.

Mrs. Rubin said, quite plainly, "What good is it for you to stay in my husband's factory collecting pieces? You could stay there forever and you won't make more than ten dollars a week. My husband is always busy. He doesn't pay attention to the passing of the years. And for you, God forbid, a year and another year and another—and you're lost here in America. After a few such years, a girl is done for. So I talked to my Harry and told him to let you work at a machine. You'll learn how to sew. He even tried to tell me about the union-shmunion, but I know that if a boss wants something, he can make it happen. So I said to him, 'If you want it, then Rivke will learn the trade, and before the union figures it out, she'll be sitting at a machine.' My Harry lets himself be convinced if you talk to him long enough. Rivke, pay attention. Sit down at a machine and pay attention. The pieces won't run away. Then we'll see. Think about it, Rivke, because if you stay, God forbid, with the pieces, then you're lost. It's good enough for an Italian, but not for Reb Mottele Zilberg's grandchild."

So, despite the fact that my grandfather, Reb Mottele, lived in the forest near Lublin, and despite the fact that he's been dead for about ten years, and even despite the fact that he probably never gave a single thought to New York, he's still more important in New York than I am, even though I'm already able to ride the subway. Rebbe Finkl and Mrs. Rubin both thought it mattered a great deal that I was Reb Mottele Zilberg's grandchild.

Maybe it would be a good idea to tell Red whose grandchild I am. If he comes, I really will tell him.

"You have no idea how easy it is to mess up your life," Mrs. Rubin said. "My sister, Golde, was a *beutee*, a real head-turner. Her braids were even longer than yours, and her eyes were—*a milyon doler*. She could have married anyone she wanted, but she took it into her head to become a doctor. 'Be reasonable,' I told her. 'Become a doctor's wife.' But, no, she wanted to be the doctor, and off she went to study. So she had to study anatomy. Do you know what that is? I would never have known if not for my sister Golde. A person has veins, this one goes here, the other one there, and this vein is called this and the other something else. Ok, so you have to remember all the veins—their names and where they lead. Who can remember so much? She would sit with her anatomy book and study those veins all day long. Summertime, when the rest of us went walking near the river, she would sit with her veins. She ruined her eyes, and her braids got shorter. By the time she figured out what was happening, it was too late. She was left with anatomy and forgot about marriage, may you be spared such a fate. This week when I was thinking about Golda and her braids, I started to think about you too, with your braids. And I'm telling you, Rivke, I was scared to see your mother before me—may she rest in peace—and that's why I asked you to come. I'm thinking about you, Rivke, and mostly about the passing years. A girl has to be careful with those years, guard them like pearls, because they're more precious than pearls."

I don't know why they're all afraid of the years here. Mrs. Shore and Mrs. Rubin say the exact same thing: "Remember, Rivke, your passing years." It seems that it's even worse to be an old maid in New York than it was in Lublin. Now I understand why my uncle is so worried about Selma.

Montsey and Bentsey

May 31

This is the first time in my life that I've heard a name like Montsey. To me, it sounds like a name you'd give a cat or a calf, but only in America can a person be given a name like that. Mrs. Shore's daughter is called Montsey and her son, Ben Tsiyon, is called Bentsey. Why they've taken on such names of their own free will, I can't understand. But even though they're called Montsey and Bentsey, I actually like them a lot.

Montsey and Bentsey are going to the mountains for the summer, so they stopped at her mother's house for a few days. In honor of the guests, Mr. Shore came too. When I went to my aunt's to see if I had any mail, Mrs. Shore wouldn't let me leave.

"I have guests, my Montsey and Bentsey," she said. "They're going to the mountains. Come see them. What a Montsey and Bentsey they are, may no evil eye find them."

Mrs. Shore was right. Montsey looked like she had just stepped out of a movie picture. She was tall and thin and blond. A pleasure to see. And her son resembled his mother as much as one drop of water resembles another. Tall and thin and blond. And both smiled. They both sang the same songs, and both clapped to the rhythm.

"It's a show," said Mrs. Shore, "a real theatrical show."

Mr. Shore calls the boy by his full name—Ben Tsiyon. He asked him what the sidra, the Torah portion of the week, was. The boy repeated the word *sidra* and laughed. He laughed loud and long at his grandfather's words. Bentsey doesn't understand a word of Yiddish, not one single word other than *bubbe* and *zeyde*.

"A total gentile," said Mr. Shore. "He needs to go to a Talmud Torah."

"What do I need it for?" wondered Montsey. "*Reelee, vat iz di yuz af eet?*"

Montsey's husband runs a wine shop with his brother in Cincinnati. They live in an Irish neighborhood.

"In my *neyborhud* you can see a Jew once in a Purim. *Vat for du ay need a talmud toyre?*"

Mr. Shore complained to my uncle. "I did all I could. No one can blame me. I provided a rabbi, a Talmud Torah, a mountain of books. Do you think it helped? What can you do?" And Mr. Shore went and brought a mountain of dusty books from which Montsey had studied.

Mrs. Shore started yelling, "Get this dust out of here."

And Montsey laughed and said, "And I studied all that junk. Terrible!"

When he had taken away all that "junk," Mr. Shore added, "It cost me a fortune, and it stuck like peas to a wall."

Later, when Mendl Pushcart came, he said in plain and simple words, "Hitler will teach us all how to pray. *Don' voree.*"

Mendl Pushcart had a lot to say about the liquor business. "Now that's a business!" he said. "Those awful drops make the best business in the world." And then he told us that when he had first come to America, he almost became a partner in a liquor store. That man became wealthy and was now living on Fifth Avenue while he, Mendl, was stuck with the Cleaning, Dyeing, and Repairing shop. Or, as he calls it, the Cursing, Dying, and Despairing shop.

This was the first time that I heard Mendl Pushcart complain about his livelihood. Somehow, I never thought of him as needing a livelihood. I thought he always told stories, played pinochle with my aunt, knew all of Grand Street inside and out as well as he knew himself. But a livelihood? I thought there was one Jew on Grand Street who could wander around without such worries. And yet here he was, working at Cursing, Dying, and Despairing.

The lost liquor business seemed to be the very worst misfortune of his life.

"I never go to Fifth Avenue," he said. "What's the point of going there, to the place where you've proven that you're a fool?"

My uncle already knew of Mendl Pushcart's troubles and tried to comfort him. "If you had been in the liquor business, it would probably have gone bankrupt. Let it go. There's no joy in what's lost."

Mr. Shore hates unhappy things. As soon as he heard about lost joy, he put Bentsey on a chair so we could hear the boy sing the Yiddish song "Mayn Shtetele Belz."

"He's like a parrot. He doesn't understand a single word," said Mrs. Shore.

"If they sent a boy like this to a Talmud Torah, he'd grow up to be a learned rabbi," Mr. Shore bragged.

Everything ends with a game of pinochle. After Mrs. Shore served some food, they all played cards. Mendl Pushcart won $1.25. He was very happy and forgot about the Cursing, Dying, and Despairing business.

Twice a Zilberg

June 4

Today was a beautiful day. As I walked out of the house, the sun seemed to wrap itself around me, warming my face and hands. It was terribly hot in the shop. The machines ran so quickly you would have thought they needed to provide livelihoods for all of New York. When it's hot, you have to spray water throughout the shop several times a day, and the *peeses* are a mess. So first I pick up all the pieces of material, and then I spray water throughout the shop. Once I've sprayed, I have to go pick up the pieces again. I thought of Mrs. Rubin's sister, Golde—she with her anatomy and me with my piecework. She stayed an old maid. And me? What's going on with me? Red's not coming. She probably also had someone who was supposed to come and didn't.

Today, I sat down next to Shirley's machine to see how gloves are sewn. It's all done so quickly that I think that if I sit and stare for the next ten years, I'll still know nothing. Whenever I try to see what's going on, Shirley works even more quickly. It's as if she's dancing with the machine: up with the elbows, and then down, left and right. Shirley is no longer Shirley. The machine is no longer a machine. It's all done so quickly that it's a blur, and I'll never know how to do it. No, I'd be better off going to Palestine, carrying bricks and mortar with Layzer rather than sitting here dancing around with the machine. The black-haired operator—the one who's as thin as a board—noticed that I was looking on and started sending me back and forth. It was dusty, and she wanted water and she wanted me to open the window and she wanted me to close it. There's a demon in that girl. On days when the demon is quieter, she's an operator like all the others. And when the demon works itself up in her, she can't sit still. I think she's so thin because of the demon inside her. In Lublin, people used to say that if imps get into a horse, they make the horse run faster and faster until it drops. What do the imps do in New York? They've gotten into the black-haired operator and she can't rest and so she makes me go faster and faster.

After work, Shirley went to a coat sale. "Come on," she said, "there's a *sayl*."

A *sayl* is nothing more or less than an extraordinary fair. The *laydees* swarmed around the coats and started trying them on. It looked like a Purim party. The coats went from one lady to another as if they were alive, as if on their own. Shirley twirled this way and that in a green coat. She decided to buy it. "*Green*," she said, "*iz miy koler*."

I wanted to buy a coat too, but I still don't have enough money. I only have six dollars, and a coat costs fifteen.

The laundress told me that she would lend me nine dollars. She knows that I'll pay her back, but I don't know if I should borrow it. I think it's better not to owe anybody anything, not even the laundress, who is so good-hearted. When it gets warm, I'll go around without a coat, and even if it gets cooler, I still won't freeze. My aunt told me that she would give me one of Selma's coats, but I told her that it wasn't my color. Here, as soon as you say "my color," people believe you. "My color" is as easily understood here as Mrs. Pushcart's "my diet." When I said "not my color," my aunt left it at that. I can now tell a lie so easily that I even forget it's a lie. The truth is that I don't want to wear Selma's coats. In Lublin, you gave an old coat to the maid to wear, so I don't want to wear Selma's here.

"You're not cold in the evenings?" my aunt asked.

"I'm never cold," I answered.

My aunt looked at me a little strangely and then said, "It's not for nothing that you're twice a Zilberg!"

My mother and father were cousins, and both were named Zilberg.

It's wrong to lie, but I still think it's better than wearing Selma's old coat.

Mrs. Koshes and the Beautiful Peacock

June 6

Imagine what a dollar can do! Mrs. Koshes owed me a dollar. When I left her to go work for Mr. Rubin, it didn't seem right to go and ask for the dollar. Anyway, I thought, with or without the dollar, I've got the same riches. Today, when I came home from work, I found Zisele, Mrs. Koshes's *aydzshentke.* I couldn't understand what she was doing there. It turned out that Mrs. Koshes had sent her with my dollar. Zisele opened her pocketbook very slowly and took out a dollar. She searched for so long I thought she must have been looking for the very same dollar bill that Mrs. Koshes had given her. And then she said, "Mrs. Koshes is sick. She has a swollen leg, and she's in bed. She asked you to visit her."

I wanted to see Mrs. Koshes and went downstairs with Zisele. Why did she suddenly remember about me and send me the dollar? It was strange that she had thought about me. Mr. Shlivke, the laundryman, stopped me for a minute and said, "Rivke, I have a note for you."

My heart was beating fast. I know that Eddie is the one who writes notes, but . . . maybe? Maybe this time the note was from Red?

The laundryman handed me the note. It was a short letter in a small envelope. I recognized Sheinfeld's handwriting. Inside the envelope there was a check for fifteen dollars and a note: "Dear Rivke, Return it to the Messiah. Sheinfeld."

What a strange day. Everybody was bringing me money. Mrs. Koshes remembered the dollar she owed me. Sheinfeld remembered the Messiah's fifteen dollars. But there was nothing from Red. Red has hidden himself away somewhere in one of the many buildings in New York.

Mrs. Koshes really was sick. She motioned me to her bed with one finger and said, "Sit down, Ray." She didn't forget that my name was "Ray," even though she's the only one who calls me that.

I never saw Mrs. Koshes talk with her hands, but now I see that the cane kept her from doing it. Today, lying on her bed, she kept motioning with her hands.

She said, "I brought nine people to America. I've married off four girls. Now that I'm lying here they call me up on the telephone. *'How ar yu, Ent?'* When I hear "How are you?" I know that they want to be rid of me and *dat's awl.*

Mrs. Koshes has a habit of stopping in the middle of saying something and sighing as if she has grown tired of talking or of remembering.

"When my youngest niece was getting married, I bought her a bedroom set for four hundred dollars. I myself never had such furniture, but that *boy* of hers wanted a bedroom set. Four years I paid for it. Two dollars a week for four years. Every week, I gave her a present of two dollars. Four continuous years. Now it's too much for them to spend the carfare to come see me, so they call up and *dat's awl. 'Miy huzbend,'* she says, *'sends yu hiz luv.*' Have you ever heard of such a thing? Over the phone he sends me 'his love.' So, what should I do? Put it in a pot and cook it? Charlotte has already forgotten the time when her husband wanted a bedroom set and wouldn't get married without one. Everything is forgotten now and *dat's awl.* I'll shut off my telephone and let them stop sending 'love.' Do you hear me, Ray? You're still young. I'm telling you, Ray, we remain alone as if stranded on an island, and *dat's awl.* Why do I need the phone to ring in my ears and pound in my head? I brought nine people to America. I sent them tickets. I bought Charlotte a bedroom set and gave them presents and who knows what else. I might as well have thrown it all into the ocean and *dat's awl.*"

Mrs. Koshes talked and talked and gestured with her hands. Then she bent closer to me and whispered secretly, "That Charlotte, with the bedroom set, once forged a thirty-five-dollar check of mine. She signed it and took the money. And when I figured it out, she said, 'Well, what could I do if I needed it? Should I have stolen the money I needed? Should I have?' And she looked me straight in the eyes like the awful thing she is and then said, 'Why does my aunt need money?'

"I didn't want to get burned again so I stayed as far away from them as from a fire."

Mrs. Koshes talks about a fire too, just like my uncle about Selma's wedding. What's going on here with all this burning?

Before I left, Mrs. Koshes said that she had a favor to ask of me. "There's a package lying in white canvas wrapping here." She pointed to the chest of drawers, and when I opened it, I recognized the beautiful peacock, wrapped in a white cloth and pinned on all sides to protect it from dust. "Take it home, Ray. In case . . ." And she didn't say in case of what. "If Charlotte comes here, she'll wreck it. What do any of them understand about this? They'll sell it for ten dollars. Take it home. If I get well, you'll bring it back to me. And in case . . ." Once again, she didn't finish her sentence, but there were tears in her eyes.

I didn't want to take the beautiful peacock out of her room. I knew that she wouldn't be able to sleep afterward. I spread a sheet on a bench so I could sleep there and put the beautiful peacock back into the dresser. Mrs. Koshes's face lit up and her tears disappeared.

"You're not like today's youth, Ray," she said. "They would have been three blocks away already. They don't care about anything as long as they can take something and *dat's awl.*" Mrs. Koshes shook her head a long time, until she dozed off.

A *Plezshur*

Eddie's mother isn't just one woman but a whole wagonload of them. First of all she really is, may no evil eye find her, huge in every direction, as if she was made up of a mountain of pillows. There's a pillow here and a pillow there, and all the pillows together are covered in a black silk dress with a large, golden brooch at its heart. That's Eddie's mother! When I came to my aunt's house and saw her, I thought the room was full of women, but when I looked more closely, I saw that there was only one woman. Still, I thought I was making a mistake.

Just then, Mrs. Shore came in and told me that Red was there yesterday and asked about me. And, of course, she said it with a wink. The room started spinning, and I couldn't hear anything for a while. I just wanted to think again and again about Red's having been there. Suddenly, the whole apartment wasn't filled by Eddie's mother but by my longing for Red. I walked through all the rooms, thinking that he had been in all of them. Maybe he did just what I was doing and walked through all the rooms? Only later did I begin to hear what was said to me. Eddie's mother was talking about a *bedrum set.* I remembered that, just yesterday, Mrs. Koshes had told me that she bought a bedroom set for her niece, Charlotte, and that without the furniture, her bridegroom wouldn't have been at the wedding. To me, all of New York seemed full of bedroom sets—white ones, yellow ones, brown ones, cherry ones—and if they were all taken away, all the bridegrooms would stay away from their weddings. I thought about how Eddie had stood near the laundromat, leaning on the handrail and whistling. I was really sorry that I had gone to the movies with Mr. Sheinfeld on the very Friday when Red had come to the apartment. Who knows when I'll see him next? He has once again hidden himself away in New York, and New York is so big.

Eddie's mother was talking about the bedroom set. "A young couple's bedroom set should be like a doll. It should be a *plezshur* to see." She says *plezshur* with a sharp *p*, smacking her lips together. Everything is a *plezshur* for her. Eddie's character is a *plezshur*. The wedding in the Hotel Royal is a *plezshur*. My aunt's cake is a *plezshur*. And her visit is also a *plezshur* for her.

When she left, my uncle wiped his forehead with a handkerchief and said, "Here you have it: a *plezshur* of a mother-in-law." As usual, he smiled and undid his tie. "The pleasure and the bedroom set will cost an additional few hundred dollars. We're lucky to have only one daughter, Ida. Otherwise, we'd need to go begging from door to door."

My uncle looked pale and very tired. He seemed upset about Eddie's mother and her *plezshur*.

When I was getting ready to go home, Selma came in. Everything on her was blue: her dress, her hat, her shoes, her pocketbook. The large white flower on her dress seemed to be calling out to tell everyone that Selma was a bride.

"Did you *kvorl* (argue) with Red?" she asked. And I noticed that her eyes were also blue.

"I haven't quarreled with anyone," I said.

"But he's not coming to see you?"

I thought that Selma was pleased with the idea that Red wasn't coming to me, although later she added, "*But hee liyks yu eneevay.*" And she smiled. Selma didn't say that Red had been there and had asked about me. It's a good thing that Mrs. Shore told me. She's a good person.

Selma really was wearing a white flower fit for a bride, but still, Eddie was standing and waiting for me. It was too bad that it was Eddie standing there and not Red. My heart started pounding.

"I saw your mother today, Eddie," I said.

Eddie asked if his mother had talked about the bedroom set, and he laughed about it the way he had laughed when my uncle had called Selma's beauty parlor her house of study. I don't like it when Eddie laughs like that. He looks like someone who makes fun of people. But who was he making fun of? It's hard to imagine that he was making fun of Selma or his mother. Maybe he was making fun of me? Then why does he keep coming here? I never invited him.

"Yeah, your mother was talking about the bedroom set."

"I would like to go with you to Palestine," Eddie said, and he took the string of white beads that I was wearing around my neck into both of his hands. He seemed to me like a little boy who wanted to play cat's cradle with me. That's how he was holding the beads on my neck. Now I understand why Eddie told Red that I have a fiancé in Palestine.

"Eddie," I said to him, "in Palestine there won't be any bedroom sets."

"All right," he said, still holding my beads as if it was easier for him to stand if he held onto them. I gave him two little slaps on his hands.

"You'll rip my necklace, Eddie. That's all I need."

"I'll buy you other ones," he said, and I thought I saw tears forming in his eyes though his eyes were still completely dry.

Never

June 10

Today, I broke a glass and a saucer, and today, Red came. He came so suddenly it was as if he had just dropped from the sky. As I was coming back from work, I decided to be done with Red, to stop thinking about him, to throw out his cigarettes and the dried roses and Ruth's letter and absolutely everything else. Enough. Everything has to come to an end sometime. I can't always go around thinking about Red. I could become a flame and burn out as my mother—may she rest in peace—would have said. As I was standing there and deciding to do all this, I heard familiar steps on the stairs and I thought, Red. Red's coming! And then I thought that it was really the fire in me. I see Red everywhere. But then I heard, "Hello, Rivke," and Red came in. I was so flustered by his unexpected visit that the glass of tea and the saucer fell from my hand, and both of them broke. And Red saw it all. He didn't say anything, but he bent to pick up the pieces of glass. So maddening! He comes as if he had never gone away for six weeks. When he had picked up all the glass, I handed him his pack of cigarettes and the dried roses and Ruth's letter.

"Here, Red, I understand that you've come for your cigarettes. Here they are."

I don't know why I was angry. I was in the mood to be contrary. What am I? A stray at his beck and call? One minute he's gone, and then he's back?

Red took the cigarettes and put them in his pocket. He put the roses back in my cabinet drawer as if it were his own. He read Ruth's letter, said nothing, and put it back on the table. I looked at Red, not understanding what was going on with me or with him. He took out the pack of cigarettes I had returned to him and smoked one. He didn't speak but just stood and smoked, and I didn't ask him to sit down.

Let him stand, I thought. It's all right. He stayed away for six weeks. Now he can stand a little.

But I saw that it didn't bother Red at all. Instead, he was strangely pleased.

Then he said, "Rivke, Italy has entered the war." I saw that Red really was crazy. I couldn't understand why he was saying that to me. But he explained: "You won't be able to go to Palestine. Rivke, you'll have to stay in New York." And Red started speaking English: "*Iy'm so gled, Rivke, iy'm so gled, so heppee*" (I'm so glad, Rivke, I'm so glad, so happy). My heart was pounding. I was sad and happy at the same time. I felt as if I was about to cry, and I wanted to leave the room, but my tears came too quickly. My eyes were burning, as if they were on fire.

I was embarrassed to be crying like that. I wanted to protest to Red. I felt as if I had something to complain about, but I didn't know what to say, and I later regretted what I did say.

"You came to tell me good news—that Italy has entered the war. You came for that, but where were you for the last six weeks? You promised *awlvays* to bring me fresh roses. Did you bring them? I'll never believe you again. Never."

"Are you joking, Rivke?"

"No, it's no joke. I'm telling you the truth. Who asked you to come? You went away. Who asked you to come back?"

I thought that Red would leave and never return again. But I had to tell him these things. I just couldn't do otherwise.

Red didn't leave. He sat down on a chair and asked me to sit down too.

The laundress came in and saw Red. Warmly, she said, "Oh, a guest! It's been so long since you were here."

"I've been *bizee*," he answered right away, and looked at her happily. "And how are you, Mrs. Shlivke?"

Red was so pleased that Italy had entered the war that he was beaming at everyone. I don't understand him at all.

We went down to the East River, which was again lit by many lights and had large boats full of carefree people. Red took my hand and said, "Rivke, is it true that you'll never trust me again?"

"It's true."

"Are you making a joke, Rivke?"

"No, Red, it's true. You lied to me, Red."

Red looked startled and said, "I've never lied to you, and I never will, Rivke. Never."

I heard the clatter of machines and the rush of the water, and I thought that everything was saying "Never, never."

I wasn't hungry, but I still wanted to tell Red that I hadn't eaten yet or even had tea.

We took a bus to some luncheonette. I don't remember what Red said to me, but it had something to do with Ruth's letter. He held my hand. I remember only one thing of that evening: the word *never, never, never*. What an odd word!

Today it felt like summer. And summer is good.

Blintzes

June 12

My aunt made blintzes for Shavuos. She invited Eddie and asked him to bring Red too. Eddie visits nearly every day, but today he was officially *invi-yted*, and he came with a flower in his lapel. Red had one too, and Selma was wearing a dress with large flowers. When I saw how dressed up everyone was, I went to Mrs. Shore and asked her to give me the velvet flower.

"What for?" she asked.

"Everyone is all dressed up for the blintzes."

Red was struck by the velvet flower in my hair. He recognized it and asked if I was wearing the lucky flower. When I said yes, he asked *viy* and laughed.

"Because you've got a flower in your lapel," I answered.

Meanwhile, Mrs. Shore came in and said that she wanted to taste the blintzes too, and Red asked her why I had put on the lucky flower today. "With this flower, girls become brides," she said, with a wink.

Then, Red insisted I tell everybody whether or not I wanted to be a bride.

"I do," I said.

Everybody laughed, including me, and Red loudest of all. Eddie was the only one who barely smiled. I felt bad that I had worn the flower.

"Who do you want to marry?" Red went on lightheartedly. "Tell the truth, Rivke. Please tell the truth."

"With whoever," I answered.

"In that case," Red said, "be my bride."

As soon as he had spoken, Mrs. Shore started to applaud, along with my aunt and Selma and even Red himself. I was so flustered. They all seemed to be in agreement, but my heart was heavy. I thought that I had really become Red's fiancée. Suddenly, I remembered Layzer. Red said that I wouldn't be able to go to Palestine because Italy entered the war. Red was really happy this evening. He danced with Selma, with my aunt, and with Mrs. Shore.

When Marvin came home, he brought up a letter for me from my brother Chatskel. He's no longer in Antwerp. He and his family fled to Paris. His daughter, Janet, had two eye surgeries already. When they fled Antwerp, she was hit hard on the head by a chunk of something that was kicked up from the ground. It fell right into her eyes, and they still don't know if she'll ever be able to see again. Chatskel needs money. When I told my uncle that I would send Chatskel the six dollars I had saved in order to buy a coat, he suddenly turned red and said, "If you're saving for a coat, then buy a coat." Then he gave me ten dollars. "Send this to Chatskel," he said, sighing just as he had that morning when he talked to me about Eddie. I took the ten dollars and started to cry, so I went into another room and wiped my eyes. Red came in, and I saw that he was annoyed that my brother's letter had disturbed our happy little party.

"Don't cry, Rivke, please. What can you do?"

He's right. I can't do anything. I just took the velvet flower out of my hair. I no longer wanted to be wearing it because I didn't want the flower to stop bringing good luck.

The Fire Can't Be Put Out

June 15

"The worst conflagration is the one you can't put out," my mother, may she rest in peace, used to say. If my brother Chatskel is asking me to send money, then he must be in the middle of a real inferno. Our family hates to beg. All we need now is for poor little Janet to become blind. My uncle gave me ten dollars to send Chatskel, but when I remembered the accounting for Selma's conflagration—the wedding—with the master of ceremonies and the flowers and the invitation cards and the tips and the Hotel Royal, I thought that my uncle hadn't added things up correctly when he gave me ten dollars for my brother. In the end, maybe it's a good thing that my uncle was an insurance agent on the east side and not a rabbi in Novogrudek. I'll send Chatskel the six dollars I saved for my coat, too, and then he'll have sixteen dollars. Maybe I should also send the fifteen dollars that Sheinfeld gave me to return to the Messiah? In order to save a person's life, you can even desecrate the Sabbath and holidays, so maybe it's all right to send Sheinfeld's money too.

Sheinfeld has really come up in the world. He sits in a well-lit room, and there are books on his table that are most likely the accounting books for the Loan Society. His floor shines just like it does in Mr. Shamut's office. Sheinfeld was busy when I came in, but he gestured to ask me to wait for him. He was talking with some tall man, and even though they were both sitting down, it looked like the tall man was dancing. His chair never stopped moving back and forth and from side to side. And, in addition to the chair's movements, the man was also jumping up and down. I thought he would fly away together with his chair. He'd lift up off the shining floor and . . . poof! He was a nice-looking man who resembled a government minister except when he reminded me of the horse thief who used to hang around my grandfather Reb Mottele's yard. When the tall man turned himself completely around and left, Sheinfeld said that he was the Lodz compatriot, Mr. Karelin, who he had once told me about. "Whenever he comes in to chat about something, I always end up with a full-blown headache. He's not a bad person. On the contrary, he's a good man who likes to do favors, but I still get a headache whenever he comes. He wants me to sign his book with my professional name: Professor Doctor Sheinfeld. He doesn't demand it. He just advises me that it would be better for him and nicer for me. And he asks if I think it will matter to anyone if I do that."

I told Sheinfeld about the fifteen dollars I wanted to send to my brother Chatskel, and I told him that Janet's eyes have to be treated by a doctor so that she doesn't go blind. Sheinfeld thought about it and said: "Well, you're the one who got the money, but it was on my behalf, and I really don't want to owe your Messiah anything, especially now when the book is coming out. I'd really rather not."

Here was Sheinfeld sitting in such a nice room with a floor that was as shiny as the one in Mr. Shamut's office, and he didn't want to owe the Messiah anything. What should I do about Chatskel and Janet? I promised Sheinfeld that I would return the money in a month's time and that meanwhile I'd send it to Chatskel. I won't buy a coat. It's warm now anyway and, even in the evenings, I won't freeze. Why do I need a coat?

Red brought me large, shiny beads today. I'm embarrassed to wear them. Why, in the middle of nothing at all, did he bring them and then beg me to put them on?

I know that it's silly on my part. I should have put them on, but I just couldn't convince myself to do it. Maybe if I hadn't gotten Chatskel's letter . . . I tried to explain it to Red. "You know that I'm not wearing any jewelry. It's not even a year since my mother, may she rest in peace . . ."

"Why do you wear a lucky flower then? If you want to put something on, you do."

"It's all right to wear a flower. It's not jewelry."

Red was silent. I wound the beads around my hand like a bracelet.

"I'll wear them on my wrist. They're not so visible there."

Red closed the clasp and said: "*Yu hev yur ohwn vay*, Rivke. You're a little nutty, *bot iy liyk yu.*"

I don't know if Red was upset, but he seemed disappointed that I had put the necklace on my arm instead of around my throat. Layzer was different. I thought about him a lot today. I didn't tell Red that I had to send money to my brother. I would certainly have told Layzer. My head was spinning thinking about all this. Or maybe it's the shiny beads that cloud my vision.

The Expensive Dolls

June 17

Two new students came to school today. They're a brother and sister whose last name is Machlis. These lucky people came from Paris, while poor Chatskel is stuck in the middle of the war. The brother wears a checkered suit, just like Layzer's. And he looks a little like Layzer too, especially when he smiles. It made me think about Layzer and Red. Will I always think about them? I don't know. The Machlises saw that I'm a greenhorn like them, and they walked me home. I asked them what kind of work they do, and it turns out that they make dolls. They paint faces on the more expensive dolls, they said, and every doll needs to have a unique face. One doll laughs, another cries, one is young, another old, and they paint them all.

What a job! They paint dolls. Ruth is a model. There are some strange jobs in this world. I used to think that the only kind of skill that existed in the world was that of a shoemaker, a tailor, a carpenter, a cap maker, a watchmaker, or a baker.

The brother and sister speak French to each other, and it made me think of my little niece, Janet, who must also be speaking French by now.

As we were walking home, we met Red, who was coming to pick me up from school. I introduced them to one another and noticed how Red was looking at the brother.

"Who are they?" Red asked when we left them.

"They're in school with me. They're refugees who paint dolls."

"Artists?"

"Maybe."

"I don't like artists," Red said. "Why do you need to go with them?"

I was disappointed in Red. He acts like he's my boss, and then he disappears for six weeks. I was so upset that my notebooks fell out of my hands. My mother—may she rest in peace—also used to drop things whenever she was upset. Once, when she was mad at my brother Mikhl because he came home to the Sabbath meal with muddy shoes, she dropped the fish platter. He really got it that time! I remembered the story and didn't answer Red at all.

It seems that Red couldn't forget Layzer's photograph because a little later he said, "I thought that your friend from Palestine had come. They look alike."

I couldn't stop myself and said, "So, do you want to disappear for six weeks again? This time, don't forget your cigarettes."

Red started laughing. "You're wicked, Rivke. As my father says about my mother, "*a bitere yidene*.""

Then Red looked to see if I was still wearing the beads. "Do you like them?" he asked, and took my hand.

"Very much. I really like them a lot."

Red was once again happy. He combed his fingers through his red hair and held my arm. "Come on, *bitere yidene*. I'll take you to the movies."

In the movies, we saw a black man dancing very nicely, and I heard Red tapping his feet to the music. He knows the steps to that dance. I'll never know how to dance like that. Is that even called dancing? It's really leaping as though, God forbid, jumping straight into hell. Maybe that's what I'll learn to do instead.

The Young Years

June 20

Mrs. Koshes disconnected her telephone. She can't conduct any business now, and she figured there was no point in paying for a phone just to have Charlotte call three times a week and ask, "*Haw ar yu, Ent?*"

"What do I need it for?" she said. "Now it's nice and quiet in my room. I can lie here and remember all the things I loved. When the phone was near me, all my nieces would call to ask how I was. I have, may no evil eye find them, a total of nine nieces. Five of them are in New York, so my phone rings all day long and gives me a headache. But the door never opens unless you or Zisele come." Mrs. Koshes smiled and continued. "You know, somebody came to see me this week who I hadn't seen for eight years. All of a sudden, he showed up. He remembered me, he said. He has an office somewhere on Broadway. He's a builder who owns half the hotels in the Catskill Mountains. Very rich. When I came to America forty years ago, he asked me to marry him. He used to wait at my door evening after evening when I lived on Rivington Street. Do you know what he said to me once, Ray? Forty years ago he said, 'Just as the sun cannot be extinguished, Betty, so will I never forget you.' And he kept his promise. I never heard of a man who kept his promise, but he did, to this very day. He became rich and is now a magnate with a chauffeur to drive him around. He's built synagogues throughout New York and even—though they shouldn't be mentioned in the same breath—a church. You know how it is with such people. It doesn't matter whether it's one or the other; they have no God anyway. But, still, he's a man of his word. He used to disappear for four or five years and then come back again suddenly and ask me if I wasn't sorry. Once he came in the middle of a storm that threatened to tear the roofs off of houses. 'Betty,' he said then, 'I bought a hotel for half a million dollars. Maybe you're sorry now?'

"Yesterday, as I was lying here, the doorbell rang, and there he was. He no longer asked me if I was sorry. He just said, 'I've come to relive my young years on Rivington Street. A person grows old. I'm too rich, Betty, just too rich. Sometimes I think that all my houses and hotels and even the chauffeur are mocking me, daring me to try and buy back Rivington Street. There were two things I couldn't buy in my life: the Rivington Street of forty years ago, and you as my wife. Other than that, a person can buy everything, Betty, absolutely everything, including a synagogue, a church, a hotel, friends, wives, kind words, blessings, clothes, everything.'

"He sat here for over an hour and then left. He didn't try to offer me any money. He knew I wouldn't take it. I wanted to give him the golden peacock, but I thought he already had too many things. He wanted to send me to a resort, somewhere warm. What for? It's good to find a mate when you're young, and it's good to accept a favor when you don't need one. I'll tell you the truth, Ray, he would never come again if I had given in to anything, even to going to the warm springs. *Dat's awl.*"

Mrs. Koshes's eyes opened wider, and I thought they were once again pretty. Stubborn and pretty.

Before I left, she again asked me to take the golden peacock. "I won't worry about it if it's in your hands. My nieces will *fiks* it for sure. They'll sell it for ten dollars. *Dat's awl.*"

I took the golden peacock home, wrapped in a sheet, and I felt as if Mrs. Koshes's soul was chasing after me to make sure that no speck of dust fell on it. Where should I put it? And how should I protect it? After all, it isn't just some piece of cloth; it's Mrs. Koshes' life, her beautiful peacock.

Like a Mother

June 22

Nothing seems to work out. When I came to my aunt's Friday night for fish, she handed me a letter in an envelope that was so big you could have packed a whole chicken into it. At least that's how Mrs. Shore described it. The letter, though, was very short. Edelshtein's firm has a job for me that pays twenty dollars a week. The letter wasn't signed by Edelshtein but by somebody named Mack Lehigh. Why did such a short letter need such a long envelope? I guess that's how the rich do things. And why was it signed by Mack Lehigh? Mendl Pushcart had an explanation: Edelshtein doesn't write any letters. First of all, because spelling is hard, and second, because as soon as a Jew from Lublin gets rich, he hires himself a flunky.

If I earned twenty dollars every week, I could send Chatskel a lot of money, and maybe it would help Janet. But they all kept quiet about the job; nobody seemed excited about it.

My aunt tried to explain Edelshtein's letter too. "Maybe it's because he's from Lublin. Do you think that the wealthy can't be decent people? They can be, and they may think about a fellow Lubliner now and then."

Selma said, "*Evreebodee liyks her*" (Everybody likes her), and with that she ruined the whole thing.

"If that's the case, it would be better for her to collect the pieces in Mr. Rubin's factory. Twenty dollars a week doesn't buy happiness. It's no million dollars," said my uncle. I was surprised because I had never heard my uncle say so much about anything. He must really dislike the idea of my taking Mr. Edelshtein's job.

The worst blow came when Red arrived and was shown Mack Lehigh's letter. When Red gets angry, he forgets entirely that he's a Jewish boy, and the English words pour out of him so quickly that I can't even begin to understand the strange words he uses.

First he said, "*Vat de hel*" and again "*vat de hel*." And then he kept saying more and more that I couldn't understand at all. But I saw that he was furious.

The only one who didn't make a big deal out of the letter was Mendl Pushcart. He said, "*A dzshob iz a dzshob*. Who cares if it's Edelshtein or Mack Lehigh? What's the difference? Are they going to eat her up there? Girls aren't eaten up in America. If I were the greenhorn, I'd certainly take the job. *Viy not? A dzshob iz a dzshob*."

"You'll never see me again if you take that job," Red said when we went downstairs.

"Don't threaten me, Red, please."

"I'm not threatening you. It's my *adviyz*."

"*Adviyz* is different than a threat. Why didn't you say so in the first place?"

Sheinfeld also gets "*adviyz*" from Mr. Karelin, and it looks to me like *adviyz* is something you must obey. You can take a suggestion or leave it, but advice is something entirely different.

Mrs. Shore came to see me unexpectedly this morning. "Rivke, I've brought you excellent cookies. They'll soon disappear, so I brought you some."

But she really came to talk to me directly and simply. Tears came to my eyes when she spoke. "Rivke, *beleev mee*. If your mother were here, I wouldn't come to you like this. But I have to tell you: don't argue with Red over a *dzshob*. What will you get for the twenty dollars a week? There are lots of Mack Lehigh jobs in life, but a boy like Red doesn't come along every day. You're already twenty years old, Rivke. Before you know it, people will start turning up their noses, calling you an old maid. Eat the cookies, and forget about Mack Lehigh. *Dat's awl*."

The cookies really were excellent. At home, we called them butter cookies, and when I ate them, I imagined that it was my mother who had made them. That's how Mrs. Shore's kind words made me feel.

Mendl Pushcart Jokes Around

June 23

Man proposes, and God disposes. The saying is as true in New York as in Lublin. Today, my aunt, Mrs. Shore, Selma, Eddie, Red, and I all set out to go to the mountains. My uncle couldn't come with us because on Sundays, when people aren't at work, he talks to them about insurance policies, and so he's busier than on any other day of the week. Selma wasn't happy with the *bontch* of people going, but she agreed because Eddie wanted to go. As he had done so many times, Eddie wrote me a note that said (in English, of course) that he was going because of me. Why was he writing me notes? Who knows? That's his way. He's a writer.

Mrs. Shore and my aunt made *sendvitches*. No matter what's going on, there are *sendvitches*. It's really something, these sandwiches. You can always find them on a walk, at a party, or at a wedding. We had dairy sandwiches and meat ones. Mrs. Shore made two cheese sandwiches, so my aunt made two with chopped liver. Mrs. Shore made two with eggs, so my aunt made two with salami. Mrs. Shore made two with herring, so my aunt made two with chicken. Mrs. Shore made two with lox, so my aunt made two with meatloaf. Mrs. Shore made two with mayonnaise and green peppers, so my aunt made two with chicken gizzards. And whether the sandwich was dairy or meat, every one came with half a cucumber covered in salt. I looked at that mountain of sandwiches and saw Chatskel and Janet before me, dragging themselves around who knows where and who knows how long it's been since they've had any food in their mouths.

When everything was ready and Selma had put on her eye makeup and checked her nails, and everybody was standing around in their hats checking to see that we hadn't forgotten anything, the telephone rang. We heard the terrible news that Mendl Pushcart had barely escaped with his life. He hadn't felt well last night, and they took him to the hospital and operated right away. If they had waited another day, he wouldn't be here anymore. He was lying in a hospital bed and asked us to come to him.

Selma was very unhappy because he chose such a terribly hot day to go to the hospital. Our group divided into two: Selma and Eddie went to the mountains anyway and without the *bontch*; my aunt, Mrs. Shore, and I went to the hospital, and Red was left hanging and went along with us.

Mendl Pushcart was very glad to see us. "Yesterday I thought there would be one Mendl less in the world. It wouldn't make any difference if there was one less in such a big world. Still, I really, really didn't want to leave it."

Mrs. Pushcart said that her legs turned to bricks. She had been so scared that she couldn't move at all. Mendl had closed his eyes and was no more. He hadn't spoken a word. Done. It was a miracle that Minnie ran for help and he was taken to the hospital and they went to work on him right away. By *work*, she meant the operation.

Their daughter, Minnie, was at the hospital. She was the violinist in all those stories that Mendl Pushcart told. She really did have long, white, thin fingers, and everything she wore matched her fingers. She wore a thin blue dress with white stripes, a long, narrow collar with a white border on her neck. Her hair was combed back with a straight part in the middle, but it was so straight it looked like she had drawn a white line to divide her hair. Even her eyes were narrow and long with eyebrows as thin and straight as arrows. I thought that even her name—Minnie—was also somehow thin and birdlike. She didn't say anything to us. I don't know if that's because professors ask her opinion about music or because she was worried about her father. Mendl Pushcart looked terrible. Only his eyes seemed alive, and I wondered at his constant joking about "one Mendl less." Before we left, Mendl asked whether I had taken the job.

"No, I didn't."

"Too bad. In this world, if you're given something, you should take it. That's what you do in this world."

Red was waiting outside for us, sitting on a bench and reading the comics in an English newspaper.

"How is he?" Red asked me, although he seemed to be thinking of something else.

"All right," I answered, but I didn't tell him what Mendl Pushcart had said about Edelshtein's job. I didn't want to mention it to Red.

A Magic Spell

June 26

I can't get used to the heat in America. If the temperature rises, it's hot everywhere: on the street, at home, even in the shade. America doesn't begrudge you coal in the winter or sun in the summer. There was a run on water in the factory today. I must have gone downstairs at least ten times to bring the machine operators soda water, Pepsi-Cola, and just plain cold water. It was also hot in the evening. You could feel the heat beating up from the ground. The laundress went up on the roof, spread a blanket, and lay down to get some air. I went up to the roof too.

"Do you see that sky, Rivke?" she said. "You can get a sky like that only in New York. All the stars are reversed. The ones that were on the left side at home are on the right side here; those that were high in the heavens are low here. It's a backward sky, but a lovely one. Do you think it's astronomy? No. It's America, Rivke! Sometimes I look at you and Red. I'm talking to you as to a sister, and to a sister, you tell the truth. Red is a fine *boy*, but whenever I see the two of you together, I think that you're walking and he's riding an escalator. He enjoys himself. That's what they're like here. My husband hates it when I read a book. 'Made-up stories,' he says. And they hate made-up stories here. Do you know what they like? 'My steak.' And it needs to be both 'steak' and 'mine.'"

I told her about Layzer's letters and that he was waiting for me to come to Erets Yisroel.

She laughed. "It's possible that life is better in Erets Yisroel. Maybe people live more with their hearts than their wallets there, but no one leaves America. Do you hear me, Rivke? That's the whole trick. It's a magic spell, truly magic. It's an upside-down world here, but no one wants to trade it in for another one. I'm telling you, it's magic."

Red called me, and I went downstairs to him. He was dressed all in white. I remembered what the laundress had just said about him and me— that Red was on an escalator, and I was on foot. Red took me out. We went on a ferry floating on silvery water. Opposite us, we saw the lights of other boats. I thought it must be a holiday and Red was dressed in white in honor of it.

Red looked at me and said, "Rivke, you're always wearing the same dress. Don't you want a new one?"

"I don't think about that, Red."

"What do you think about?"

"Red, do you love your mother and father?"

"*Shur.*"

"I'm thinking that it's such a silvery summer evening. My father and brother aren't freezing in Lublin now. That's what I think about, Red. Do you understand?"

"*Shur,*" he answered, putting his arm around me as we stood at the ferry's railing.

When I came home, I found a box on the table. Red left it before he called me to come down from the roof. In the box there was a light, green dress covered with large flowers and a slip of the same color in addition to stockings and handkerchiefs and a note from Red written in Yiddish with lots of mistakes: "*Rivke, dos iz a gift fon miyn moder.*" I laughed at all the mistakes and then I kissed the note and the dress.

At night I dreamed that Layzer came to my room and took back all his letters. He opened the drawer, took them out, and put them into his pocket. I saw him leave again on a Greek ship with a masthead of a bird with a long neck. It was the kind of ship you see in pictures. First, the ship swam through the middle of the street, and then it turned, and I couldn't see it anymore. I woke up with a start and ran to see if Layzer's letters were still in the drawer. They lay all bound together just as I had left them. The box with Red's gifts was on the table. In the open drawer I saw Mrs. Koshes's beautiful peacock wrapped in the bedsheet.

My head was pounding. Everything was all mixed up, as if the parts of my life were colliding in my room. I couldn't sleep anymore, probably because of the heat.

I Learn How to Sew Gloves

June 27

I tried to sew a glove today. There was a machine that wasn't being used because Blonde Bessie hadn't come to work. The girls said that she quarreled with her fiancé and that whenever they fight, she gets sick for a few days and doesn't come in to work. Blonde Bessie has thick lips and quick hands. Her hands are like birds; they dance on the machine so easily that you'd think Bessie wasn't working at all but just came into the shop to play a bit. Still, if she moves her lips, you can tell how hard she's working. She smacks and smacks her lips so much that you don't know what she's saying, and in the end, it turns out that she's only saying two words: *it's raining*.

Blonde Bessie has been going out with her boyfriend for ten years. He's up there in years, and she's also no youngster, but they still haven't gotten around to getting married. In the shop, they say that Bessie's fiancé is a musician, and he says that if he gets married, it will affect his music.

Minnie, Mendl Pushcart's daughter, the violinist, is also unmarried. Maybe that's the way it is with musicians. If you want to play music, you don't need to get married. Why does Blonde Bessie need a man like that? At home in Lublin it was the exact opposite. Musicians had wives and many children. Naftali, who played the bandura, had eight children—four boys and four girls—and they were called the "Polska Army," the Polish army. But it looks like New York is different. What is it that the laundress says? "It's a backward sky, but a lovely one."

When I sat down at Blonde Bessie's machine, I was afraid it would carry me off. I turned it very slowly, and it began very slowly to make a sound and to sew. I thought about Bessie's hands and how they flew around like little birds, and I began to feed the machine more material. I made a seam! It's true that it had four little holes, but it was still a seam. In the afternoon I went back to sewing, and the forelady said, "*Yu'll be awlriyt.*"

I felt that my hands had become lighter and faster. If Blonde Bessie quarrels with her boyfriend again and stays home for another few days, I'll learn how to sew gloves.

Everyone Already Knows

June 30

When I went to my aunt's Friday night for fish, I was wearing my new dress, and everyone said: "*O, shee haz a gud tayst!*"

"Who's this *shee*?" I asked.

"Your mother-in-law."

"I haven't even gotten married yet, but I already have a mother-in-law?"

"As you can see."

How did they know that the new dress and slip and the stockings were a gift from Red's mother? At first I thought that the laundress had told them. Then I thought that Red had told Eddie and Eddie told Selma and Selma told everyone else. It turns out that it was Eddie's mother who told my aunt. And how did Eddie's mother know? She had met Mrs. Levitt, Red's mother, who told her that she liked me and she sent me a present. My aunt had come home all excited and told Mrs. Shore and my uncle about it, and then she told Selma and Mendl Pushcart and even Marvin. Ever since Marvin started to earn money for his dancing and to have his picture in the papers, my aunt considers him "a real mentsh, may he be spared the evil eye" and tells him everything.

"Thank God, we've almost gotten Rivke married. It was a little easier than with Selma." That's what my aunt said when she brought home the news.

Mrs. Shore told me to remember that, despite whatever I may think, she's my aunt, my family. My aunt was excited and happy when she talked about meeting Mrs. Levitt. It's also true that it didn't cost her anything.

Selma said it was *imposibl* (impossible) to wear my new dress with black shoes. I must wear white ones. "*Dat's funee,*" she added.

What good does the new dress do me if I look *funee* in it? What's so funny about it? I won't buy white shoes now because I have to save money so I can repay the fifteen dollars to Sheinfeld's Messiah.

Mendl Pushcart made an even greater to-do over my dress. He came back from the hospital the same Mendl Pushcart he had been before. "*A kveen*," he said. "She looks like a real queen in that dress. I wish I had a fine boy so she could be my daughter-in-law." It ended with several glasses of tea that I made for him, wearing my new dress.

Red Can Also Speak Capriciously

July 3

Red can do strange things sometimes. When we took a bus to a luncheonette, I saw that Red's mother was there. She hadn't come over to us but seemed to be checking me out from a distance. Red said she was there because she was hungry, and so she went in to get something to eat. I asked Red how it was that she had chosen that exact place and time, and he said it was because it was a good restaurant.

I saw that Red could go on "becausing" the whole night and always come up with a new excuse. It's not just me who answers capriciously; Red is even better at it than I am.

"What would happen, Red, if your mother didn't like me?"

"That's impossible," he said. "It never even crossed my mind."

Red is in love with his mother. She's a *bizneslaydee* he says, and he says it with as much respect as my mother used to say that her grandmother was a religious, honorable woman.

I almost quarreled with Red again today when he talked about his mother and said, "*Iy liyk tu vimen.*"

"Who?"

"Guess," he said, just the way that I say to him.

"Your mother . . . and . . . that's all I know."

"*Tu bad*," he said, "that you don't know."

"Maybe Ruth."

Red was as mad as if I had said the worst possible thing to him.

"*Pleez*, Rivke," and then he added bitterly, "you don't want to show me your letters from Palestine." So Red hadn't forgotten about Layzer and the photograph, and today he just had to talk about it.

It's true that I think about Layzer a lot now, especially ever since Red brought me the dress that was a gift from his mother. Maybe I need to write to Layzer, but what should I write? Can I write to tell him that Red brought me a dress? Can I write to tell him that Red is teaching me English? Can I write to tell him that I went to a luncheonette with Red? I can't write those things. If Layzer were to know about them, he might never think about me again. Maybe I should write that it's impossible to travel to Palestine now. But he must know that himself. It's a good thing that I'm working in the shop and am so busy that I don't have a lot of time to think about such things. Still, that's probably what I should be doing.

Mendl Pushcart Wins the *Sveepstayks*

July 6

My mother, may she rest in peace, used to say that good and bad go hand in hand. I see that it's true. Mendl Pushcart and his wife came all dressed up today and so happy that you would have thought it was Purim. My aunt supposed it was because Mendl Pushcart's operation went well and he's as healthy as if he'd never even had an operation.

She said, "We can really say mazel tov to you. Thank God you're back to your old self."

"How do you know that you should say mazel tov to me?"

"What do you mean? Didn't we come see you in the hospital?" My aunt was rather insulted.

Mendl Pushcart lifted his arms up high, as if he wanted to raise the ceiling. "Who even remembers the hospital? We won the *sveepstayks*!" My aunt didn't even wish him mazel tov for that. She didn't ask how much he had won or what he had won. She just jumped up and went to Mrs. Shore, and before she had even opened the door, she yelled, "Mrs. Shore, may you live and be well. Come, come quickly and you'll see them!" Mrs. Shore ran into the apartment wearing her apron and only then did my aunt finish telling her the good news. "They've won the sweepstakes!"

Mrs. Shore took her hands out of her apron pockets as quickly as if she was holding them too close to fire. She still couldn't believe that my aunt meant Mendl Pushcart and his wife, and she asked, "Who won? They?"

"We, we! What do you think? Rockefeller needs to win? Although I'd still switch places with him even now."

After all the uproar, it turned out that the winnings added up to three hundred dollars. "It could have been more," said Mendl Pushcart, "although three hundred dollars doesn't walk up to you every day on Grand Street. But the number just next to mine won forty-eight thousand dollars. I couldn't sleep the whole night. The man who sold me the ticket asked me to choose one slip of paper or the other and, of course, I went and chose this misfortunate one and left the fortune for somebody else."

"What are you complaining about? Did you invest your grandmother's inheritance?" his wife asked consolingly.

Still, even though he had chosen the misfortune and left the fortune for somebody else, we raised a glass, and Marvin, who had just come in, danced a lively dance that only he and Goodman and no one else in the whole United States knows how to dance.

Mrs. Pushcart told us that they had another stroke of luck. The doctor in the hospital warned her husband to stop smoking. And since stopping, he's become a new man. His mind has become clearer. Even his business is doing better. The smoke fogged his brain, and now it's cleared up.

"If you become rich, you become smart too," Mendl Pushcart announced. "If I had won the forty-eight thousand dollars, I'd be so smart that I'd put Einstein to shame. *Beleev mee.*"

So, you can argue about whether he would have put Einstein to shame, but it was certainly true that Mendl Pushcart was a new man after his operation and winning the sweepstakes. That's as clear as day.

It's an Old Story

July 10

At home, people used to say, "You have to be careful in the month of Tammuz. The heat can make people crazy." I'm saying this because of Eddie. What's with him? I really can't understand it.

Today, when I left to go to work in the morning, the laundress said, "Rivke, you can start putting all your *boyes* up for *sayl*. Somebody's been waiting for you since early morning."

Eddie was pacing around near our house. I was so surprised that I didn't know what to say.

"Eddie, what is it?"

"In the evenings, you're *bizee*," he said, as if it bothered him.

"You're busy too," I answered.

"Yeah, me too."

He walked to work with me, and on the way he took two white handkerchiefs out of his pocket and said, "Rivke, this is for you."

I took them and thanked him.

"I want you to keep them in your pocketbook."

"Good, Eddie, thanks."

He walked with me and was silent. When the streetcar came, Eddie asked me not to get on but to wait for the next one.

"Today is *sutch a niys day*," he said in his broken Yiddish. "*Tu bad* that you have to go to the *fektoree*."

I got on the next streetcar, and Eddie stood on the sidewalk and lifted his hand to his forehead.

On the streetcar, I took out the handkerchiefs. They were thin and white and on each of their corners one word was written. On each handkerchief, the words were "I LOVE YOU, DEAR."

I hadn't noticed the words when he gave me the handkerchiefs. Who embroidered them? Did he order them? Or maybe they're ready-made? Who knows? In America, almost everything can be bought ready-made, even "I love you."

All day, I kept thinking about Eddie and the embroidered handkerchiefs. In the evening, when Red came, I couldn't stop myself, and I showed them to him.

"I got this gift today."

"Who gave it to you?"

"Eddie."

"Do you know why?"

"No, I don't."

"Eddie thinks that if a boy is in love with two women, then he's a *reel man*. It's an *owld storee*." And Red started to laugh.

If so, then maybe my uncle was right about Eddie. When he saw Eddie's note that time, he said that Eddie was no great prize. It's a strange world here. The laundress says it's a backward sky but a lovely one. I think it's the other way around: a lovely sky but a backward one.

When Red left, he took the handkerchiefs with him. He just opened my pocketbook and took them out.

"What are you doing, Red? They're mine."

"I don't want you to have them in your pocketbook," he answered, without a smile, as if the whole thing upset him. "You shouldn't have taken them," he added, putting the handkerchiefs into his pocket.

Now there are two things I don't know: why Eddie brought them and why Red took them away.

Now, That's What You Call Luck

July 11

I don't know what Red thinks he's doing. Yesterday he took the handkerchiefs that Eddie gave me out of my purse and preached to me, saying I shouldn't have taken them. And today he was unhappy that the Machlises were walking home with me.

I'm really happy with the Machlises. Until they came to the school, I was the worst student in class. When everybody else had started writing, I still didn't know what to do, and Mrs. Schwartz had to come over and help me out. Now it's the Machlises who are the greenhorns. They don't know any English, and it makes me happy to know that I look like a learned woman next to them. It's not good to be the worst student in class or the worst at anything else. I'm always smiling at the Machlises because I'm so glad they're here. Today, they walked home with me. They told me that the sister found work. She now sews doll's dresses and is already earning ten dollars a week. She'll soon be earning even more. They both live on that money. How is it that she has white shoes to wear? I was embarrassed that I hadn't yet bought myself a pair of white shoes, and so I couldn't wear the new dress that Red had given me. As I was walking with the Machlises and thinking about the white shoes, Red came to meet me because he wanted to walk me home from school. I know that when Red is unhappy about something, he starts to comb his fingers through his hair as if it was the hair that was bothering him. Red said hello to the Machlises and then said good-bye right away. I didn't like that. He treats me like a child. It's as if he needs to pick me up from school and take me away from bad influences. And that's exactly what he said to me.

"I don't like the company you keep."

I wanted to tell him off, and I said, "They're very nice people, and I like them."

"*Tu bad*," he said, putting his hands in his pockets.

I was less upset with his answer than with the fact that he'd put his hands in his pockets. It looked to me like the gesture of somebody who thinks he's above it all. Since I didn't have any pockets on my dress, I couldn't do the same thing, and it made me out of sorts. I couldn't let it go.

"You don't like the Machlises. You don't like Eddie's handkerchiefs. You don't like the letters from Palestine. You don't like Edelshtein's job. What *do* you like?" I laid it all out for him and felt like a stone had been lifted from my heart. Red can do whatever he wants. He can go away for another six weeks, or even for six years. I had to tell him that he was bossing me around too much.

Red didn't answer me, but his lips turned pale.

I could have done without all this quarreling. What was the point of it? Red's cigarettes were sticking out of his pocket, and I took them out and handed them to him.

"Red, don't forget your cigarettes," I said, laughing.

Red smiled, took my arm, and said what his father probably says to his mother when they're arguing: "*Yu'r a* bitere yidene, Rivke, *beleev mee*, biter vee gal."

Red had said that before, but I hadn't expected him to know so much Yiddish, and I asked him how he knew the expression *bitter as gall.*

"My father says it to my mother. *Evreebodee hez to no eet.*" And he smiled.

It's just my luck that when the Machlises walked home from school with me, Red took it into his head to come at the same time. Now, that's what you call luck.

Stories

July 14

Every summer, Mr. Shlivke—the laundress's husband—goes to New Haven for a day to visit his mother's grave. He leaves early in the morning and comes back the next day at 10:00 a.m. after spending the night at his sister's house. She lives in New Haven and has her own laundry business there. He's as punctual as a clock.

Mrs. Shlivke said he wouldn't be back until tomorrow at ten o'clock. When he left, she opened all the drawers, took out all the photographs, and laid them on the table. Some of the packets of photos were tied together with red ribbon. She told me that those were the ones from her youth. She undid all the packets and looked at every one of the photos, shaking her head over some of them. And then she put them back in the drawers, taking out one photograph to show me.

"This girl, Tillie was her name, killed herself over a love affair. She had a wonderful fiancé, but just before the wedding, with no warning signs, Tillie took poison. People said she did it to spite her fiancé, who had started looking at her younger sister more than he should have. Once, Tillie saw them leaving the theater together. It was on an evening when he said he was going to visit his mother, and her sister said she was going to the doctor because she didn't feel well. And then, when Tillie went out for a walk, she saw them both coming out of the theater. She poisoned herself and left a note that said, "I'm dying because there's no honesty in the world."

I thought a lot about Tillie, who had found no honesty in the world. I imagined her with large, dark eyes, very curly hair, and full lips that were pursed as though about to kiss someone. All the features of her face were a little too much. My heart ached for her as though I had known her or as though the whole thing had just happened.

"She was a good person," the laundress said of Tillie. "She would give the shirt off her back if somebody needed anything."

When all the photographs were back in their drawers, the laundress got up on a chair to dust Tolstoy's portrait and to put a fresh branch on top of the frame. She covered the credenza with a clean white cloth and dusted the *Mayflower*'s sails. It looked like she had set things up for a long voyage, and the *Mayflower* was spreading its clean sails.

I couldn't forget about Tillie. I couldn't fall sleep for a long time because I saw Tillie's full lips and I thought I could hear her saying, "I'm dying because there's no honesty in the world."

White Shoes

July 17

Every woman in New York is walking around in white shoes, and they keep looking at my black shoes as if I had forgotten some very important thing. The forelady in the factory looked at my shoes and didn't say anything. She just looked again. Selma also took a long look at my shoes and then lowered her eyebrows just like the movie stars who lower their eyes and raise them back up slowly.

On Friday, my aunt said, "Rivke, if you don't have any white shoes, I'll buy you some." My aunt has a habit of saying something and then forgetting about it. It's not because she's cheap, but she's just plain addled, probably because of Selma. In Lublin, I wore black shoes all summer long and never gave it a second thought. Here, when I get up in the morning and put on my black shoes, I remember that in an hour's time, the forelady will look at them a little too much. When Red takes a walk with me, he also looks at my feet, and I know what he's thinking. He's thinking of a pair of white shoes. When I was in Lublin, the Warsaw mademoiselles used to come with white shoes. In fact, that's why they were called mademoiselles. Mademoiselle or not, here you need white shoes.

I think that I'll take the money I've been saving to pay back Sheinfeld's Messiah and buy myself a pair of white shoes first. Then, I won't feel like such an outcast. What about Sheinfeld's honor? I'll make it right a few weeks later. I didn't spare my own honor when I went to find him the money. When I have the white shoes, I'll be able to wear the dress with the large flowers that Red brought me. As Selma says, it's *imposibl* to wear it with my black shoes. And, when it comes to these things, you can rely on what Selma says. I think that Selma knows more than all of New York about what does and doesn't go together. Once, she said, "I'd rather die than wear a blue coat with a brown hat." She said it in English: *"Ay vud rater diy."*

Yet, here it is, less than a year since my mother's death, and I'm already thinking about wearing new, white shoes. But, still, if all of New York does it, it's probably all right for me too. I really want people to stop looking at me and my shoes.

Lubliners

July 21

There are lots of regions in America, but none is as famous as California. I still don't know if California is a good place or not. When I buy apples or oranges, the saleslady tells me their quality right away: "They're Californian." And, once it's Californian, it needs no more praise. So that must mean that California is good! But on the other hand, if a man wants to run away from his wife, he heads to California, and once he's there, it's all over. When

Blonde Bessie quarrels with her musician and stays away, the girls say that one day he'll run away from her and go to California. When Ruth was angry with Red, she left for California. When Mrs. Shore told me that Ruth had gone to California, it was as though she had told me that Ruth went off to another world. But it turns out that it's not so easy to get to California. Take Ruth. She traveled and traveled and got as far as Baltimore. Today, Mrs. Shore said mazel tov to me. "The bride is back. She got to Baltimore, and she came back yesterday. She looks like a doll and is as thin as a rail. That's what happens when you're *krayzee* about a boy."

I think to myself, Who am I crazy for? Layzer? But I write to him so seldom. Maybe I'm crazy for Red? I don't know if I would have gone to California and come back because of him.

I said all that to Mrs. Shore. She knows a lot. When her fiancé fell in love with the Bessarabian woman with the cheese, Mrs. Shore looked around and figured out what to do. Now, she thought about my situation and said, "Rivke, it's bad to be tested. Do you know why you wouldn't have gone to California? Because the *boyez* come to you. Not everyone can behave so well if they get knocked around. I'm telling you, it's all because of your braids. And anyway, if you're a Lubliner, you can turn heads."

It made me laugh to hear what she said about people from Lublin—"if you're a Lubliner"—as though there was another sort of people back home.

I told her that, but she said there was nothing to laugh at. "I've noticed that with all of you. Your aunt is a clever woman. But does she show her cleverness? No, never. She keeps it to herself. She hears what she needs to hear. If she doesn't need to hear it, she turns aside and doesn't hear a thing. She remembers what she needs to remember and forgets what she needs to forget. Do you think I don't like her? I like her very much. She's a dear woman. But she sure is a Lubliner. And you?" Then Mrs. Shore took my chin in her hands the way you do with a child. "You're a Lubliner too. I see how it is. You put your braids on top of your head, like a crown, as though all of New York was about to come see you. Other girls run too much, laugh too much. But not you. Everything will come to you, and all you have to do is wait. That's some luck . . . but only the Lubliners can be like that. They have such clear eyes. Lucky." She stopped for a while and then asked, "Do you ever cry, Rivke?"

"Who else do you think cries? Of course I cry."

"Maybe. But it doesn't show on you."

"So maybe we're real people after all, like everybody else."

Mrs. Shore laughed, and I remembered Mr. Edelshtein and his gray, clear eyes that laughed and may have even been laughing at me when he gave a hundred quarters for a dance during the ball.

I've been thinking about two things all day: that Ruth came back and that I finally have white shoes. When Red came over, I put on my white shoes and the new dress that he gave me. Red was so happy, but I couldn't understand why. All he said was, "Oy, Rivke," and he took me in his arms and didn't say anything else. I'd give a lot to know what he liked so very much. I could have sworn it was my white shoes. In the end, I couldn't stop myself, and I asked him: "*Pleez, Red,* tell me *di trut.*"

When Red heard "*di trut,*" he opened his eyes wide and then quickly started to comb his fingers through his hair. God knows what he thought I was going to ask him. Maybe he thought I was going to ask him to tell me the truth about Ruth.

"Tell me *di trut,* Red, the whole honest truth. Do you like my white shoes?"

Red laughed with a mixture of delight and disappointment.

"Tell me, Rivke, the truth. Did you want to ask me something else?"

"There is no '*somting els*' if you're wearing white shoes," I answered. I really was so proud of my white shoes and of being more like everybody else.

I didn't ask him about Ruth. What's the point of asking when "it's bad to be tested," as Mrs. Shore says?

Those Times Are Gone

July 24

Red hasn't come for several days. I had a note from him with just a few words: "Dear Rivke, I'm busy today. Larry." Red's real name is Layzer Yosl, and he's called Larry here. How strange it is that Red's name is the same as Layzer's.

I don't understand why he's so busy that he can't even come tell me himself but has to send a note. Is it because of Ruth? Because she's come back from California? Who knows? If Eddie can give me notes that say "I love you" even though he's about to get married, maybe Red is like that too. I never thought about such things when I was at home and went with Layzer to the forest. But those days are gone. Now I'm in New York and, as Mrs.

Koshes says, "we remain alone, as if stranded on an island." That's how I feel today. I thought about Tillie, who died because there's no honesty in the world. Who is meant by that? Red? Ruth? Eddie? Maybe me? Certainly not Selma. She's filing her nails and waiting for the conflagration.

The best thing to do on a day like this is to go to school. After class, the Machlises invited me to go to a movie with them. I saw something odd there. There was a family in which everybody was cheating on somebody. The husband had a lover and so did the wife. Their only son was cheating them out of all their money. The only faithful one in the family was the dog. Why did I need to go to the movies today and see that the most faithful being is a dog?

The Machlises are strange people. He talked the whole time about the dolls he made. One of them, he said, was exactly like a live person. It was a clever doll, with long eyebrows and a beard. What nonsense! Although, maybe if that's your job, that's what you think about. Still, it was good that I spent this evening with them, when Red was *bizee*.

Charlotte

July 25

I came home late today. Red had been here and left a note. It's good that he didn't find me at home. He shouldn't think that he's the only one who's *bizee*. In his note, he drew a mountain and a tree and a bridge. In short, a whole painting. He must have waited here for a long time. Let him wait.

After school, I went to Mrs. Koshes to see how she was doing. One of her nieces was there. It was Charlotte, sitting in her hat like a guest. She was wearing seven gold necklaces, one under the other, so that her whole chest was covered in gold. She wears even more makeup than Selma: on her cheeks, her lips, her eyebrows, even her nose. She must work at it for three or four hours a day. Mrs. Koshes was silent the whole time, just shaking her head now and then.

Charlotte didn't stay for long. Before she left, she winked at me as if to say that Mrs. Koshes was very sick. She made a big deal out of saying good-bye. "*Gut bay, Ent*" (Good-bye, Aunt), and "*Tayk ker an yuself*" (Take care of yourself), and "*Eet, mume*" (Eat, Auntie), and "*Triy to sleep, Ent*" (Try to get some sleep, Aunt). It must have been ten minutes before she finished saying her good-byes, and when she left, the chains on her throat and the bracelets on her wrist clanged, the clasp on her pocketbook clicked when she put her handkerchief into it, and finally, the door screeched when she closed it. I thought she was one big noisemaker. When she left, Mrs. Koshes started to talk.

"She's the one with the check that I told you about. Why do you think she was here? She told me that her husband needs money. He needs at least three hundred dollars. Ray, if I were young now, I wouldn't bring anyone to America. I'd live differently, behave like people do nowadays."

I felt so sorry for Mrs. Koshes. She was lying on her sickbed and regretting the favors that she did when she was young. It's a good thing that her leg is getting better. Maybe she'll be well again and think about how you can use colors to make the heavens.

Janet Is Blind

July 26

I'm almost able to sew a glove, but according to the black-haired Mary, if I don't have a union card, I might as well lay down in the street and die. She thinks there's nothing else I can do. When she saw me working at the machine yesterday, she started to click away with her tongue. *Click, click, click.* I heard her talking about a union card, and in the end, she went and called the union organizer. He came today and talked to the forelady and then to Mr. Rubin. They called me into the office, and I heard Mr. Rubin say to him, "She already knew how to do this work a long time before coming here." I felt, in the depths of my heart, that sometimes a lie can be kosher too. When the organizer asked me how long I'd been in this trade, I really played it up: "It's been seven years. I was already working at it in Poland." The organizer looked at me, and I don't know if he believed me or not, but he asked me to join the union.

"Are you a refugee?"

"Yes, a refugee."

The fact that Mr. Rubin lied for me, and that I came out with "seven years in the trade" will help me become a factory worker, just as Layzer wrote. The black-haired Mary looked at me today as though I had stolen something from her. She didn't even ask me for water. She went and took it herself. Let her go. She's not crippled.

Coming home, I found another piece of "good news." There was a letter from Chatskel saying that Janet is now blind, poor girl. She doesn't see a thing out of one eye and almost nothing out of the other. She can't go anywhere without somebody guiding her. The poor child has lost the war she was fighting. She's only seven years old, and Chatskel writes that she doesn't even want to get out of bed. She doesn't want to be led around. She cries, begging them to call a doctor. She wants to walk by herself. "Don't ask, Rivke," Chatskel writes, "what we're going through. It's better for you not to know."

Mrs. Shlivke saw that I was lying stretched out on the bed with the letter on my face. She brought me a glass of tea and asked me what was the matter and I told her that my brother's daughter had been injured when they fled Antwerp and she was now blind. Mrs. Shlivke sat down on the bed next to me. She didn't say anything, but I felt better having her sit there.

"Drink your tea, Rivke," she said later. It seems that people can go on despite everything. I drank the tea. I was very cold, and Mrs. Shlivke covered my legs with a blanket even though it's summer. I think Janet has suffered the worst fate of all, even worse than my mother's, may she rest in peace.

Red didn't come today. Either he's mad that I let him wait yesterday, or he's once again *bizee*.

The Blind World and the Lonely World

July 27

For the past several days, I've been trying to figure out how to talk to Red about what had kept him so *bizee* last week. My mother, may she rest in peace, used to say that you have to test a thread to see if it will hold or tear apart. I think you have to test devotion in the same way.

It was hard for me to ask Red about it, and it was completely impossible for me to sit and wait to see if he would come today or if he would be *bizee*. I decided to take a walk to Mrs. Koshes to see how she was doing. I like to hear her stories, and she always knows what to do even though she's so old and sick. If she were in my place, she would certainly leave her apartment and not sit there waiting for Red. I was all set to leave when Red came in, and I burst out with, "You're not busy today?"

Red started speaking in English, as usual. He must have been unhappy with my question. "*Viy yur esking mee?*"

I don't know why my heart starting pounding, but it was so loud that I was afraid Red would hear it. I answered Red without thinking. "Red, Ruth came back from California. You went out with her for a whole three years and four months. You should go with Ruth, Red." I said *and four months* for no good reason, because I wanted to get back at Red for his *bizee.*

Red spoke in English again: "*Yu vant mee tu doo so,* Rivke?"

I thought Red was making fun of me, teasing me. He went over to the window and looked out at the streetlights just as he had done when he asked to see my letters from Palestine. And, instead of answering him, I saw little Janet before my eyes. I saw that she was blind and sat on her bed and didn't want to go out. I felt such pity, but I don't know if it was for poor Janet or for me. I closed my eyes and saw many red rings circling around and turning green and blue. The blind world is a world too, and the lonely world is a world too, and why do I need to answer Red if he's teasing me? When I opened my eyes, Red was standing bent over my chair.

"What are you thinking about, Rivke?"

"Nothing. I'm thinking of the fiery rings that I just saw."

"I don't understand."

"Nothing, Red. It's not important."

I wouldn't care if Red left. At that moment, nothing mattered to me. I wasn't happy or sad or anything. But Red didn't leave. He has some strange ideas. He sat down on the floor and took off my shoes.

"Lie down, Rivke. You're tired. I'll bring you some coffee." I did what he said and lay down. I felt as though I wasn't in New York but in my grandfather's house in the forest near Lublin. It started to rain and thunder. Red brought me coffee and sat down next to me. He said: "Rivke, it's true that I used to go out with Ruth. She cried. I'll never go out with her again."

The only thing I heard was the word *never.* I believe him when he says never.

The Visit

August 1

I had an important guest today. Ruth came, all dressed up as usual. But this was a different Ruth. I saw it as soon as she walked in. Her head was bent forward, as if she was carrying something on her back. I gave her a chair, thinking that she needed to sit down. She started to talk to me in Yiddish, and maybe that's why I thought that a different person was sitting here.

"I'm twenty-four years old. I was twenty when I met Red. We should have already been married, but I did something foolish. I wanted to save money for a place to live and for furniture. Now I have six hundred dollars. And you came along."

Ruth started crying quietly. She kept catching her breath as though she wanted to see if she still had any left to breathe. "Selma says that you have a *boy* in Palestine. *Awl miy liyf—*" she said but I didn't hear anything else that Ruth said. I just saw how she was holding her head bent forward and the green feather on her hat was shaking. I imagined it was my blind niece, Janet, crying and asking for a doctor. Ruth spoke some more and then became quiet. She sobbed and caught her breath again, as if trying to take in air. That must be how Janet cries. I said to Ruth, "I'm not a doctor. Why did you come here?"

Ruth jumped up. "Not a doctor? What do you mean by a doctor?" She was red in the face, and she stopped crying and began speaking English. "*Ay taut yur a hyuman being, bot yul kom tu mee som dey*" (I thought you were a mentsh, but you'll come to me some day).

I heard Ruth running downstairs, and I thought that she would fall down the steps because she couldn't see a thing. I wanted to run after her to help, but her footsteps became quieter, and I was left sitting in my spot.

Mr. Edelshtein

August 6

Sheinfeld wants to be entirely above board. It matters a lot to him that I return his fifteen dollars to the Messiah. I had a note from him today that said, "Please, Rivke, send the fifteen dollars to the person from whom you took it. I don't want to owe anything to anyone if I don't have to. I sacrificed a lot to be able to do this. If you don't have any money now, I'll send you another fifteen dollars."

When I got his letter, I went out to see if I could get another four dollars to add to the eleven I already had. My aunt didn't have any money with her. Mrs. Shore wasn't home. Who did I get four dollars from? Mr. Edelshtein! I wanted to go home and borrow four dollars from the laundress, but just opposite me I saw somebody walking who I could have sworn I had seen somewhere. I finally recognized him when he smiled at me and I saw the gray clear eyes that laugh a little and take pity all at once. It was Mr. Edelshtein, the wealthy man from Long Island. What was he doing here?

He recognized me and stopped.

"How are you?"

"I'm *awlriyt*, thanks."

"Where are you going?"

I wasn't thinking that I was talking to a rich man, and I told him where I was going. "I'm going to look for four dollars to repay a debt."

Mr. Edelshtein took out his wallet and handed me four dollars.

"Take this," he said, "and don't go looking."

What a mess I've made of things, I thought. How could I take four dollars from Mr. Edelshtein? It looked like a handout coming from such a rich man. I told him just what I was thinking.

"I don't want to take your money. You're wealthy; it will look like I'm . . ."

I didn't want to add the word *begging*, but Edelshtein understood what I meant, and he said, "You met me here by accident. You didn't come to ask me for money. Take it."

He's such a strange person, this Edelshtein. He's completely straightforward, and I felt like I had known him for ages. I told him about poor little Janet. And it seems I made another silly mistake. Edelshtein said, "Give me your brother's address. I'll send him ten dollars every month."

That's just what he said: "ten dollars."

Mr. Edelshtein walked with me, and I saw that his shoulders were a little bent. He's not so young anymore. He talked to me about Lublin. "I used to eat at your grandfather's, Reb Mottele's, table every week before he went to live in the forest. Those were the best meals I had all week. He would ask me to sit down at the table and say the blessing over the bread. He was a religious man, your grandfather, and a very busy one. In the middle of a meal, he would jump up and start yelling at your grandmother: 'Give him something to eat. Why aren't you giving him?' He was so distracted, he'd say it for no reason, sometimes even after I had finished eating. In order to obey her husband, your grandmother would move the saltshaker over to me. He was really a busy, distracted man."

So it looks like my grandfather was also "topsy-turvy," as Edelshtein tells it.

I gave Mr. Edelshtein my brother's address. Maybe it wasn't such a nice thing for me to do, but it's better than letting my brother go hungry. And, again, that's just what I said. "Maybe it's not so nice that I'm giving you his address . . ."

"Of course it's not nice," he answered. "You think it would have been a lot nicer if you hadn't wanted to give me your brother's address?" He laughed and added, "Who taught you this 'not nice'?"

I walked him to his car. He looked at his watch and said, "I've got a free half hour. Come, I'll show you New York."

I got into the car, which was wide, with soft seats that felt like velvet. New York whizzed by. Tall buildings, then Central Park, swans swimming in the middle of a lake. I thought it was all a dream. Mr. Edelshtein brought me back to the laundromat.

"Why didn't you want to take the job I offered?"

"Thank you. I have a job."

Again, his eyes laughed as they looked at me. "Good-bye," he said, shaking my hand and leaving.

So, Mr. Edelshtein ate at my grandfather's table. I felt sorry for my grandmother. Nobody ever talks about her. It's always about my grandfather, Reb Mottele.

Blonde Bessie

August 12

I'm done with the pieces. I'm working at a sewing machine now. Blond Bessie shows me what to do, smacking her lips loudly and saying, "Ease up on your hands; make them lighter."

I don't understand how it's possible to make your hands lighter or heavier, but it's certainly easier to have Blonde Bessie willing to help me. And when I see her smacking her lips, even my soul feels like it's getting lighter. She got into trouble with Black Mary today because of me.

Black Mary is simply evil. Instead of saying that she begrudges the fact that I can work a little on the machine, she makes herself into God's emissary. She's protecting the union, and since I don't have a union card yet, she really went all out complaining and making those clicking sounds. And when Blonde Bessie kept on helping me, Black Mary said that she was a *skeb* (a strike breaker), and *a dertee skeb* at that.

Blonde Bessie started smacking her lips, but that didn't settle anything, so she went over to Black Mary, placed herself opposite, pretended to draw a moustache over her lips, and said, deliberately and slowly: "Philip left you. Good. You don't even want to help a refugee. Tfu, you witch."

Black Mary didn't say a word. You could see two shiny spots in the corners of her eyes. They didn't look like tears, but like sparks. She was thinking about what to say to Blonde Bessie, and she thought a long, long time, because after fifteen minutes, she went over to Blonde Bessie's machine and, in English, said loudly, so everyone could hear: "And your musician has wanted to get rid of you all these years. All these years."

Blonde Bessie didn't even look at her. She just spit in Mary's direction and said, "Witch."

Later, the union called me, and I saw the organizer. He has a round face, just like Mr. Shamut. Where did they all get such faces? The union organizer gave me an application to fill out and, once again, I wrote down the whole story: that I had worked in the trade for seven years. I paid a dollar for the application. The organizer gave me a receipt, and I went back to the shop.

Blonde Bessie took the receipt and said, "I wish you good luck." Then she added, "You'll slave away at the machine, don't you worry." But that wasn't the end of it. She got up and took the receipt over to Black Mary. Smacking her lips a lot and loudly, she finally said, "Here, lick the union's receipt. You'll get fatter."

Black Mary didn't answer her. She just stuck her tongue out, and I couldn't help wondering how such a little thing could have such a long tongue.

Blonde Bessie took me under her wing. She's not helping me, but every now and then she reminds me, "Ease up on your hands, Ruth."

They call me Ruth in the shop. So, now I have three names in all: Ray, Ruth, and Rivke. And all this in less than one year of being in America.

It's Not for Nothing That a Place Like New York Was Built

August 18

It was a lot harder for me to return the Messiah's fifteen dollars than it had been to get them. And yet people say it's hard to get money, easy to give it back. It's not always like that. When I brought the fifteen dollars to the Refugee Aid Society, Mr. Shamut looked at me as shocked as if I had come into his office with no dress on, God forbid, or without a head.

"Why are you bothering with these fifteen dollars? What for?" he said unhappily, scratching his head. Then he seemed to realize that he was being too hard on a person who was returning money, and he smiled and said, "Ay, Lublin, Lublin! When will you become America already?" And then Sheinfeld's money was carried from one person to another. It turns out that the money was from the Messiah, but he had borrowed it from the Aid Society, and they hadn't yet put it in their accounts, so nobody knew who should get the money I brought back. Mr. Shamut was in a sweat about it.

"So, why did you bring the fifteen dollars? Have you ever heard of such a thing? Returning money?"

Later, Mr. Fishman came, and that's when the real to-do started. He took me by the hand and led me from one door to another. At each one, he said, "I told you that you can trust them. A refugee is a mentsh. They would all return what they borrow. If you don't believe me, here's your proof."

He didn't put the fifteen dollars into his pocket. He carried it around like a flag held high in one hand, and with the other hand, he led me around as living proof that "a refugee is a mentsh." We walked around for almost two hours, going from person to person. I was dripping with sweat, but the elderly Messiah wasn't at all tired.

"I'm always telling you," he argued, "we don't need all this furniture. We need to trust people." And he mentioned the oak table that he himself had finished. His last stop was at Mr. Shamut's door. Mr. Shamut was sitting at his green table and looking around for a way to save himself from the Messiah. In the end, he grabbed the clock that was always sitting on his table, and clutched his head. "I completely forgot. I have a meeting." He stood up, took his hat, smiled, and shook hands with the Messiah. "Be well, Mr. Fish. You're right."

To me, he said, "Ay, Lublin, Lublin. *Gud biy.*" And he was gone in a flash.

The Messiah brought the fifteen dollars to the cashier, and to me he said, "May you be successful in all you do here. It's not for nothing that a place like New York was built."

I left the Aid Society and saw New York, a place not built for nothing, but for me. The street was all lit up and noisy and bustling. The cars that stopped to give other cars the right of way seemed to be dancing a polka mazurka. I was absorbed in the noisy street, and I thought that the elderly Messiah was standing behind me and making sure that I would be successful here.

A Summertime Meeting

August 20

Mr. Edelshtein really did send ten dollars to my brother, and he sent me the bank receipt. It was actually Mack Lehigh and not Mr. Edelshtein himself who sent it. What do I care? Let it be Mack Lehigh as long as my brother gets ten dollars. I left the receipt on the table because my aunt called me to go to a meeting of the Lublin Ladies' Society. I went, as always, with the hope that maybe I'd hear something about my family in Lublin.

The meeting was about Mr. Shamut's birthday party. It wasn't well attended because it was summertime and only a few of the women could come. The *kepten* of the celebration, Mrs. Tkatsh, came to the meeting from Mountaindale. She was dressed for summer, with short sleeves. She has fat arms that look like big blocks of wood, and they're as flabby as kneaded dough.

"Nothing in the world could drag me into the city in such a heat except Mr. Shamut's party," she said.

Mrs. Rabkin was back from her vacation. She was as dark as if she had been visiting the sun instead of the Catskills. My aunt didn't go away this summer because of Selma's "conflagration," but she told the women that she had stayed in the city because of medical treatments. I guess, for some reason, that's a better excuse. Mrs. Rubin never goes away for the summer. Her husband can't go because of his business, and she doesn't go because of her husband. During the weekends, they both go away. There were only a few other women there, so it was a quiet meeting. They decided to put an announcement about Mr. Shamut and the celebration in the papers. All the women except Mrs. Rubin took out their pens.

"I can't write anything," she said. "It's bad enough that my sister, Golde, was ruined because of her learning."

Mrs. Rabkin is the best writer in the Lublin Ladies' Society. She wrote and every now and then scratched her nose, and in the end, she read her *kompozishen* aloud.

"We're proud to have an important personage such as Mr. Shamut as our compatriot, and we are honored to celebrate his fiftieth birthday."

Everybody was very pleased with the beginning, and they applauded, agreeing that Mrs. Rabkin was a talented writer. Even Mrs. Tkatsh, the "captain," applauded. Mrs. Rabkin continued writing and erasing and writing some more, and then she again read aloud what she had written.

"In these times, when Jews are suffering throughout the world, we're happy to be in America, and we're proud to have such personages as Mr. Shamut."

It got late, and we chose a committee to complete the announcement for the newspapers.

It was silly of me to leave Mack Lehigh's bank receipt on my table. When I came home, I found Red there, once again standing at the window looking at the streetlights. That's always a bad sign. I know that when Red starts looking at the lights, it means that he's angry. He spoke in English.

"*Rivke, vat kiynd of reseet iz eet?* (What kind of receipt is this?) I asked you not to go to Mr. Edelshtein."

At first I was sorry that I had left the receipt on the table, and then I thought that, after all, I'm not married to Red, and I don't owe him an explanation or a lie.

"How do you know that I went to him?"

"What about the receipt?"

I told Red about running into Mr. Edelshtein on the street and that he said he would send ten dollars to my brother every month.

"It's too little, Rivke," Red said, laughing.

I don't know what happened to me, but suddenly I felt a pain in my chest as though I had been stabbed, and I couldn't speak for a while. I must have turned pale because Red realized I was upset and held my shoulders and said, "Rivkele, don't be angry."

"You never think about my brother, and it doesn't bother you that he's starving. And Edelshtein . . ."

"I'm not as rich as he is," Red answered.

"And you're not starving either."

Red was silent. He sat with his head bent, and I saw that he had decided something. But he didn't tell me what it was.

If he won't, he won't, I thought. Sometimes I just can't figure him out.

We made a date to go out tomorrow, and Red asked me to wear the new dress his mother had sent.

Where does Red want to take me? And why do I need to get all dressed up? I couldn't fall asleep for a long time after Red left. And then I dreamed about the receipt, and Mack Lehigh's signature was written in stone. In my dream, I tried to touch the signature several times, but it hurt my finger. Then I thought that it wasn't my finger that hurt but rather my brother Chatskel's. When I woke up, I saw that my finger was red. I probably jabbed it somewhere yesterday. That's bad because it will make it harder to work at the machine.

I Go to Meet Red's Parents

August 21

At home, when people had arranged marriages, they would go to meet their intended husband, but today I think I went to meet Red's parents. I've never gone to meet a potential husband, but it's certainly even stranger to go meet the parents. Red's father looks like the papa bear, and his mother looks like the mama bear. When I was riding on the bus with Red, I imagined that his parents would take hold of me with their big paws and the world would turn upside down.

Today Red told me that I needed to go thank his mother for the dress. That must have been what he was deciding when he was sitting so silently in my room yesterday.

Red's parents have a luncheonette. Red works there during the day, and his mother works in the evenings and then he's free.

Red's mother, Mrs. Levitt, shook my hand. She's "English," which means she speaks English. His father is "Yiddish"; he speaks Yiddish. His mother calls Red Larry and his father calls him Layzer Yosl. (Again Layzer.)

I thanked Mrs. Levitt for the dress, and she said: *"Iy'm gled yu liyk eet."* She wears red nail polish, and she looks a little bit like a rich lady.

Cake and coffee were served on a small table, and I had no idea what to say. Mr. Levitt came over and said, "How many hours did you spend in the beauty parlor today with those braids?" At first, I thought he wasn't talking to me, but when I looked around, I saw that he was looking straight at me. I didn't know what to say. Red stuck up for me, but so fiercely that I didn't know what in the world was going on.

"Vat du yu meen?" Red angrily said to his father, and in a flash, he took out the four hairpins that were holding my braids in place and they fell down, one behind me and one in front.

Mrs. Levitt said, *"Leree, yu'r krayzee."*

Mr. Levitt looked at my braids with smiling eyes and said, "She's the real thing, this girl of yours."

"Shur," Red answered. I saw that Red and his father had the same eyes. You could see the twinkle in both of them as they stood looking at me. I wanted the ground to open up beneath my feet so I could sink into it together with the table, the cake, the coffee, and the loosened braids. But everything stayed in place. I barely heard a word that Mrs. Levitt was babbling at me in English. I don't even remember how I put my hair back up. Everything was spinning around me until Mr. Levitt handed me a bowl of ice cream.

"Take this," he said. "You'll enjoy it."

When we left the luncheonette, Red was very pleased. My heart was still pounding, and I was annoyed with Red for undoing my braids. I couldn't stop myself from saying, "Red-Shmed, what did you do to my hair?"

"Eet vaz vonderful" (It was wonderful), he said in English, and he laughed as he always does when he's pleased about something. I stopped walking, looked at him, and slapped him on both cheeks.

"This is a nice engagement," he said, and he kissed each of my hands.

The Anniversary of My Mother's Death

September 3

What the earth covers up must be forgotten. That's what my aunt said today when she saw that I was crying because it was my mother's yortsayt, the anniversary of her death.

"Why must it be?" It's the opposite for me. Even when I don't think about my mother, I never forget her. And I never forget that my father is in Lublin sleeping on the ground in a barn or that Janet is blind. How can anyone forget all these things? But I've learned to keep quiet about it, to cover it up with white shoes, with factory work, and with living on Grand Street. Sometimes, if I laugh too loudly, I hear my laughter and I'm amazed. And in an instant, I'm more in Lublin than in New York.

Today, of all days, a letter came from my father. It took seven weeks to get here, and in the end it arrived on the day of my mother's yortsayt. He asks me not to forget the day. So today I went to work in my black shoes. Our forelady must have ten pairs of eyes. She sees everything. As soon as I came into the factory I saw that her eyes were already on my shoes! The factory is the best hospital in the world. Nothing matters in the factory except the factory itself. There's no yortsayt there, no headache, no tears.

My father's letter was so short that it scared me. He writes that he's well and that Mikhl is not in Lublin, but he doesn't say where Mikhl is. He writes that I shouldn't forget my mother's yortsayt. And his last sentence says that God will help us.

Red came to pick me up from work today. I think it's because I had told him that today was my mother's yortsayt. He looked at my black shoes too, but he knew why I was wearing them.

Is one year such a long time? Instead of Lublin, there's New York. Instead of my mother, there's a yortsayt. Layzer is in Palestine, and Red came to pick me up from the factory. And my father, who has remained all alone in Krasulye's stall, writes, "God will help us."

Stars

September 15

Everything was whirling around last week because of Mr. Shamut's birthday party. My aunt had black circles under her eyes from working so hard. Mrs. Rabkin had to lie in bed for two whole days because she was exhausted. First she had to finish the whole description of who Mr. Shamut is and then there was the project of getting his picture into the newspapers along with everything she had written about him. Tuesday, when she reported to the membership of the Lublin Ladies' Society, she said, "I've been to all the editors, and they have *gepromisd* (promised) me that they'll put the picture in a good spot." After the meeting, Mrs. Rabkin took to her bed for two days so she'd have strength for the event itself.

The real fuss came on Sunday morning because that's when Mr. Shamut's picture appeared in all the newspapers. In the picture, Mr. Shamut was sitting in his office, with a cigar in his mouth, looking at papers on his desk. The members of the ladies' society each bought two newspapers, one to bring with them to the event and the other to put away as a souvenir. Under the picture it said, "Mr. Shamut, prominent Jewish leader in New York." The women were very happy with that sentence, especially with the word *prominent*. Mrs. Rabkin said that she searched through hundreds of lines under all sorts of pictures until she chose that one for Mr. Shamut. "I couldn't do more than I did," she said, spreading her arms wide in front of her as she stood in the middle of the hall in her blue evening gown.

Opposite Mr. Shamut's picture, there was another picture in the newspaper. It showed Mr. Karelin and said, "Y. H. Karelin: His Biography and Social Welfare Activities, edited by Professor Dr. Sheinfeld."

Even though the "captain" of Mr. Shamut's celebration was Mrs. Tkatsh, it was Mrs. Rabkin who took charge of the whole thing. When Mr. Shamut came into the hall, the guests threw confetti, just like we do in Lublin for brides. And it wasn't Mrs. Tkatsh but Mrs. Rabkin who took his arm and led him to his chair in the place of honor. He was given a golden pen with the inscription "From your Lublin compatriots with appreciation." All the guests cheered when Mr. Shamut took the pen, and they were excited when he made a speech. "This is not a time for celebrations," he said, "but since you all remembered that you had a fellow Lubliner who was turning fifty and you made a celebration, I would like to express my deepest appreciation. It's a great honor for me and also a great pleasure to be with you all today."

After the speech Mr. Shamut took out a ten-dollar bill and gave it to the Lubliner Ladies' Society as a gift in honor of their important work on behalf of the misfortunate people in "the old country."

The audience sighed. Mr. Rubin also gave ten dollars, and Mr. Tkatsh—the captain's husband—brought a third ten-dollar bill. And then Mr. Shamut sold autographs for a dollar a piece. In the end, they collected a hundred dollars for the Ladies' Society. When people started dancing, I left. Even though it's past my mother's yortsayt (may she rest in peace), I couldn't dance because I kept seeing Janet before me. I went home and went up to the roof.

Around me, the New York sky was spread out full of stars above and the streets of New York below. But in my heart, there was only darkness. I was happy to remember that tomorrow is Monday and I'll be going to the shop. In the shop you forget everything, both happiness and sadness.

My Grandfather, Reb Mottele, and My Engagement

September 23

Yesterday, Sunday, was Selma's wedding. Red's parents came too, just as if they were really in-laws. Red came to my room in the evening. He brought a diamond ring and said that we should announce our engagement tonight, at Selma's wedding.

"The Zilbergs don't eat cake off others people's plates," I answered.

"*Vat?*" he asked. "*Iy don' understend yu,* Rivke."

"You don't understand?" I said. And I repeated what I had said about the Zilbergs not eating off others' plates. And he asked me again what I meant.

"You see, Red, my grandfather was . . ."

Red interrupted me to say "Reb Mottele Zilberg. I know that already. He was a terribly important and good man."

"Yes, Reb Mottele Zilberg was not an arrogant man. Before Passover, when he would go from the woods to Lublin with a wagon full of flour for the poor, he would take the reins into his own hands and ride into the city like an ordinary coachman. He would take the sacks of flour on his back and carry them himself even though he had plenty of people working for him.

"'Flour,' he would say, 'can only be given by someone who has what to give. It can only be given by the rich. But everyone can make an effort to do whatever he can, and I want to do what everyone can do so that if I become poor I'll still be able to be a righteous man.'"

"That's philosophy," Red interrupted me to say.

"But that's what my grandfather would say, even though sometimes he would hold himself so above everyone else that it was impossible even to talk to him. He was a timber merchant. Once, other merchants asked him to come to them to discuss a business deal. Pagode, the richest man in the area, was going to sell his woods, and it was a bargain. My grandfather went to the merchants, where he saw Hirsh Frampoler wearing a gold chain across his stomach, Itshe Mayer Tarnapolski wearing a pince-nez, Shimele Milner with a yellow beard that made him look like a plucked chicken, and Yokhe's husband (that's what we called him) panting like a goose. They were all sitting waiting for my grandfather. He was annoyed that they had talked things over among themselves first because they were richer, and only then had they sent for him. When they told him about the bargain, my grandfather stood up and rejected their offer. 'Zilberg hates bargains,' he said, and off he went. When he came home and said he had turned down the bargain he had been offered, my grandmother went straight to Lublin and brought all their daughters and sons-in-law and sons to talk him into becoming a partner in the business. But my grandfather had said no, and no was no.

"'Zilberg doesn't eat cake off other people's plates. Let them keep their bargain.' No one could make him change his mind.

"Pagode had an assistant, a young man with long whiskers and tall boots who rode around on a bicycle. He thought the world of my grandfather. And without hesitation he told the merchants that he wanted to sell them the forest, but he wanted Zilberg to be the guarantor. He trusted only Zilberg. So they all went to my grandfather: Hirsh Frampoler with the gold chain on his belly, and Itshe Mayer Tarnapolski with his pince-nez, and Shimele Milner with the yellow beard that made him look like a plucked chicken, and Yokhe's husband who panted like a goose. All of them were there. Still, my grandfather was stubborn and absolutely refused.

"'And what about the fact that Lublin Jews will lose so much money because of you? It's a sin,' they said, threatening retribution in the world to come.

"'So Volhynia Jews will buy it. Jews from Volhynia are also Jews.'

"And my grandfather stuck to his word. He wouldn't eat cake off rich people's plates."

"Well, I understand you a little bit," Red said. "But what about the engagement ring?"

I stretched out my finger. "Give it here. My grandfather used to take what was given to him; otherwise he wouldn't have been a rich man. But he didn't always take."

"I know that you have your own ways. *A bisl tsedreyt*. A little mixed up, *bot iy liyk eet*."

Red walked around the room happily. Then he came over to me, picked me up, and said right into my ear, "Rivkele, your *zeyde* was *awlriyt*."

With the engagement ring on my finger, I went to Selma's wedding with Red.

There's a Mendl Pushcart in the world, and he already knew about the engagement ring. I don't know what's with him, whether it's foolishness or goodness, but when the guests were seated and we had liquor in our glasses and we had wished the bride and groom mazel tov, Mendl Pushcart erupted with: "Let's also say mazel tov to Ray Zilberg. She got a nice present today, an engagement ring from Larry Levitt."

Everybody applauded and congratulated us. I think Mendl Pushcart did it because he wanted to thank me for the glasses of tea that I had always given him. And, in honor of the gathering, he didn't call me Rivke but Ray.

I thought I would faint, but it was done. It seems that Mendl Pushcart had given little thought to my grandfather, Reb Mottele, and his pride.

Red's father danced with me. He speaks like a Jew, but he dances like an American, and as smoothly as a young man. While we were dancing, he said, "Layzer Yosl is our only child. If he loves you, so do we."

Red's mother was wearing a black velvet dress. Her hair was done up with large, tall curls. She looked like quite the aristocrat.

My aunt and Mrs. Shore insisted that we had a double celebration today, and Marvin danced that dance whose steps no one in the whole United States knows except for Benny Goodman and Marvin.

Ruth didn't come to the wedding. She sent a telegram: "Congratulations and best wishes." Instead of bringing gifts, many of the guests gave my aunt envelopes with money and wished them all *gud luk*.

I was at the wedding, but I was seeing Lublin, my father in Krasulye's stall, Chatskel, and poor, blind Janet. It was as if they were all standing near me, behind a curtain.

I danced with Red. "You have to learn how to dance the modern dances," he said.

The floor was slippery, and I felt as if I was rocking back and forth, as though on a ship.

I still think that what happened yesterday was a play and that Mendl Pushcart told a story about America and a girl from Lublin who had long braids and was given an engagement ring.

Who Knows?

October 6

It's been a long time since I've written in this journal. Everything I am experiencing now has no beginning and no end. Once, I saw a fire in Lublin. A house was burning, and the fire made it so transparent that through the burning walls you could see a tree that was growing behind the house. That's exactly how transparent everything seems to me now. What was once, and all that happened to me in New York this past year, and my destroyed home—all these things stand before me as transparent as if I were seeing them through the fire.

Today I received a letter from Layzer, as always, in a blue envelope. Layzer wrote:

> We are now living in darkness. There's a blackout here every night, but we hope that after this darkness will come the lightness of day. However long the war lasts, Rivke, I'll wait for the day when you come to Palestine. Everything is terribly expensive here now, and it's very difficult to make a living. Shimshi helps me a lot with money and work, although the necessities are still often missing. But it's not hard for me. I have a great deal of hope, and with hope it's easy to live. Please, Rivke, write to me often. Even if I don't get all your letters, I'll feel that you're writing to me. You write so seldom.

I didn't know where to put the letter. What if Red were to see it? I wanted to tear it up, but how could I do that to a letter from Layzer?

I gave the letter to the laundress to keep. She opened one of her drawers and put the letter there. She closed the drawer, put the cloth back on top of the cabinet, and straightened the *Mayflower*.

When Red came, he said, "My father says that you should leave the factory and come help us in the luncheonette."

Red is very good to me. He doesn't let me worry about anything. "Don't think so much," he says.

I wear the engagement ring, and I think that Rivke Zilberg no longer exists. In New York, someone named Ray Levitt will soon be walking around. Rivke Zilberg remained in Lublin. Someone in Palestine is waiting for Rivke Zilberg. And Ray Levitt lives in New York.

Can it be that everyone in the world lives like this? Who knows?

KADYA MOLODOVSKY (1894–1975) was one of the most well-known and prolific writers of Yiddish literature in the twentieth century. Born in Bereze, a small town in what is now Belarus, educated in Poland and Russia, Molodovsky was an established writer when she came to the United States in 1935. With the exception of three years (1949–52) when she lived in Israel, she spent the rest of her life in New York. Known primarily as a poet, essayist, and editor, she published over twenty books, including poetry, plays, and four novels.

ANITA NORICH is Professor Emerita of English and Judaic Studies at the University of Michigan. She is author of *Writing in Tongues: Yiddish Translation in the 20th Century, Discovering Exile: Yiddish and Jewish American Literature in America During the Holocaust, The Homeless Imagination in the Fiction of Israel Joshua Singer*, and editor of *Languages of Modern Jewish Cultures: Comparative Perspectives, Jewish Literatures and Cultures: Context and Intertext*, and *Gender and Text in Modern Hebrew and Yiddish Literatures*. She translates Yiddish literature and teaches, lectures, and publishes on a range of topics concerning modern Jewish cultures, Yiddish language and literature, Jewish American literature, and Holocaust literature.